THE OUTCAST PRINCE

SHONA HUSK

sourcebooks
casablanca

Published by Sourcebooks Casablanca, an imprint of Sourcebooks, Inc.
P.O. Box 4410, Naperville, Illinois 60567-4410
(630) 961-3900
Fax: (630) 961-2168
www.sourcebooks.com

Printed and bound in the United States of America.
VP 10 9 8 7 6 5 4 3 2 1

For my children. You're never too old for fairies.

Chapter 1

CASPIAN TRAILED HIS FINGER ALONG THE WOODEN mirror frame. Was the piece an antique or a clever fake?

One touch was enough to confirm the mirror was old, made by hand well over a century ago. As he examined the Rococo workmanship, he caught a brief movement beyond the sky that was reflected in the glass. If he looked closer and concentrated on the shadowy movements that normal humans didn't see, he'd be able to glimpse the fairy world of Annwyn. Now there was a surprise. Was the glass enchanted or fairy-made? Was it the mirror the fairies were looking for?

Caspian drew his hand back casually so as not to attract attention. The garage sale wasn't the place to examine it further. He deliberated for a couple of heartbeats, then decided acquiring it would be worth the risk.

A blue fairy wren fluttered around him and then landed on top of the mirror, drawn by the magic.

"What can you tell me about the mirror?" he asked the seller. He tried to sound only vaguely interested. He glanced at his watch, making sure he still had time to investigate and haggle—although for a mirror like this he'd make time and be late to his meeting. Not that he liked showing up late.

The woman shrugged. "It was my mom's. I thought

she'd gotten rid of it years ago. But no, it was shoved in the back of her wardrobe, along with shoes she hadn't worn for twenty years."

Caspian's eyebrows rose. "She didn't like it?"

"Said it gave her the creeps." The woman shooed the wren off the mirror.

He could understand that. Having a mirror that looked into the fairy world was bound to be unsettling. "I'll give you four hundred even for the mirror and these iron sconces." He grasped the metal, ignoring the jolt of pain the iron sent through his system. No wonder fairies hated the stuff. Given the uncertain situation in Annwyn at the moment, having a bit of extra iron around the house wouldn't be a bad thing.

The woman gave him a closer look. "Who are you buying the mirror for?"

Caspian smiled. There was a touch of the fairy in the woman's family even if they were trying to bury it. "My ex-wife's birthday."

It wasn't her birthday, and he wasn't buying it for her, but if the woman knew what the mirror was really worth—both in human and possibly fairy terms—she may not want to sell it so cheaply.

The fairy wren returned and danced along the top of the frame, hopping and turning. Their name didn't come from their diminutive size the way most people thought; their name came from the fact that they were drawn to all things fairy.

This time, the reflection on the mirror showed a tall, thin man standing on the other side of the road. Beautiful but gaunt, fairy but not one of the Court—a Grey. Caspian blinked and glanced away. He turned a fraction, expecting to see the man still watching, but the Grey was gone.

A wren, a Grey, and a mirror with a connection to Annwyn. He should be walking away. But he'd heard of a hunt for something called the Window. According to rumor, it was a portal between the human and fairy worlds—and it was right here in Charleston. Every time he saw a mirror, Caspian checked to see if it was fairy-made. As much as he hated getting involved in fairy politics, even he knew how disastrous it could be if the Window fell into the wrong hands: a Grey's hands.

He forced his gaze back to the woman as if he'd seen nothing to worry him. As if he'd never noticed the banished fairy. He'd learned long ago to pretend he never saw them. His gaze would drift past, but never stop. His heart, however, responded to the surge of adrenaline kicking through his system.

There was nothing more dangerous, or desperate, than a Grey. A fairy banished from Court had nothing to lose, and banishment was a slow way to die, a wasting of strength and beauty until he literally faded away. As a changeling, Caspian got to live and die like a mortal.

"Four hundred and fifty," the woman said.

His phone beeped a reminder about his meeting. Caspian briefly considered trying to bargain her down, but he didn't want to stand around waiting for the Grey to come back.

He nodded. "Okay."

She smiled at her win, no doubt wishing she'd asked for more.

He hadn't come here expecting to find anything quite

so valuable, or so dangerous. Would it be ethical to sell an enchanted mirror to an unsuspecting buyer?

The skin between his shoulder blades prickled with cold despite the sunny spring day, and the little blue wren came back to dance on the furniture in the woman's driveway. Was it heralding the return of the Grey? If so, was the Grey drawn to the woman or him or the mirror? God, he hoped it was the woman, not the mirror. He didn't really want anything to do with a fairy, banished or otherwise. Those of the Court were just as much trouble, if not more, and infinitely more powerful. He gathered his purchases and walked back to his car, but he didn't see the Grey again.

The drive across town was uneventful. No wrens, no Greys. Just him and the mirror and the whisper of music that came straight from the Court and made him want to pull the car over, peel back the layers of wrapping, and gaze into its surface. But the prospect of viewing the infamous Callaway House urged him on.

It was a job he'd almost turned down. After his divorce, he'd needed any extra money he could get doing valuations for insurance and estates to get back on his feet. These days, he could pick and choose. And normally he chose not to value estates because inevitably he felt like an interloper. But Callaway House was more than a bunch of antiques. With just one touch, the house would come to life again. He'd be able to see the parties, the dealmakers, and the intimate moments that went on behind closed doors in the former plantation home. Like all fairies, he had a vicious streak of curiosity that couldn't be ignored—that was why he had a mirror connected to Annwyn in his car even though he knew better than to get mixed up in anything fairy.

The wrought iron gates to the estate hung open, but they looked like they hadn't closed in years. The whole house had an air of decay about it: a faded Southern belle trying to hang onto her looks and failing. It had been many decades since Callaway House had been respectable. He parked the car and took a moment to gather his thoughts and make sure that when he walked in he wasn't immediately overwhelmed by the past.

He ran his fingers through his hair and took a deep breath. It was time to find out what was rumor and what was truth.

———

Lydia walked through the house, still expecting Gran to call out or appear around the corner. But the house was silent. Not even its colorful history could bring life into the empty rooms. Her chest tightened. She couldn't do this. She couldn't let a stranger wander round and itemize everything and assign a value. While the will had clearly stated the shares and other funds were to go to her mother, everything still had to be assessed. Damn it. In Lydia's mind Helen didn't deserve anything; she had denied her family long ago. But Gran had obviously felt differently about her only daughter.

Lydia swiped at a tear that trickled down her cheek. The house was all that was left of Gran, of her whole family. She stood frozen in the front room. This was where she'd found Gran sitting on the sofa, glass of wine on the coffee table, TV on, not breathing.

A knock on the front door forced her back to reality.

Lydia took a moment and a breath before opening the door, then braced herself for the greedy eyes and half-hidden glee at being allowed inside Callaway House.

The man on the doorstep was nothing like she'd expected. After talking to him on the phone, she'd imagined the deep voice belonged to an old man—yet he wasn't old. He was tall—they were eye to eye even though he was down a step, with dark hair that wasn't quite curly or straight. However it was his eyes that were stunning, the palest of greens, but not cold like ice.

"Caspian Mort," he said as he offered his hand.

She blinked. He had a serious kind of beauty that made her want to see him smile. She clasped his hand. "Lydia Callaway."

Callaway. The name that had haunted her all her life.

For an awkward moment they stood there. Then she took a step back. "Um, come in."

"Thank you. I know letting a stranger in can't be easy. I'll try to make this as un-invasive and painless as possible."

Lydia shut the front door. "You do this often?"

"When required. I prefer valuing for insurance, but…" he shrugged. "It's what I do."

For all his cool demeanor there was something going on behind his pale green eyes. His gaze flicked over her, then over the hallway. Was he imagining what had gone on in the house? Picturing the wild parties? Imagining what used to happen upstairs? "How about you show me around so I can get an idea of the scope of work?"

"Yes, I'm sure you're just dying to dive in." Lydia didn't mean to sound brusque, but years of curiosity-seekers had eroded her patience. She'd spent most of her life trying to defend the family name against all the rumors of wild times in her family's past. For generations, the Callaways had been prominent in Charelston's social scene and state politics. Even back in the nineteenth century, the plantation house had been known as a place where the rich and famous could come to play with no repercussions.

Caspian turned to her. "You know I almost didn't take this job?"

Lydia was taken aback. "Really. Why?"

"Because I didn't want to be the one putting a price on a piece of history. Then I realized if I didn't someone else would, and at least I'd get it right."

"Modest of you." Yet he hadn't said it to gloat, it was just fact. There was a quiet confidence about him as if he didn't need anyone's approval to exist.

"Honest. I know antiques… better than I know people." That admission drew a rueful smile from him that caused the corners of his eyes to crinkle.

He was older than she'd first thought. Over thirty. Her gaze dropped to his left hand. His ring finger was bare. Not that it mattered. He was here to do a job and nothing more.

"Let me show you around."

She walked through the entrance without waiting for a response. But she heard his steps behind her and was aware when he paused to look at something.

"These paintings are originals."

She turned to see him peering at the oil painting of a bridge. "Yes. Gran liked artists. She said they added to the party, and if they couldn't pay, they'd donate a painting for the walls or a sculpture for the rooms."

Caspian raised his eyebrows. "They're insured?"

"Of course. My grandmother wasn't an idiot."

He nodded and looked at the next painting, a partially nude woman who was reading a book while lying in a bed of flowers. Obviously posed but she looked like she was about to turn the page.

"Amazing." He touched the frame ever so delicately. "Your Gran must have known many brilliant people."

Lydia smiled, her first real smile in a week. "She used to talk about the parties that went on in the fifties and sixties and the things they'd get up to. Sometimes some of the old girls would get together for lunch." Those old girls had been rich men's mistresses that had been housed here so the men could pretend to be respectable in town then come out here for a weekend of entertainment. The precariousness and lack of respectability had created friendships that had lasted a lifetime. Most of them were dead now. She turned away and opened the door to the parlor.

"When it was the mistress hotel?" he said.

"Yes. You've done some research?"

"Not much; call it general historical knowledge of Charleston."

"Ah." Well, then he probably knew that in the seventies Gran let hippies camp on the grounds and grow weed. Every so often she still found a plant in the backyard. "This was where most parties began." She swept her hand out and tried to imagine the room full of men in suits and the women in dresses. All of them knowing that the wives were at home with the kids—and no doubt the wives knew where their husbands were too. From what she knew, Gran had been the house matron—too old to be a mistress and too in need of the money to turn her nose up at the source.

Lydia was pretty sure Gran would have sold her soul to keep Callaway House in the family. The thought made Lydia queasy. She didn't know what she was going to do, or even if it was possible to hold on to the house. Over two hundred years of family history gone because she couldn't afford the repairs. At least if she sold, someone would refurbish and Callaway House would go on. Maybe it would even become a tourist attraction like some of the other old places—because Charleston needed another historic house open for viewing. Or a scenic wedding location; Gran had tried that in the eighties but then decided it wasn't worth the hassle or insurance costs. Or perhaps someone would try to market it as a haunted bed and breakfast. She wouldn't mention the ghost to Caspian. Not yet anyway.

She walked through the parlor. The doors on the other side opened up onto the patio and backyard. In summer, the old parties used to spill outside and people would disappear into private corners of the yard. But as the years went on, men tired of their mistresses or they no longer could afford to keep them, and most of the women left. A couple had stayed on because they'd had nowhere else to go. One had been the nanny and housekeeper for years until she'd married. Her husband never suspected she'd once been the mistress of a criminal lawyer. But even that was decades ago now.

Caspian stopped in the middle of the room and looked around, turning slowly as if taking in all the details. To her everything looked dusty and neglected. Gran had let things slide as she'd gotten older, but to Lydia it was still the house she'd grown up in, a place where anything had seemed possible. What did he see?

Chapter 2

CASPIAN WALKED AROUND THE ROOM, CAREFUL NOT TO touch anything. He could feel the history pressing against him as if the house were bursting with secrets ready to be revealed. Keeping his talent shut down was difficult considering he wanted to reach out and run his fingers over everything. To keep his hands busy he pulled a notepad out of his jacket pocket and started writing down the details of each room. He'd use the list when determining how long it was going to take him to assess everything.

He glanced at Lydia. Despite the suit and the sleek twist of her dark blond hair, she looked brittle, as if she might crack at any moment. He wasn't sure what he could do to give her comfort. It was never easy going in and placing a value on the things that were left after a loved one had passed on. He couldn't even offer the assurance that the afterlife was pleasant.

Maybe the King of Annwyn would think Madam Callaway's life well-lived and grant her peace on the other side of the river beyond the fairies. But she could just as easily be drowned in the river of damned souls or eternally trapped in Annwyn, watching the endless party but never able to participate in it—what mortals knew as purgatory. Who knew how the King judged? Guessing the mind of a fairy was a sure way to go mad. Would delving into the secrets of Callaway House have the same effect on him?

"I'll take you upstairs, and then we can finish off in the kitchen and do any paperwork." She didn't wait for him to answer.

He followed her up to the second floor. His hand alighted on the mahogany bannister for only a second. A semi-clothed couple embracing filled his mind.

The man kissed down her neck as she arched her back, her leg lifting to reveal the tops of her stockings.

Caspian jerked his hand back, but the image lingered, with the promise of everything else he'd see. That was just a taste. The raw sensuality of the vision burned in his blood, rousing a hunger he'd pushed aside after Natalie's betrayal.

He'd never told her he was psychometric, and she'd never told him she had a lover—he'd found out because she'd made the mistake of bringing him into their home. They'd both lied by omission and in the end they'd both had too many secrets.

He paused halfway up the sweeping staircase. He'd made a mistake. He couldn't do this job. Not without losing himself in the lives of the women who'd lived here.

"These are the bedrooms, but most haven't been used in years." Lydia's voice drifted back to him.

With his hands by his sides, Caspian walked up the last few stairs. Lydia was opening doors as she went down the hall. The walls were hung with paintings, and a sculpture of a seminude woman playing a harp overlooked the entrance below. Caspian glanced up at the chandelier hanging from the center of a very ornate ceiling rose. While it was in need of a serious dusting, it was also worth some serious money.

"The rose and decorative cornices are all original," Lydia said as she came back to his side.

"I can see that." He was beginning to think that there was going to be a whole lot of original in Callaway House. He'd expected most of it to have been sold off or destroyed. "It's a beautiful home."

She nodded, her lips twitching in a sad semblance of a smile. "It needs repairs."

That was the problem with old houses. They were old and needed to be maintained. He made a couple more notes. In the silence he listened to the house creaking and for a moment he felt more than the history. The hair on the back of his neck prickled, but even as he lifted his gaze and glanced casually around he knew there was nothing there. But he'd felt it. A Grey. The one he'd seen earlier or a different one? Neither option was appealing. He turned around and faced the row of doors as if nothing had happened. Lydia was watching him too closely for him to slip up. Maybe he was just being overly paranoid about fairies.

In the first room a wrought-iron bed covered in a frilly quilt took up the center. To the side was a matching dressing table and mirror. None of it looked cheap. Against his better judgment, he crossed the threshold and touched the wooden top of the dressing table.

A young woman cried as she packed away makeup. But there were other women before her. He skipped past those impressions without stopping, back to the piece's creation at the turn of the century.

Slowly he drew his hand back. If Callaway House had antiques in every room, he was going to be here far longer than he'd expected. He looked more closely at the glass in the mirror, but nothing moved beyond the surface. What were the odds he'd find two fairy-touched mirrors in one day? One should be enough for anyone. And two Greys? Dylis hadn't been joking when she'd mentioned the increase in fairy activity in the area because of the hunt for the Window.

"Is all the furniture original?"

"It may not all be totally original, but most if it's quite old. We haven't altered anything since closing to the public."

"That was nearly thirty years ago." His eyebrows drew together but only for a moment. Probably around the same time Lydia was born.

"My grandmother didn't use these rooms and saw no reason to change them."

He looked at Lydia again, this time seeing the expensive suit and the careful grooming. She looked like a businesswoman—but not any businesswoman; she looked like one at the top of her game who'd eat for breakfast anyone who flinched in her presence. Madam Callaway would've been the same, he was sure. She'd taken serious risks to keep the house. A widowed woman opening her house to other men's mistresses? While he could almost hear the scandalous conversation that would happen in town, the house didn't give off that vibe at all. It seemed empty when it wanted to be full, hanging on the memories of when it was in use and the parties were in full swing.

"What do you do for a living?"

She glanced at him. "Public relations."

He smiled, seeing the connection immediately. "You learned from your grandmother."

"It's all about presentation. Callaway House was always spoken about as the place to party. Everyone knew what really happened, but it was the guests and the entertainment that kept people coming back for more. Once the mistresses left, people still came. Musicians and poets, artists—it was always a gathering place for… interesting people."

"You're very open about it."

"I can't really hide that I'm a Callaway." She glared at him as if daring him to challenge her. Her dark brown eyes weren't nearly as fierce as she thought. He could see the sadness and the many hours spent fighting to prove herself respectable.

He knew because he fought those same battles, only he could never talk about his family secret. Fairies didn't exist. It was much, much safer for the average person to believe that instead of the truth.

He walked past the other open doors, glancing in and making a quick assessment. He knew he'd have to spend more time up here to assess properly. Time would have dulled many of the everyday impressions, but the stronger emotional ones would linger. They were all around him. He let the back of his hand touch the wall experimentally.

She wrapped her legs around his hips as he lifted her against the wall. Her back arched as her lover pressed closer, unable to wait until they reached her bedroom.

Caspian drew his hand away, but the memory of lust was hot in his blood. The house groaned around him as if reluctant to let him forget. He drew in a slow breath and tried to clear his head before moving on.

Lydia led him up the next flight of stairs. When she

glanced over her shoulder at him, for a moment he was seeing someone else, someone younger, but no less aware of what she was doing as she led him upstairs. He blinked and Lydia was back, one eyebrow raised—but she wasn't leading him up the stairs for an illicit liaison. He swallowed hard as the idea took hold with far too much ease. The house was sliding under his defenses and blurring reality with the impossible.

He wasn't going to be sleeping with anyone in Callaway House. But it was just another reminder of everything he'd been missing since his divorce. Of course, if it weren't for the fairy blood in his veins, he wouldn't be in this situation in the first place. He'd be able to have a nice, normal relationship. Yet when he glanced at Lydia's back, he couldn't shake the image of exploring these rooms in a far more intimate fashion. His fingers curled, and he pressed them against the still tender iron-burn to help tamp down any further visions.

On the third floor the grandeur disappeared and was replaced with a homier feel. She opened two doors. One room looked lived in. This must have been Madam Callaway's bedroom. But instead of talking, Lydia just stood back, her face a little paler. As with the other bedrooms, it was beautifully furnished in a matching suite. He turned and faced the other room, unwilling to ask anything when Lydia's loss was so fresh.

The other bedroom was different. He crossed the corridor and went in. This one only had a single bed. The white suite looked much more recent than the rest of the house. He touched the bed for half a heartbeat.

"This was your room." His words were little more than a whisper. Lydia had grown up here.

"Until I went to college. After my mother left me here, Gran stopped the parties."

"How old were you?"

"Three months."

He opened his mouth but didn't know what to say. It wasn't like his childhood had been conventional, but at least his had been private. People had thought he was imaginative when he'd mention seeing fairies, but Lydia had grown up in the shadow of her grandmother's business and without a mother. That couldn't have been easy.

"I'm sorry."

"Don't be. I don't remember her. She had me at seventeen and took off. I had a nanny and Gran and that was all I knew until I went to school. Then I realized how different my family was." She crossed her arms as if shielding herself from the cruel barbs kids made. But there was no defense.

He knew he shouldn't pry—he was here to assess the estate, not chat up its owner—but he couldn't help wanting to know more about her, wanting to melt her cool façade. "And your father?"

"No idea. I think Gran blamed herself and that's why she shut down the parties. Helen had started joining in, but Gran didn't realize until she was pregnant and then it all fell apart." Lydia leaned against the door as if she needed the support. "And they're just the recent skeletons. Wait until you start digging." She forced a smile. "Still, I loved growing up here." Her voice softened as if she was remembering happier times. "The stories, the dress-ups—there is a whole wardrobe of fancy clothes—I was surrounded by people who loved me. It could have been worse. She could have taken me with her."

They looked at each other for a moment, but he didn't know what to say. He couldn't change her past no matter how much of it he could see. He wouldn't assess the room that had been hers—not by using his talent, anyway. The furniture wasn't antique; he could just make a visual judgment the way a more human assessor would.

Lydia broke the silence. "Shall we go downstairs?"

"Is there much more to see?" Already he was tallying the hours.

"Not much. The kitchen, the yard, and the old stable building that hasn't been opened in too many years. Plus the three cabins on the verge of collapse—rumor is they were used to make and store whisky during Prohibition." She closed the doors and they began walking down the two flights to ground level.

"Are any of them full of antiques?"

"That would depend on your definition, Mr. Mort."

"Caspian." The decorative light fixture in the stairwell looked as though it had been installed around the same time electricity was connected. "I think assessing the house is going to take me longer that I thought."

"You sound dismayed… Caspian."

His name on her lips sounded nice. He wanted to hear it again. The walls seemed to sigh around him, the slow languorous sigh of a satisfied lover, reminding him there was a reason he hadn't dated since his divorce. He saw too much and could never be honest. He wasn't going to repeat the same mistake; the next person he was with would know the truth.

"Not at all. I love old furniture and looking into its past." Spending more time with her wasn't going to be difficult at all.

"But?" She paused on the landing, one hand on the railing.

Caspian stood opposite her and let his fingertips brush the wood. He didn't have to imagine the parties that went on below; he could see them. Laid over each other in a haze of alcohol, perfume, and skin. If he closed his eyes and concentrated, he'd be able to separate them all instead of just feeling the rush of excitement and the heat of desire. The yearning that lingered long after everyone had left. Just being in the house was crumbling the walls he usually put up against getting lost in the past.

Could he do this job without drowning? He didn't need it, but he wanted it. There was so much here—and then there was Lydia. This close he could smell her floral perfume, something soft and almost faded that she'd probably put on in the morning, and he wasn't sure if the heat in his blood was entirely from the past.

She was watching him. He needed to get a grip and focus on the present. She tilted her head a fraction, a small smile on her lips as if she was appraising him and liking what she saw. If only she knew... she'd run.

"But it's going to take time." This was not a one-evening job, or even a one-weekend job. And if there was furniture or items in the outbuildings it could really drag on. Although there were worse places to be working.

"I know. But it has to be done."

He nodded. He didn't want anyone else to do it, even though he wasn't sure he could do it without getting lost in history. "Has the house been valued?"

"It will be. Once that's done and you're done, the

carve-up can begin." Her words caught in her throat and she turned away to walk down the last flight of stairs.

He felt the shock as a physical blow, breaking apart the pieces that made up Callaway House would be like destroying any artifact. He suppressed the urge to voice his objections. This wasn't his house, and he knew nothing about Madam Callaway's will, only that Lydia obviously didn't want that to happen either.

"You're selling?" was all he managed to say as he followed her to the rear of the house and into the kitchen.

"Hopefully not. But the will may be contested, so I have to be prepared." Her lips turned down, but she lifted her gaze to him. "Still, it's got to be done and it's not your problem. So, when will you start?"

Caspian looked at the notes he'd made, then back at Lydia. Her eyebrows were slightly raised as she waited for his response. He wanted to be something else, someone else so she wouldn't see him and think of her grandmother's death. No matter what he did, death surrounded him. The joy of being fairy.

He should finish this job as fast as possible because an attraction to Lydia would only end badly. Yet he wanted to see her blond hair loose and without the suit she wore like armor. When he blinked, the image of her leading him up the stairs to the bedrooms remained. A taunt? A glimpse of the future? Or the past teasing him with things he couldn't have?

"Did your grandmother have any of the furniture valued previously? Or did she keep a list of items for insurance?"

Lydia pushed a black folder over the kitchen table.

"This is everything I could find. But I don't know how complete it is, or how accurate. I know it's not recent."

He picked up the folder without touching the table. He was very used to not touching surfaces. Usually his defense against unwanted information was better, but the sheer weight of history around him was unavoidable.

Caspian flicked a couple of pages and saw the hand-written list. Spots of water had stained the page. Tears. He didn't need to see the past to know that. "I am very sorry for your loss."

"Most people won't be." She forced a smile that held no warmth, and he knew it was one that got well used. "Once the press finds out…" She shook her head.

He could imagine. The house's history would be in the news again, and Lydia by default. "You don't have to be here while I work if you'd rather keep your distance."

Her eyes flashed, hard as stone. "I want to be here. This is my house."

"I'd like you to be here too, to answer any questions I have." Now he would have to ask some questions, otherwise she might ask a few too many of her own about why he insisted on touching everything. Everything but her, even though he wanted to reach out and run his fingers over skin instead of lifeless wood and metal. Old memories of other people's lives were a hollow reminder of everything he'd walked away from. "Evenings?"

"Weekend?"

"I have a shop to run on Saturday."

She pressed her lips together as she thought. "You don't mind coming here for just a few hours at a time?"

"Not at all." He was sure that would be all he'd be able to handle of the past, and of being near Lydia.

Maybe it was the house causing such a strong reaction. It wasn't easy being surrounded by lust and not feeling something. His blood warmed at the acknowledgment. He would not be driven by instinct like a sex-crazed fairy. It was the house getting to him. Next time he would be better guarded.

"Great. Six o'clock tomorrow? I'll try not to get caught up at work."

"And if you are?"

"You'll have to wait." She neatly put him back in his place with a few words and a smile.

If he hadn't glimpsed the heat in her eyes that sparked for just a second he would have thought the attraction was only going one way. Instead his heart kicked over again as he shook her hand and said good-bye. The heat of her skin seared into his palm, and her fingers trailed over the back of his hand for a moment too long.

As he slid into the seat of his car, he couldn't be sure whether it was Lydia's lingering touch or the lure of the fairy-touched mirror in the backseat that had his pulse racing. Both were dangerous. And yet he couldn't help wanting more of each...

Chapter 3

CASPIAN PULLED INTO HIS GARAGE, THE CALL OF THE mirror humming in his blood. It was almost as if he didn't have any choice but to pull it out and do a further examination from his workbench. He hesitated, not wanting to give in to the lure. But the sooner he could give the mirror a proper assessment, the sooner he could get rid of it, and the trouble it would bring.

He'd worked too hard for too long to avoid all politics of the Court. No one needed to know he was the Prince's son. The father who'd raised him certainly hadn't guessed Caspian's real heritage, and he had a feeling his mother had never said a word about her affair with the irresistible fairy Prince. The Court of Annwyn was dangerous, and the less he had to do with it, the better. If this was what they were looking for, they were welcome to it. The four hundred and fifty dollars was a small price to be free of fairies—yet still in their good favor.

He carefully pulled off the wrapping he'd put on the mirror to protect it during transportation. His finger trailed over the carved walnut frame. The detail was beautiful, the scrollwork smooth and even. A well-made piece even without the fairy influence. He kept his gaze on the wood and not the glass, yet even at the edges of his vision he saw the shadows move, thickening and becoming clearer. He closed his eyes against the distraction and let the wood's past form pictures in his mind.

Caspian saw a middle-aged woman, then a younger version receiving a gift. A wedding gift. The house where it had hung for one hundred years and back to the man who'd carved the frame. His first impression had been right. The frame was authentic, which made it worth far more than what he'd paid. It also made him doubt it was what the fairies were looking for. This was human made, not fairy crafted. Merely enchanted, and not the Window.

Keeping his eyes closed, he let his fingers drift to the glass, not sure what he'd see in the enchanted pane, only that the magic was in the glass, not the wood. Darkness, storage. The back of the wardrobe where it had been kept. He went deeper, older. Something shifted and the glass cooled beneath his skin. Then he saw the fairy who'd placed the enchantment on the human-made mirror. A pregnant woman—a fairy—who smiled as she stared and Caspian knew she was seeing the Court. She had charmed the mirror so she wouldn't get homesick. Images skipped past and he saw she was in lust with a human man, and to satisfy her desire she was playing his wife and in return he was giving her what a fairy man couldn't—children.

Caspian's lips twisted in a bitter smile. The fairies sneered at humans unless they wanted heirs; then they used magic to lure and seduce the unfortunate human to their bed. Fairy men took human women, and fairy women took human men. It was the only way fairies could breed and usually the children were born in Annwyn, ensuring continuation of the line.

Somehow his mother had convinced the Prince to let her go and give birth to him in the mortal world. Not a fairy and not quite mortal yet bound by the rules of both worlds. Still, it could have been worse; he could've actually been a fairy.

He looked at the beautiful woman in the mirror. She would have gone home to give birth. How long had the woman remained in the mortal world before growing bored and returning to Annwyn for good? Had she left behind a heartbroken husband? And what of her child? The mirror didn't have those answers.

Beyond the old images the shadows moved. Caspian opened his eyes. The fairy Court was before him as if he was looking through a window, not through the veil and into another world. The clothes glittered in silver and gold, a glittering rainbow of velvets, brocades, and silks cut in styles no human had ever worn. One man drew all attention as he danced to music Caspian could almost hear. Changing partners and spinning them around. Elegant and graceful in a way no human could be. For a heartbeat he wanted to join the dance instead of just watching. Heads turned as if he'd spoken the thought aloud. Eyes as pale as ice and twice as cold stared.

Eyes exactly like his. His father.

Caspian yanked his hand away, his skin stinging like he'd been holding snow. He flipped the blanket over the glass, his heart racing to get away. It was too late. They'd all seen him. His father had seen him. Caspian stepped back, but the temptation lingered to glance again at the beauty no living human should see. If a human danced, or drank, or ate the food, they'd be trapped in Annwyn forever or until the King decided to release them.

And he was human enough that the rule applied to him.

He swallowed and took another step back. Then another. Each pace was a victory of willpower over seduction. The more distance he put between himself and the enchanted glass, the more its power waned. When he closed the connecting door between the garage and house, the lure was almost gone. At least the mirror was only enchanted, not fairy-made. Fairy-made objects were a whole other bundle of trouble. The memory of the Grey from the garage sale rose in his mind.

He leaned against the door and closed his eyes. Images of the party in Annwyn flickered past and longing rose in his blood. Only it wasn't the fairies who turned and looked at him; it was Lydia, beckoning him to dance at Callaway House.

Reality was blurring. He needed to ground himself in ordinary tasks. He opened his eyes, but his house was quiet. There were fairies here, but he never saw them. Brownies had taken up residence after his breakup with Natalie and they kept the house clean. As in immaculate and far cleaner than any human could manage. In exchange, he left out tea and cookies as was the proper thing to do.

The tiny porcelain tea set—an eighteenth-century Minton children's set—that sat on the corner of the kitchen counter was empty, so he topped it up with a little milk in the jug and a little sugar in the bowl, some tea leaves and water to the teapot, and a wafer on each of the plates. He had no desire to be sharing his house with an angry Brownie who felt disrespected. When dealing with fairies, he'd learned if they couldn't be avoided they should be respected… in the same way people respected any dangerous wildlife: keep a good distance where possible, don't make eye contact, and run.

In addition to cleaning, the Brownies kept the Greys away. Because the power of the Court ran in his blood, fairies flocked to him like moths to a light. A fairy banished from Court became a Grey; cut off without access to the magic, they began to lose energy. Some chose stature and lost their looks, becoming skeletal ghouls of nightmares. Some chose to remain beautiful and became the tiny imps or pixies of children's tales that would shrink to magnificent nothing over time. Others chose power and became ugly, small, and spiteful boggarts. He'd seen them all and everything in between. Brownies, however, either chose not to live at Court, or they had been exiled to the mortal world, which was a social death instead of actual death. Since he never saw them, he'd never had the chance to ask, and they probably wouldn't tell him anyway.

Caspian made himself a cup of coffee and waited. As much as he avoided fairies, Dylis was an exception. She'd been charged with his care at his birth and would kill to protect him. After thirty-five years of her company, he was used to having her flit in and out and he'd learned to ignore her in public. He expected she'd breeze in any second.

Halfway through the coffee, Dylis appeared. He sensed her a heartbeat before he saw her, a blur of sliver and purple as she jumped onto the counter and helped herself to one of the cookies he'd left out for the Brownies. "Nice mirror," she said between bites.

"If you like that kind of thing."

"Oh, come on. Don't you even want to peek at the party? I do. It's been ages since I was at Court." She fixed her glacier blue gaze on him, like a sullen doll. A slash of silver passed for a skirt and was topped with a purple frock coat. Dylis enjoyed a flair for the dramatic. But this doll was armed; wherever she went, a short silver sword hung at her side. Dylis was more deadly than she looked.

"You went last weekend."

"That was business."

"Reporting back."

Dylis laid her hand on her heart. "Never. I was getting the latest gossip." She shook her head. "You didn't hear it from me, but there's been a major falling out and things are very unbalanced."

"I don't care for Court politics." The games, the scheming, and the cutthroat—literally—behavior made human politicians look like kids playing dress-up.

"You will if it bleeds through the veil."

Caspian put down his coffee. "What do you mean?"

"The river isn't flat." She lowered her voice further so he had to strain to hear. "It has ripples."

The last time the river of damned souls had rippled, millions had died of the Spanish flu. If it broke its banks, death would spill into the mortal world and plague would just be the beginning.

"Does it have to do with the mirror they want?"

Dylis shook her head. "That's a separate but related issue."

Of course it was, because fairies never did anything the easy way. There had to be layers of intrigue and dealings and games.

"But there are whispers a Grey is after the Window." She was frowning at her cookie. Was she actually concerned?

The memory of the tall Grey chilled his blood. A banished fairy, an enchanted mirror, and ripples on the river. He didn't believe in coincidences, not when the Court was involved.

"And by talking about them you're feeding them." He would not be dragged into Court intrigue.

"It can't be allowed to fall into the Grey's hands. With it he could get back into Annwyn and cause all kinds of strife." She looked up at him. "Your father is concerned."

His father. His fairy father. The man he'd never met and whose sole contribution to his life was to assign Dylis to his protection.

"I said I'll keep an eye out." And even though his gut was telling him to run, he knew he would check any mirror that came across his path. The idea of a Grey sneaking into Annwyn and causing trouble didn't sit well. That there were already ripples was a concern. What was going on?

"You swear?"

Caspian shook his head. He wasn't going to be drawn into making a deal and agreeing to help.

"You're no fun." She kicked the teacup.

Caspian smiled and straightened it up, knowing she wouldn't really do anything to anger the Brownies. He knew she liked to socialize with them. He'd heard the music late at night when they'd thought he was asleep.

"You need to come to Court. It's so much more fun than," she waved her hand around, "this place."

"And when I fall into step and get caught in the dance? Or if I sip the wine? Taste the food? What then?" He knew. He'd be stuck until the King or his father chose to release him, but the cost would be his soul.

"Fine." She crossed her arms and turned her back as if she was angry.

Maybe she was. Maybe she'd been asked to convince him to visit Court. Or maybe she was just trying to get her own way. Sometimes she was worse than his ex-wife. Dylis had hated Natalie. She'd never trusted her. He should've listened and saved himself the heartache.

Dylis's back straightened. If she'd been a cat her fur would've been standing on end; as it was he could sense the shift in her energy. Caspian followed her line of sight out the kitchen window.

His heart forgot to beat. In his yard was the Grey he'd seen earlier. He tried to act like he was casually looking out of the window, but the Grey raised his hand in greeting.

"He's seen us," Dylis whispered.

"Oh yeah, and he knows we've seen him."

"Where did you get that mirror?" She spoke without taking her gaze off the tall fairy.

"Garage sale."

"The one time you go without me and you come back with a Grey on your tail." Her teeth remained clenched together.

The Grey vanished as if he'd never been there, and Dylis moved as if freed from a spell.

"I need to see the mirror."

"It's not the Window, only enchanted. And if it's his, he can have it." Losing the money was nothing compared to what the Grey could take. A banished fairy would do anything to get home, and the soul of a changeling would be a sizeable bargaining chip. If the Grey suspected which fairy was his father, it could be an even bigger problem.

If one enchanted mirror brought a Grey to his house, what kind of trouble would the Window bring? Getting caught up in fairy problems never went well for humans, and he didn't think it would go much better for changelings. Yet he was already involved. Even if it was as simple as examining every mirror, if the Court wanted to they could force him into a deal to find it or pay the penalty. A Grey could do the same.

"It may not be that simple."

No, it never was with fairies. "You can look at the mirror. I've seen enough of the Court for one day."

Dylis opened her mouth, but he turned away and she didn't press the point. Instead she flung the garage door open with more magic than necessary. He flinched as the door handle slammed against the wall and left a dent. The Brownies would fix it, but that wasn't the point.

With the door open and Dylis unwrapping the mirror, Caspian needed to put some distance between him and the glass. He needed to do something human and mundane. So he went upstairs to work. He needed to tally his hours and send an estimate for his work at Callaway House. As he waited for the laptop to wake up, he could almost hear the tune of the music coming from Annwyn. In his mind he could see the dancers. Their beautiful clothes and unearthly faces. It was unnatural and yet he could feel the lure the same as any fairy. The call to go home.

A shiver raced over his skin and produced a shudder. He was home. He was human; this was where he'd been born and this was where he was staying.

Chapter 4

LYDIA LAY IN BED LISTENING TO THE PERKY CHATTER of the breakfast radio hosts. In another minute or so the daily horoscope would come on. While she didn't believe in their predictions, imagining the outcome was an interesting start to the day.

"Capricorn, break free of routine and embrace change."

Embrace change. If change looked like Caspian, she'd gladly embrace it. She smiled to herself.

When was the last date she'd been on? She frowned. Four months, five months? It had started off well enough, but then he'd expected her to spend most evenings with him and she couldn't. She had work and Gran, and she just didn't have time to squeeze in a relationship.

Now she was about to inherit a crumbling plantation house, had a mortgage on her apartment, and a job that wouldn't stretch to pay for repairs. Her fingers scrunched the sheets.

Embrace change!

Maybe it was time to sell. She could move to another city. She could travel. She'd stayed because of Gran, but she no longer had that tie. She could do whatever she wanted. She opened her eyes waiting for a sense of freedom or something to jolt her into action. Nothing. She felt as empty as Callaway House. Even when it had just been Gran living there, the old place had lived and breathed. Now it was a shell.

Except Caspian hadn't seen it that way. He was fascinated even as he tried to remain impartial. He hadn't asked leading questions about the house and it's colorful past. He was genuinely interested... and interested in her.

She hadn't missed his glances. She'd stolen more than a few herself. There was something different about him, but she couldn't say what. However, she was interested enough to want to find out more. She flipped back the covers and sat up. She had a day at the office to put in before meeting Caspian at Callaway House. The weather forecast came on, another patchy day of undecided spring weather. Dress for summer but add a jacket, and take an umbrella just in case. She reached out to turn off the radio, but the announcer's next words slammed into her.

"Madam Callaway has died at age eighty-nine. No doubt there are some relieved power brokers this morning knowing the secrets of the mistress hotel are safe with her."

Lydia drew in a breath and held it. She'd expected something two weeks ago, been braced for a story then, but when the media hadn't picked it up she'd relaxed. She rubbed her hand over her face as her eyes stung. She wasn't going to cry. She'd done enough of that before burying Gran in a small private service—one her mother hadn't bothered to attend. Some daughter Helen was.

Lydia took a deep breath. She was in public relations. This is what she did for a living. First rule, control the situation.

She needed to come up with a statement that seemed

to give the media information but that told them nothing, certainly nothing salacious. She'd been hoping Gran's death and sorting out the will would happen quickly and quietly so she could stay well clear of the gossip, but Gran would have wanted to go out in style. Maybe a big party was just the thing after all…

Maybe a very public memorial would be enough for people to sate their curiosity while reminding them that Gran was a much loved person, someone who'd made a difference in many people's lives. Lydia nodded to herself. Yes. That was how she'd respond to the media. She'd lay down a challenge and see who was brave enough to show their face and mourn Nanette Callaway.

And in the meantime, she'd figure out who tipped off the press.

Something hit his bedroom window with a thump and a flutter. Caspian opened his eyes, awake and alert even though morning was still thinking about arriving. For a moment all he heard was the pounding of his heart. Then the flutter-bump happened again. He turned to face the window and saw a small bird against the pane. The bird's wing caught in the streetlight and shone iridescent turquoise. A fairy wren.

Flutter-bump.

The bird was on the inside trying to get out.

Cold filled his gut. If a wren was in his house…

"Shit." *The Brownies*.

He threw back the covers and ran down the stairs two at a time. Ice pumped in his veins, fueling a panic he hadn't felt in a very long time.

He skidded into the kitchen and stopped as if he'd hit a wall. The antique tea set was scattered across the floor. Sugar was everywhere. A broken saucer had sent shards of porcelain over the tiles. His eyes widened at the wanton destruction of an irreplaceable one-hundred-and-fifty-year-old tea set. It might have been worth hundreds of dollars, but to him it was worth more. He'd purchased it especially for the Brownies. He'd taken their arrival as a sign of good fortune and protection.

The skin on his back prickled as if a ghost was running its fingers down his spine. Caspian slowly lifted his gaze from the floor, aware he was being watched. The gaunt man from the yard sale stood in his kitchen, sipping from a tiny teacup. The echo of fairy beauty still clung to the Grey like an extra shadow. The man's lips turned up in what could only be called a victory smile.

Caspian did a quick threat assessment. The Grey looked pretty enough to have only been recently banished.

But still Caspian was out of his depth.

For several heartbeats neither of them moved. Caspian looked away first. If it hadn't been five in the morning, he might've been smarter and pretended as if he hadn't seen the Grey. Although the smashed tea set had already given away that he could see fairies. He really hoped the Brownies were safe.

The Grey set the cup down on the saucer. "I appreciate your hospitality, Caspian ap Felan ap Gwyn ap Nudd."

The use of his fairy name to the fourth generation was a sign of respect, but coming from this man it was more of a threat. The Grey knew exactly who he was, and no doubt knew exactly how the fairy blood in him had manifested in the mortal world. The Grey had watched him touch the mirror at the garage sale. He knew he shouldn't have bought it.

His heart hammered, rattling his ribs. Where the hell was Dylis? Caspian inclined his head but didn't speak. Fairies could twist words to their own advantage better than any human lawyer.

"You have been well schooled. Be assured I'm not after your soul. In my present state I have no use for it." He flicked his hand dismissively as if he were used to being obeyed.

But that didn't mean he wouldn't take Caspian's soul to trade later. Caspian waited. Running would serve no purpose.

The Grey walked around the kitchen counter. His clothes were finely made and highly decorated. Velvet and brocade in muted shades, a memory of their past color. They had yet to show signs of wear from being cut off from the power of the Court. He'd obviously been a lord, and yet he wore no sword of fairy silver. Whatever he'd done had been bad to be cut off and cast out without a weapon.

Caspian's initial adrenaline-fueled panic gave way to something much colder. A bead of sweat rolled down his bare back. It was one thing to see fairies but another to have one break into his house and confront him.

The Grey's boots crunched over the pieces of china. Caspian tried not to wince. The Grey was doing it deliberately and enjoying every pace. Each grinding step was another insult to the Brownies. He was acting as if he were still at Court looking down his nose at those who chose to live in the mortal world. But here, fairies, like

Dylis, and the Brownies outranked a Grey no matter how recently banished.

Even a changeling like him outranked this Grey. Pity there was no one here to enforce the rules and protocol. Caspian willed himself to remain still and wait, trying to think of ways to get rid of the Grey without it being construed as an insult or a sign of weakness. He drew a blank.

"While I don't want your soul, I do want something from you." The Grey smiled the way a fox would smile at a cornered rabbit. His pale eyes glinted in the predawn light.

Caspian was as good as dead. If he refused he was as good as dead, and if he helped he was as good as dead. It was simply a matter of time and a question of who would kill him first. The Grey or his father—the Crown Prince of Death, guardian of the veil between worlds—for breaking the rules and making a deal with a banished fairy.

Caspian watched the Grey but said nothing.

"I'm looking for a mirror, one lost in your world centuries ago." The Grey paused as if waiting for a reaction and got none. "It's very valuable, and you shall help me find it."

Caspian was willing to bet that the mirror he'd picked up at the garage sale wasn't the one the Grey wanted, otherwise they wouldn't be having this one-sided conversation. The Grey would have merely taken it and left. This Grey knew about the Window. Was he the one Dylis had warned about? However, the Grey didn't know that Caspian knew as much about the Court as he did.

"What does it look like?" If he spoke carefully and gave no real answers, perhaps the Grey would leave, perhaps Dylis would show up… hell, perhaps his father would show up and kill the Grey. All unlikely outcomes. The best he could hope for was politely refusing and hoping the Grey left without doing more damage.

"If I knew that, I wouldn't need you, would I?" The Grey took a couple of paces and kicked a chipped cup. It spun across the tiles and smashed against the wall sending shards across the kitchen floor.

Caspian's fingers curled at his side, but he forced himself to remain still. He couldn't react. The Grey was trying to goad him.

"What makes you think I'll help you?" Caspian knew he was on dangerous ground, baiting the Grey, but he wouldn't stand for such a blatant invasion in his home.

Before Caspian could even track the movement, the Grey had closed the distance and snagged a handful of Caspian's hair.

Caspian bit back a curse but didn't struggle. If he got angry, he'd make mistakes and he couldn't afford to make mistakes with this Grey. This close he could see the fine lines of desperation etched around the man's eyes. The too sharp jut of his cheekbones. Recently banished but trying to hold onto his looks and power.

A human would have looked into those pale bottomless eyes and done whatever was asked of them. The magic slid over Caspian's skin and fell away without leaving a trace. He drew in a breath and looked steadily back. He wouldn't show even a glimmer of fear, even though his stomach writhed with ice-cold snakes.

"You will help me because you don't have a choice." The Grey glared at him, and again Caspian felt the shimmer of magic as the Grey tried to enchant him.

This time the magic didn't roll away quite so easily. If the Grey kept going there was a chance Caspian's defenses would crack. And he'd thought all that time with Dylis learning how to be safe around fairies was a waste. Now he wished he'd paid greater attention and been a better student instead of just doing enough to get her off his back. As he stared down the Grey, Caspian was sure he could see subtle changes; a deepening of the lines, a dulling of his skin, and a fraying of his clothing. Every time the Grey tried to enchant him, every time he used magic, he was losing a little more. Soon he would have to choose. Stature or looks or power—and even then a Grey couldn't live forever. Cut off from the magic of the Court, they were condemned to a powerless and slow and ugly death. The thing all fairies feared.

Caspian waited until the Grey stopped trying to enchant him, then he crossed his arms and smiled like he hadn't noticed the magic gliding over his bare skin. "I need more information."

He had no idea where to even start looking.

The Grey's jaw worked as he considered what to say next.

Caspian was just as curious about how much the Grey would reveal as he was about the mirror. It must be something very special for a Grey to come to him for help. Did he not fear that Caspian would go directly to Court with this news—or was he aware that Caspian never went near Court?

With a snarl the Grey released Caspian and stepped away as if touching a human would infect him with mortality. "The mirror is fairy-made and very old. It hasn't been seen in over a century. I hope to find it and return it to your grandfather." The Grey folded his hands in front of him and tried not to look desperate.

The act would have worked better if he hadn't started off by destroying the tea set and being haughty and rough.

While he would have liked to laugh and tell the Grey no outright, he didn't. He was having a conversation with a Grey and so far hadn't agreed to anything and he still had his soul. He was winning, and hopefully he could end this his way and with no nasty side effects.

"You hope to buy your way back to Court."

"You're a little too perceptive for a human."

"I'm a little too fairy to be human." Every word out of Caspian's mouth was carefully spoken so it couldn't be misconstrued.

"You have psychometry, you can read objects. Find me the Window." The Grey thumped his fist on the kitchen counter.

"Why?"

The Grey blinked, startled as if no one had ever questioned him before. "Because I said."

Caspian shook his head. "You have no authority over me, and I don't make deals with fairies."

The Grey nodded, his pale eyes cold and calculating. "Not today. Maybe not tomorrow. But you will help me find the mirror I seek." Then he turned and walked down the hallway and out the door.

For several heartbeats Caspian didn't move. His breaths were shaky as he let the tension go. He'd survived—that was a small victory. He curled his fingers and forced movement though his limbs. Slowly he picked up the larger pieces of the tea set and placed them on the kitchen counter, then he swept up the shards and spilled sugar and put them in the bin. As he worked he became aware he was being watched.

Dylis. She could go back to Annwyn and stay there. He ignored her the way he wished he'd ignored the Grey as he filled the little teapot. A hairline crack ran up the side. It wouldn't last. Dylis was silent for once, as if she knew that speaking first would be the wrong thing to do. He took a breath and forced calm into his voice.

"Who was he?" Caspian didn't turn to look at his godmother.

"Shea ap Greely."

"And who the hell is he?" Caspian rounded on Dylis.

Dylis cast her gaze over the damaged cups as if debating how much to tell him. With a muttered curse she sat on the counter. "The ripples in the river of souls were caused by the Queen's not-so-subtle affair with Shea."

Now he was getting the full story out of Dylis instead of a hint designed to spike his curiosity. "And he got banished for it while she still gets to be Queen."

Dylis nodded. "Annwyn needs both King and Queen."

Caspian's jaw tensed. "So she gets away with cheating."

"Don't put your values on us. She and the King have both had lovers. When you live as long as we do, being faithful literally is an eternity. What matters is love. The very idea of sharing power is enough to make most of us swear off the very mortal affliction." Dylis glittered with fury as if all her power was trying to burst out of the tiny body she chose to wear in the mortal world. "Shea stole her heart from the King."

The Queen was no longer in love with the King; she was in love with Shea. That was what caused the ripples on the river of damned souls. Caspian didn't want to be caught in a power struggle between the King of Annwyn, the Queen, and her lover. No wonder the Prince was concerned. There was no way that was going to end well for anyone.

A sigh slipped past his lips. If the river broke its banks, there would be plague the likes of which the world hadn't seen since the Black Death.

A squabble and a hundred died.

A fight and thousands died.

If the King and Queen separated, the world was fucked.

"Finding the mirror will calm the river?" While he could turn his back on fairy politics, he couldn't walk away when their bickering bled through and started killing humans.

"It will help."

He nodded. "And where were you while Shea was trying to trick me? I thought you were supposed to help me with this stuff."

"I saw no reason to reveal myself," Dylis said. "You obeyed the rules. If you'd done something stupidly human, I'd have stepped in."

He considered the beautiful and annoying fairy and how little he knew about her. How little she told. "Shea knows you, that's why you hid." It was a bold assumption, but maybe she'd reveal something

"Everyone at Court knows everyone worth knowing."

Getting a straight answer from her was going to be like pulling out his own teeth. But she obviously had some standing when she was at Court. What a comedown it must be to spend time with him. "What do you know about the Window?"

It certainly wasn't the one he'd bought, but had that been bait laid out by Shea? A chance to watch and see what he was capable of? If it had been, he'd fallen for it.

He watched Dylis carefully; she'd been the one to alert him to the Window's existence, and the probability that it was in Charleston. She could be on Shea's side. And Shea's side wasn't the King's side. And while he may not be fairy, he knew which side he was on and it wasn't with a fairy banished for sleeping with another man's wife.

"Nothing more than I've already told you." That sounded like the truth. "I'll have to ask some careful questions. The Queen will have supporters and spies. And I'll need to let your father know Shea is actively looking for it."

"You do that." The words were harsher than he intended. He sighed. If Annwyn was in trouble, Dylis was right—whatever side she was on she was in danger. "Take care at Court."

"I always do." She stood and gave a half-bow. And then she was gone.

―⁓―

As a precaution Caspian took the enchanted mirror to work with him. He didn't want it in his house attracting anymore Greys. While it had seemed like a good idea at the time, after spending several hours in its company all he wanted to do was throw back its covering and gaze at the Court. He found things to do to keep himself busy and distracted. He prepped the till even though most people paid with credit. Gave everything a dust. Just because the furniture was old didn't mean it had to look like it came straight out of a museum. People had to be able to picture the Victorian armchair in their house and the art deco vase on their sideboard.

He paused at the china. He desperately needed a new tea set to woo back the Brownies. While he had some beautiful pieces in the shop, he had no children's sets. He'd have to stop by a toy store and hope for a china set. If he didn't get something today they wouldn't be happy and might disappear altogether—if they hadn't already.

The music of the Court filtered through his shop at the edge of his hearing. He couldn't sell the mirror as it was, it was too dangerous for anyone with a touch of fairy blood, and he couldn't keep it for the same reason. He should have known the bargain was too good to be true.

With careful footsteps, Caspian made sure he didn't follow the beat, no matter how tempting. That would be the first step in falling into the lure of the Court. He pulled a screwdriver out from under the counter and walked out the back. The mirror lay on the workbench still wrapped from being transported to the shop.

His fingers tightened around the plastic screwdriver handle even as he wanted to pull back the wrapping with his free hand and peek into Annwyn again. Before he could do something stupid, he slammed the screwdriver into the center of the mirror.

Glass cracked and for a second he smelled heady floral perfume like a garden in full bloom. Then it was gone and so was the music that had taunted him. Caspian swallowed down the sudden sense of loss. With his next breath he knew the threat was gone and he was free of the desire to see the Court once more.

He peeled back the wrapping to examine the damage. He'd devalued an antique as well as broke the enchantment. The old glass cut his reflection into pointed shards. Pale green fairy eyes looked back. But at least they were his own eyes.

But what about the mirror Shea wanted? Would he have the strength to shatter that one when the time came? And even if he did, what would be the price?

Chapter 5

CASPIAN PULLED INTO THE LONG DRIVE OF CALLAWAY House at dusk. In the fading light, the dark house almost looked forbidding. Yet he was eager to get inside. Eager to see Lydia.

He locked the car and knocked on the door, a faint echo of laughter lingering beneath his fingers. He couldn't help himself from looking over his shoulder. Were there any banished fairies living in the graveyard down the road, or following him? How far did Shea's power reach?

He shivered. People who couldn't see fairies didn't know how easy they had it.

The door opened and Lydia stood limned by light. Dressed simply in skinny jeans that showed off her long legs, ballet flats, and a shirt that hung down to her hips, she looked like she was dressed for a casual evening in. The jolt of raw attraction caught him off guard. He'd been expecting corporate Lydia. Not sexy-stay-at-home Lydia.

Caspian blinked to break the spell she'd cast. This wasn't her house, nothing he'd touched had indicated she lived here, and it sure as hell wasn't a date. Would it be wrong to ask her out for dinner? He should've grabbed something on the way over, but he was already late.

She smiled and stood to the side to let him in. "I didn't think you were coming."

"I, er, lost my keys." Caspian stood on the step, unwilling to push past in case he touched her and slid into the enchantment she didn't know she was casting. Bewitching. Lydia wasn't fairy; her power was far more potent.

She raised her eyebrows. "You don't seem like the disorganized type."

"I'm not usually." *Get a grip. She's not interested in you.* But she held his gaze for a moment too long for him to believe the lie he was telling himself.

"Ah." She nodded. "And I thought you were immune to Callaway House." Her lips curved in a small smile that made his chest constrict.

Caspian glanced down for a second and tried to find something to say. He didn't want her thinking he was flustered by the house's history; that would be worse than letting her think she affected him. He met her dark gaze. Chocolate brown, a color no fairy would have, yet no less mesmerizing. "It's not the house."

That was probably the wrong thing to say. He'd never been good at these things. Even Natalie had thought him eccentric, something she'd found endearing at first.

Her eyes widened for a second so fast he could've imagined it. "Come in."

He followed her into the hallway and was once again surrounded by the weight of history. This house had lived even before it had stopped being a family home. The Callaway name had once been respected. Rumors of gambling debts followed by the gradual fall from grace had tainted the name. He spent some time earlier doing a bit more basic research. Sometimes using the computer was easier than sifting through years of history—plus he didn't always get the full story by touch.

She closed the door, giving him a view of her butt. At least when she was in a suit and being cool or upset he could ignore the attraction that kept rising up. Now he could almost taste it in the air. If he'd met her anywhere else... he'd have done nothing because he'd have been too afraid to start anything because he knew where it would end up. He couldn't handle that again.

Keep it professional. "So, where did you want me to start?"

Lydia was studying him as if searching for something. If she looked too closely, would she realize that he wasn't quite human? And if she did, that flicker of desire would die.

"Someone released the details of Gran's death to the media." Her gaze never left him, and he knew this was a test. She suspected him.

"I heard the news. I understand why you'd want to keep it quiet." Again he was grateful that his life and troubles had all remained very private.

She nodded. "It wasn't you."

"No. I don't divulge details; it's not good for business." Neither was standing around chatting. If he hadn't been here for work, he'd have gladly spent hours talking to Lydia about anything and everything. It had been a long time since he'd felt at ease around someone—not enough to be himself and tell all, but enough to relax a little and enjoy her company. If he let himself slide down that path he could almost picture himself sharing the details about his life that he'd never told anyone. He'd vowed to be honest next time. To not get into a relationship without at least mentioning the psychometry... it was best for everyone that he never mentioned fairies.

She smoothed her hands over her thighs in a move that drew his gaze for longer than it should have. "You're all about business?"

"I run my own, it's only me, so yeah, it takes up a lot of time. But I like it. It's interesting to find out when a piece was made and working out what it's worth." His work had stopped him from drifting after Natalie. He'd thrown himself into it, partly out of necessity as he'd needed to eat and get another house, and partly because it was familiar and something he could control.

Now was the moment to explain how he worked and to see how she's react, before he let himself get too caught up in the idea of asking her out or thinking she'd accept. He looked at her and the way her lips curved, inviting and tempting, and the words that he should say failed to form. Asking her to believe in psychometry was as bad as asking her to believe he was a changeling prince.

"Every day something new to explore?"

He'd never thought of it that way. "Yeah… except for the paperwork."

She laughed, and warmth filled her eyes as if she was seeing him in a new light. "I think Gran would've liked you."

The tension in his shoulders eased and he smiled. He'd passed whatever test she'd set, even as he failed his own. The longer he went without telling her of his gift, the harder it would become to reveal. "Thank you."

He meant it; it felt like he was one step closer to Lydia seeing him as something other than the vulture valuing her grandmother's things. Small steps; after all, they weren't even dating. Maybe family secrets could wait until after the job was finished. Except in his heart he knew that would be too late. She would look back at this time and know he'd kept things from her. Would she even want to know the things he saw? He didn't half the time.

Lydia put her hand on his arm. "She might have even let you into a party." She sighed. "It's nice to talk about her without the slurs that usually follow."

"It's nice to hear more about her, the real woman, not the spin." Her hand was warm against him, the heat seeping through his shirt. The simple touch was a reminder of the human contact he'd shunned. A shimmer of desire slid over his skin. It would be very easy to fall and not think about the landing. Too easy. And he knew how destructive and devastating the impact could be.

For a moment she just looked at him as if not sure what to make of him. Her eyes darkened, inviting trouble. Then she grinned. "You're something different, Caspian."

Yes he was, and it was a good thing she didn't know how different.

———

Felan leaned against a tree in the cemetery. Above him the branches swept toward the sky, muttering softly. But he wasn't here for the whisperings of trees, or to enjoy the mortal world; he was waiting for someone.

The shrubs to his left gave a rustle and then a small fairy in dull clothing appeared, the exiled fairy he'd assigned to watch his son's house. The fairy bowed low as was proper when greeting the Crown Prince of Annwyn.

Felan inclined his head. "Full stature, I don't wish to stoop."

Once he and Chalmer had drank and gambled together. Now it was more than the veil that separated them. Yet he still trusted the fairy. If he didn't, he wouldn't have sent him to his son's house to be Caspian's Brownie.

"Your Highness, thank you for agreeing to meet your most humble servant at such short notice." The man gave another slight bow that put Felan on edge. Chalmer didn't bring good news and was afraid... yet not so afraid that he wouldn't spill.

"I don't have long." He had other meetings tonight and he didn't want to be seen talking to Chalmer; it would start rumors he could ill afford.

While he'd told Chalmer to attend the changeling, he hadn't said why. He'd done everything he could to ensure Caspian's safety after allowing him to be born in the mortal world. A lump formed in his throat that was very un-prince like, and more like that of a father who hadn't seen his son in thirty-five mortal years. He couldn't.

His fingers curled as if remembering the feel of the tiny babe in his arms. Just the once he'd held his son and kissed his downy hair. That was all he'd allowed himself—any more and his son would be in danger. He knew Caspian would grow up in a loving family; he'd seen their joy and had known he'd made the right decision. From what he'd heard, Caspian was everything a father could want in a son—except the mortal part.

The Brownie inclined his head. "The changeling was recently visited by a banished lord, my Prince, Shea ap Greely. I thought you'd want to know, given recent events."

"Why does this concern me?" For how much longer would the secret of Caspian's linage be safe?

"Lord Greely is looking for something called the Window. He was... ah," Chalmer glanced at Felan before finding the right word, "quite insistent."

Felan drew in a breath. Had his son betrayed his family? "And did the changeling make a deal?"

"No, Prince. The lord was not happy. He broke the ritual spread, forcing my family to leave, as is proper."

"Hmm. Thank you for your information; it was most useful." And most troubling. He'd heard the murmurs between the measures of music and knew that Shea and the Queen were planning something. He'd hoped to have the Window by now, but it appeared to have vanished. If Shea wanted it, it meant he planned to sneak back into Annwyn and cause more trouble. Felan needed the Window, not only to protect his father from the bitterness of the Queen, but also to protect himself.

The Brownie bowed again and hesitated as if not sure if he should leave. "I am ever your loyal servant, Prince."

"I know, Chalmer." Felan glanced at the lord who'd been reduced to a Brownie. The gambling debt had been a setup, Felan was sure of it, but that didn't change the fact that Chalmer needed to pay a penalty. "What is it that you desire?"

"I'm concerned for my family when the power shifts."

Felan nodded. Many were petitioning the King to lift their exile. They could see the King's rule was ending and no one wanted to be on the wrong side of the veil when the power of Annwyn shifted from father to son. Those caught in the mortal world would die. "Your daughter is fairy?"

"Yes, Prince. Taryn merch Arlea." Chalmer used his

daughter's full name to confirm her linage, and make clear he'd broken none of his exile conditions. Taryn was his wife's child.

"Send her to Court before the vanishing of the moon. For the moment it is all I can do." At least she would be safe.

Chalmer sighed and looked at the ground as if he had expected more.

"I'm sorry, but the King is issuing no pardons." He knew his father hadn't forgiven Arlea for choosing love over duty to her King.

"I understand." Chalmer bowed, but Felan still saw the disappointment.

If he'd had the power he would have undone the exile, but he didn't. The first thing he had to do was stop Shea before he could even start making plans for his own takeover. "I will deal with Shea, you stay with the changeling."

Chalmer hesitated. "And the spread?"

Once broken that was usually the end of the relationship. "The changeling will receive a suitable setting. Report back if Shea returns."

Chalmer nodded. "An honor serving you, my Prince." He bowed again then disappeared into the now dark garden.

Felan pressed his lips together. Things were more dire than he'd thought. That Shea even knew about the Window was bad. Did this mean that the Queen had the Counter-Window? It didn't matter who had it. As long as the other piece of the portal was in Annwyn, Shea could get through. He needed to find the Counter-Window, fast.

With Caspian there, it was easier to start sorting through Gran's things. Lydia had made several attempts over the past few weeks, but each time she had been unable to do much more than cry and then go home. Today felt different. Maybe it was because she knew she wouldn't cry in front of him, or maybe it was because she was able to talk about Gran. It was just nice to be in the house and feel like she could breathe again without being crushed by loss.

She wanted to know more about him but wasn't sure how to start without seeming obvious. It was easy to talk about Gran and the house, but harder to ask questions that would reveal a little more about him, like where he grew up, did he always want to work around antiques, and what films did he like? Initial attraction didn't always last once the real person was discovered.

Lydia looked at the pictures hanging on the wall. A mismatched collection of frames and images that had been tacked up to form a collage of Gran's life. Some were black and white, others more recent. And while some were family pictures, including one that she assumed was her mother as a toddler, many were of people she didn't know. Artists maybe? Friends? Should she pack them away? If she was going to sell the house, it would be better to have all personal items removed— she didn't want strangers stopping and gawking.

"Do you need these?" She turned to Caspian.

Caspian glanced up at her from his laptop. "I'll have a quick look at the frames, but probably not."

He walked over, graceful as if he were at ease in a

strange house. Her heart lifted as he drew close and she glanced away. There was something eye-catching about him, yet he didn't act like a man who knew he was good-looking. He paused to examine each picture on the wall. Then he actually stopped; he was staring at one in particular.

"Found something?"

He tore his gaze away and looked at her. "Do you know who this is?"

She looked at the picture of a young man with a guitar. He was smiling, his pale eyes and sharp cheekbones making him look more like a model. He was almost too pretty in his flares and waistcoat. The clothing gave her an indication of the era, but other than that she had no idea. "Probably just one of the musicians who came here."

Caspian nodded. He touched the edge of the fame, then shrugged and moved onto the next photo.

"There's nothing antique or individually valuable here. You can pack them. I'll just make a note of them in the record." He took a few photos and she watched his lips move as he did a quick count. Again his gaze seemed to stick on the pretty man.

What was so special about that one?

She glanced at Caspian again. She didn't really have a clue what was going on behind those pale green eyes. She was sure he'd broken hearts with just a look. He seemed so unobtainable. Or maybe it was because he wasn't fawning over her like other men. A small part of her wished he'd show a little more interest in her, that he'd hold her gaze when she caught him looking so she'd have an excuse to start a more personal conversation with him. Gran would be having a fine old laugh; she was all for putting the cards on the table and seeing what was there.

He typed something on his laptop. "This was more of a living room?"

"Yeah, Gran used it for watching TV, said it was more comfortable than the parlor." The more time Lydia spent in the house the more she began to realize just how badly Gran had let the house go. Most of the rooms needed repainting. The garden out back was overrun, and the outside of the house was in serious need of attention, and she suspected the roof had a leak since the half-story attic smelled of mold. She hadn't been game to go in and examine the damage yet as there'd been something scuttling in the dark and she suspected it was something more substantial than the ghost.

Maybe a quick sale was all she could hope for, and then Callaway House would be gone forever. While she could feel the weight of her name lifting, she couldn't let go of the rope. If the house became a bed and breakfast, all she'd have left of Gran would be a few pieces of furniture. It wasn't enough. She wanted the house and all the memories it held. Callaways had lived here for over one hundred and fifty years. Gran had done everything to keep it in the family, and Lydia didn't want to be the one to fail.

"Aside from the two paintings and the crystal vase there's not much in here." Caspian's voice broke into her thoughts. She didn't have to decide yet.

"The vase was a gift, she never told me who from." But her eyes had always lit up when she spoke about it.

Caspian glanced at it again and smiled as if he knew

something she didn't. "Shall we move on? I'm sure you have better ways to spend your evenings."

Lydia nodded, then shook her head. This was much better than working late at the office. "I'm still sorting through the personal items in her bedroom. I never thought it would be so hard to pack everything. How do you deal with it?"

"I don't. I assess and move on. I don't like doing deceased estates because the emotions are so raw. Not everyone appreciates what I have to do." He shrugged but looked uncomfortable discussing it.

"I appreciate the way you're doing it. I'd expected someone to come in and be all obsessed with its unusual history." Maybe that would have been easier; then she would have been able to brush him off instead of wanting to know more about him.

"The sex, drugs, and rock and roll?"

It didn't sound scandalous when Caspian said it, yet she still felt like she had to defend the house as best she could. "There was no rock and roll."

Caspian raised an eyebrow. "Didn't some rock star have their wedding here and then get divorced three months later in the eighties?"

"Not everything you read on the Internet is true... it was almost four months later." And that had been the end of the wedding location according to Gran.

"Just sex and drugs then." He was smiling.

She couldn't stop her lips from curving in response. Was he flirting with her? She took a risk to see how far he'd go. "Mostly sex."

He nodded, but he was watching her as if he was trying to work out what to say next. Had she just killed the conversation? A flutter of nerves caught in her chest as she waited for him to respond.

"I read the dinner parties were something special."

Lydia let out the breath she'd been holding. "Well, I guess when you get a whole bunch of powerful men and their mistresses in one room things are going to happen. That's old though. Later it was more hippie. No mistresses, just people boarding here and partying."

"Is the ghost a myth too?"

"That depends on who you talk to. Gran believed something was here, but I've never seen anything, just lots of odd bumps." There was definitely something here; however, she wasn't about to confess her belief in the ghost to Caspian. Not yet. Besides, it would be more fun if he realized for himself that they weren't alone in the house. And if he didn't? Well, he wouldn't be the first person to logic away the ghost. But that crawling sensation that someone was watching when she was alone, or the creak on the floorboard that sounded like steps in the middle of the night—she couldn't explain them away.

"I'll keep an eye out for it," he said with a smile.

She looked at Caspian again. There was an air about him as if he was from another time and place, like he didn't quite fit. Like her. But instead of pressing forward she retreated. "Let's do the parlor. All the best parties started there, or so I was told."

She turned away but was sure she could feel his gaze lingering on her back as he followed her into the parlor.

There was dust on the shelves and on the chandelier. The two loveseats looked faded and threadbare. As a child it had seemed magical, now it just looked old.

Caspian scanned the shelves, walking the length of the room. "Do you have a list of the books? Are any first editions?"

"I don't know… is it important?" There were maybe a hundred old books and plenty of other little ornaments; china dancing ladies, ivory animals, and trinkets from overseas. On the table was an empty brandy decanter and glasses.

He nodded.

"I think some of these belonged to Gran's father-in-law." She'd kept them because it made the place look better, like they could all read and were educated. "I'll start listing the books."

He glanced at the bookcase behind the desk. "Maybe it could be sold as a bulk lot?"

"Do you think I should sell?" She meant the house, not just the contents of the parlor.

"Do you want to?" He put the laptop on the desk, his fingers tracing lightly over the surface. She'd noticed that about him—he touched an object if only for a second before photographing and documenting. He was tactile even though his job seemed cold and impersonal.

"I thought I did. I had an offer this morning from someone wanting to turn the house into a bed and breakfast."

Caspian looked over his shoulder. "Because Charleston doesn't have enough historic escapes for visitors?"

"I can't afford the repairs without taking out a mortgage that will be bigger than I can repay." She blew the dust off a book and opened up the first page. Shouldn't he be telling her to sell? Wasn't that his job, to make people part with precious things in exchange for money? She sniffed and blamed the dust, not the sudden lump in her throat. "Do you want it?"

He looked at her, then the chandelier and the rest of the room. "If I had that kind of capital, I'd buy it and pretend to live like a lord." He closed his eyes and took a breath as if he could imagine the parties the way she once had. As he opened his eyes, he shook his head. "The divorce cleaned me out."

One eyebrow rose. Divorced. That was the first personal detail he'd revealed about himself, and it was enough to make her want to know more. She bit her tongue on the more nosy questions like what was his ex-wife like and how long were they married and what had happened. Instead she went for the gentle question that would hopefully lead to more. "Recent?"

"Recent enough. It was amicable, she kept the house, and I kept the shop and started over."

Meaning he'd walked away, because he'd done the wrong thing? She frowned. How could she ask that without putting her foot in it? But it was important to know.

He continued without looking at her. "At the time it felt like the right thing." He started tapping on the keyboard. "In hindsight I was overly generous."

Lydia took the opening. "Guilty conscience?"

"Betrayed heart." He looked over his shoulder and fixed her with those icy green eyes. "I caught her cheating."

"Ouch." But he'd wanted her to know that, and that gave her hope that maybe they were at least looking at the same book, even if they weren't on the same page.

"Not quite what I said." The corner of his mouth twitched as he tried to hide the hurt.

"No kids?"

"Fortunately no." He turned and leaned against the edge of the desk. "You know this would be quicker without the twenty questions."

"But it wouldn't be as much fun. Don't you want to know something about Callaway House? People always want to know what went on." She walked over and put the book on the desk next to him. If she put out her hand, she could run it down his arm. Her fingers twitched.

He looked up from the screen. "I'd rather know about you."

She automatically put up her defenses, then stopped herself. Wasn't this what she wanted—a chance to get to know him better? The only way she could do that was if she let him get to know her. "Ask something then."

"What is your favorite room?"

Of all the questions he could've asked, he'd picked that. She wasn't sure what to say. Was there even a wrong answer? "It depends. In winter I used to like sitting in the kitchen. It was always warm and smelled of homemade treats. But in summer evenings Gran would open up the glass doors and the scent of jasmine would fill this room. I'd sit and read and pretend I was a princess in a palace. Do you have a favorite room yet?"

He blinked. His dark lashes rested against his skin for a heartbeat before he opened his eyes again to look at her. This time there was almost a sadness in his eyes. "Your gran might have let me in, but I couldn't afford a drink in here. My mother's a nurse. My father's a mechanic descended from French pirates. I don't have class, money, or artistic talent."

Lydia titled her head. Was he saying what she thought he was saying? That she was out of his league? She would've laughed except he looked deadly serious.

Her hand covered his. Skin to skin, her breath caught.

"Callaway House was never about the money or mistresses. It was about the party. Sure, the rich spent up big when they came to play and make deals, but without the struggling artists and the musicians who played for a meal and drinks—and to say they'd played here—Callaway House would've been no better than the motel that charges by the hour. It was about atmosphere. People had to want to come here."

"But they stopped coming."

"Nightclubs and bars took over. No one wanted to spend a weekend listening to poetry and getting high, or hearing some up-and-coming blues guitarist work on his next album. I wish I'd seen it in action."

"It would have been some party." His hand trailed up her arm.

Before she could second-guess herself again, she leaned in and kissed him. Her lips brushed his, testing to see if she'd like the feel of his mouth. She did. She liked the way he smelled of soap and that his cheek was rough because he hadn't shaved before coming around.

He didn't respond. His lips didn't move. She pulled back. *Awkward.* "I'm sorry. I don't usually kiss men I've just met."

"I don't usually kiss while on the job." This time there was only heat in his eyes, like someone had lit a match and held it to his soul.

She couldn't move away as she waited for his next move. If he made none, that was it. She'd go and sit in another room while he worked and pretend as if it had never happened. Then he placed his lips to hers. Softly as if the kiss was something he shouldn't be taking. Her eyes closed and her mouth opened, letting his tongue slip inside. Tasting and teasing. Her hand snuck around his waist, drawing him closer.

In return his hand swept over the curve of her butt. Pressed against her he felt good, his body was firm as if he spent his spare time keeping fit, not sitting. She relaxed into his hold as heat spread through her body. It had been too long since she'd had a man in her arms. He ended the kiss with a couple of slow ones as if he couldn't bear to pull away. That made two of them. His breath caressed her lips as he took a final taste and then released her. Neither of them moved. All she could think about was her body and the way it melted in his hands like he'd seduced her with just a touch.

"That's going to complicate things," he murmured as he tucked a strand of her dark blond hair behind her ear. His lips still felt the pressure of hers, and his skin was hyperaware of every subtle move she made, her body pressed against his in a way that was far too intimate. He wanted her, he couldn't remember wanting anyone quite so much, and he was sure she would have noticed his attraction.

A look of surprise lifted her eyebrows. "That's not what I was expecting to hear."

He let his hand fall away from the silken strands of her hair. "I shouldn't have done that."

Caspian's hand touched the desk and his head was

filled with images of another night years ago and what
had happened on the desk. *Skin and sweat. Clothing
being peeled off in a rush to find satisfaction.* Driven by
lust his heart pumped a little harder.

It was the house.

It was what he was seeing.

He looked at Lydia.

Hell, it was the woman.

"Will you get in trouble?"

He paused before answering. She meant with work,
but he was thinking about the Grey who'd been making
threats. Not that he could explain how he was mixed
up in a deadly game of fairy politics. He hadn't lied to
her about his lack of social standing… in the human
world. The fairy world was a whole other festering
kettle of fish.

"Depends. Are you seducing me to get a favorable
valuation?"

That could be a problem if someone thought he was
fiddling the figures. Surely no one could contest a will
that left the estate to the only child and grandchild?

"I didn't seduce you." She gave him a halfhearted
push. "I merely took advantage of an opportunity."

Had he looked like he wanted to be kissed? Had it
been that obvious every time he looked at her?

"Okay then." He nodded, then placed another kiss on
her mouth, taking the opportunity to kiss the beautiful
woman in his arms, before she changed her mind and
realized that he was not the kind of man she wanted.
His tongue traced her lower lip just once, then he drew
back before the temptation took hold. The echoes of
what had happened previously on the desk still filled

his mind with possibilities he hadn't wanted to explore in a while. That he shouldn't be thinking about exploring now. He didn't want to risk dragging Lydia into his problems. Maybe it was too late. He was here and for all he knew Shea had followed him. He was sure there was a Grey in the house, not that he'd seen it... but there was something. Something more than a photo of a fairy in the living room.

"Okay." She didn't move away.

He didn't care. If he had to come back here every night for the next year because they kept getting distracted, it would be worth it and much better than being in his empty house. Lydia's childhood had been odd like his, and while he couldn't talk about it, she could and it made him feel a little less strange that even humans without fairy blood could have bizarre families.

The pause stretched out as if neither of them was willing to end the moment and yet neither was sure how to move forward.

He tilted his head at the laptop. "I should keep going."

"Right." She looked at him as if she was about to change her mind. He knew if she offered he wouldn't refuse. She was under his skin and he wanted her to dig deeper. Then he remembered what would happen if she did dig deeper. He'd have to tell her about his real father, about psychometry and fairies. The heat in his blood cooled. He didn't know how to tell her the truth. He'd never told anyone.

Above them came the sound of soft, scuttling footsteps. Caspian looked up.

"It's just the ghost."

If that was a ghost, he'd give Shea his soul and

the damn mirror. He knew what small fairy footsteps sounded like. And since Dylis wasn't here, and there were no Brownies here, that only left a Grey. No wonder no one had ever seen the ghost. Only those with fairy blood could see fairies—unless the fairies chose to reveal themselves. Until now he hadn't seen or heard a thing, which meant it had been hiding. Why? And why was it here? He couldn't sense anything fairy-made here that would attract it. Usually anything that came from Annwyn had a resonance of power that all fairies would recognize. Had the man in the photo been a Grey who had decided to stay on after he'd had to stop mixing with humans? It didn't feel right. Something was... he couldn't put a finger on it, but it was that same feeling he'd had when he'd first come here. It wasn't like a Grey to hang around; they generally gathered and kept to themselves in run-down areas of cities.

"Does it usually pace the floors?"

"Yes, and sometimes it opens drawers or cupboards." She was smiling, as if she found it amusing that he could hear the ghost.

Okay, so he didn't bring the Grey. It was already here. That was an even more unsettling thought. How long had the Callaways been sharing a house with a Grey?

"It's nothing to worry about." She touched his arm. "You're not scared of ghosts, are you?"

"No." Ghosts didn't bother him at all; Greys, on the other hand... He smiled at her as if nothing were wrong. Maybe nothing was wrong. It had been here for years, maybe decades, without causing any problems. Maybe it liked the ambience, the space, and the solitude. Yeah, and maybe Shea was simply misunderstood.

"Good." Then she stepped away and picked up the book, and went back to making the list.

He watched her for a moment then trailed his fingers over the desk. The older images disappeared beneath the new impression of them kissing. The heat hit him again and left him longing. He was too human to resist wanting to get to know her, and too fairy to resist the game of lust she offered.

Double damned as usual.

Chapter 6

NEITHER OF THEM HAD MENTIONED THE KISS, BUT Lydia could feel it simmering between them. An unresolved something that could be nothing and yet it had felt like everything. Now it was getting close to eleven and they both had work the next day, yet she wasn't ready for him to leave. While they hadn't talked about what had happened, they had talked about the house and the things in it. Caspian was more than happy to talk about everything except himself.

The one thing she wanted to talk about.

She couldn't treat his time here as default dates. He was working. But he didn't seem to mind her questions and she liked to watch him work, like the way he'd look at something with a slight frown before making notes. The way the light sometimes caught his features and for a moment he seemed sharper and more beautiful than possible, then he'd turn and look at her and she'd realize it had been a trick of the light, or her mind running away with the fantasy of doing more than kissing him.

However, at the back of her mind she couldn't shake the sensation that he was hiding something, even if she didn't know what it was. She kept brushing aside the feeling. Maybe the divorce had made him gun-shy. If she wanted him, she was going to have to make it clear.

He shut the laptop. "I'm going to have to call it a night."

She nodded. "Are you sure you don't mind coming over after work?"

"Not at all." He gave her a rare smile. "You don't mind me being here?"

Lydia shook her head. No, she couldn't imagine any woman kicking him out. Yet one had cast him off. What was his flaw? Was he messy? Refused to do housework? Watched sports all weekend? Her gaze skimmed over his body—it had felt pretty good when she'd kissed him. Maybe he played golf all weekend. "More of the same tomorrow?"

"Afraid so, and the next day."

"How will I survive?"

He touched her arm. "You will. You Callaways seem to be able to survive anything and come out better for it."

She glanced at him. She'd meant it as a joke and he'd taken her seriously, and then complimented her family in the same breath. Gran would have worked out his secret over a few wines. It was a pity they had never met. Caspian was a boyfriend Gran would've approved of. Not that he was her boyfriend after one kiss.

These evenings were the closest she'd come to a date in a while and she was enjoying them. Which said more about her life than she liked.

They walked toward the front door in silence. The old house creaked and sighed around them. It had felt hollow after Gran's death, but now it was starting to breathe again—much like her. Caspian was right. She would get on with living and be okay.

"Thank you." She wanted to touch him again, to lean in and kiss him, but she held back.

"Just doing my job." He looked at her with those eyes that saw everything, yet hid whatever he was thinking so well. She wished she could read him better.

"Yes. Um, okay. I'll see you same time tomorrow?"

"That would be good."

The front door was an arm's reach away, yet neither of them moved. Her tongue darted over her lip, and his gaze lowered to her mouth. Her skin warmed as if she was burning from within. Then he brushed his lips over her cheek, his stubble grazing her skin. The scent of his skin and something else filled her lungs.

She turned her head, needing to taste his lips. His fingers brushed her neck, then threaded into her hair. Her eyes closed as she let herself sink into the kiss, her body easing closer to his, her hand sliding over his chest. She didn't need to breathe. He took a step and she moved with him, her back hitting the wall as he deepened the kiss, his tongue dancing with hers. A moan lodged in her throat. She wanted more than a kiss. She trailed her fingers over his hip, then pulled him closer so she could feel him pressed hard against her.

He didn't resist. He slowly moved his hips against hers and she wanted to start unbuttoning his shirt there in the hallway. She broke the kiss and took a shaky breath. His lips remained millimeters from hers. Again they were caught, unwilling to pull away and yet unable to go forward. She hadn't planned for this. She wasn't prepared—no matter what her body was screaming.

"It's late."

"I know." He kissed her again, softly as though hinting at what could be.

"You shouldn't be driving home this late." Neither should she.

He drew back a fraction to look at her, and the heat in his gaze nearly burned away every rational thought. "What are you suggesting?"

What was she suggesting? That they use Callaway House the same way it had once been used? Why not? "Maybe you should think about staying here, so you aren't driving tired."

Yeah, not even she believed that.

He considered her for a moment and she resisted the urge to bite her lip and act like she was nervous, even though she was. It was too fast. She almost took back the offer, but then realized that just because he was sleeping here didn't mean they had to sleep together. How else was he going to take the suggestion? This close he couldn't exactly hide what his body was thinking.

Just when she thought it was going to be a no, he spoke. "That's a generous offer."

"Yes, well, there are plenty of bedrooms." *Shut up*. She pressed her lips together and smiled.

Caspian nodded. She could almost hear the wheels of his mind spinning up possibilities, but his eyes were unreadable.

She started to backtrack, certain she'd blown it. But how many men would turn down an offer to stay and play at Callaway House? Once upon a time no one would've. Now? "If you're not comfortable staying here, I totally under—"

He placed his lips against hers to silence her. She gasped and guessed that was a yes, he'd be staying the night. The kiss made her forget about all the reasons she shouldn't and think about all the reasons she should.

As he drew in a breath she spoke. "So was that a good-bye or a yes?" She needed to know.

"Both, I think." He pulled back a fraction. "If you're sure, how about tomorrow night?"

She'd never been more sure in her life. "I'm sure." She kissed him once more to be certain. Then smiled. "I'm looking forward to it."

"So am I," he murmured near her ear before pulling away. "I'll see you tomorrow."

He opened the front door and the cool night air swept in between them. He glanced out at the night then back at her. The moonlight cutting across his face made him seem sharper and colder than he'd been a moment ago. Then it was gone as he walked down the stairs and away from Callaway House.

"Good night, Caspian," she said even though she knew he couldn't hear her. She wouldn't be sleeping well tonight. Her dreams would be full of him and the kiss and what hadn't been said, but what they both wanted. Her blood fizzed like champagne through her veins and then pooled in her belly. She closed the door and leaned against it for a moment.

She was acting like a lovesick sixteen-year-old. No. Not sixteen because she knew exactly what she wanted to do with Caspian. Her skin ached to be touched. There was a heat she hadn't imagined as he whispered in her ear as if he knew exactly how she'd be spending her night because he'd be awake too. She hoped thoughts of her would keep him up all night. As she locked up the house and turned off all the lights, all she could think about was tomorrow evening and seeing Caspian again.

—∿∿∿—

Felan lounged in his chamber. Bare feet, shirt undone. It had been a long day—even for him. Most of the lords and ladies at Court had avoided him as if they knew the anger that simmered, turning his blue blood red with fury. But he'd been calm. He'd danced and feasted as if nothing were amiss. He'd even managed not to question his mother the Queen over dinner, but then she'd been busy trying to goad his father.

"I have to return. Caspian is unprotected." Dylis stretched and eased out of bed. She'd been waiting in his chamber as he'd ordered. Her hand feathered down his back. "You have to stop calling me back to Court if you want me to do my job."

Felan caught her hand. "Do your job and I won't have to call you back."

Her smile froze in place. "What would you have me do? Kill Shea ap Greely?"

"We have to be smarter than that." He released her hand, not sure how to deal with Shea just yet.

"This is more than I agreed to do."

"You agreed to look after Caspian."

"I agreed to ensure his safety in exchange for my lover's freedom. How much longer, Felan?"

Felan stroked a tendril of her blond hair and coiled it around his finger. He drew her close enough to kiss her lips. "Do you still want Bramwel?"

"Yes. You are merely keeping me warm for him."

Felan laughed. He liked her well enough, and she

liked him. Dylis had been a secret set of eyes and ears for him ever since his mother had imprisoned Dylis's lover Bramwel as a tree and left him in her private grove. He'd found it by accident some years ago and had been horrified that everyone there was alive, just frozen in place and hidden in plain sight. Now Bramwel had to spend his life waving his branches in the breeze and hoping someone would release him—before the power shift.

"Get me the Counter-Window and I shall free him straightaway." He kissed her fuchsia lips for the last time. "If you fail…" He let the threat hang unsaid. There were too many lives at stake. Human and fairy.

"I won't fail." Her eyes glittered like palest sapphire and she drew away as brittle as any fairy. But with Dylis there were no fake formalities. They both knew where they stood in bed and out of it.

He stood and buttoned his shirt. "I value your presence more than you know." When he took the throne she'd make a fine Hunter.

Dylis inclined her head, the ever-obedient courtier. "Thank you, Prince. I will hold you to your fine words." She buckled on her blade and checked her appearance before facing him. "What do you know of a fairy called Riobard?"

Felan glanced up. He hadn't heard that name in a long time. "He left Court a very long time ago to wander amongst the mortals. Why?"

"I was doing some digging in the mortal world and his name was mentioned in connection with the Window." Dylis was watching him closely.

"Riobard, like your Bramwel, was a minstrel before

I'd reached one hundred mortal years. After a fight with his lover he left, never to be seen again." Felan picked up his waistcoat. "There were a few rumors that he took some things. A silver pipe, a set of dice... trinkets that mortals wouldn't suspect gave him an advantage."

"So he could've taken the Window."

"If he did, the loss was never mentioned." He looked at Dylis. "For obvious reasons." No one would want to admit to owning it and losing it.

"Who was his lover?"

"Sulia's mother." While Sulia's mother was dead, Sulia was the Queen's favorite lady-in-waiting.

Dylis gave a low whistle that sounded more mortal than fairy. "Do you think she still has the Counter-Window?"

Felan shrugged. "If she does, I doubt she knows what she has, otherwise she'd have handed it over to my mother." The word caught and left a bad taste in his mouth. "I could probably get an invitation to her chamber."

She pressed her lips together for a moment as if calculating her next few steps. Felan liked the way she was always thinking ahead. "Too risky; besides, you told me once you'd rather cut it off than sleep with her."

He laughed. "I'd make an exception in this case."

"Better I arrange something."

She was right. Dylis had reach in places he didn't— including with his mother's ladies. He put his hand on her arm. "Watch yourself in that den of wolves."

"I will." She inclined her head and pulled away.

Felan walked over to the desk and picked up a box. Made of sandalwood and lined with delicate fairy-made velvet, the box itself was a work of art no human could match, but the gift was inside. "A gift for my son."

Dylis looked at the box, and then at him. Her eyebrows were drawn down. "Am I to say it's from you?"

Felan nodded. It was time to let Caspian know he hadn't forgotten him and that his father knew of the son's dealings with the banished Shea.

Chapter 7

CASPIAN WALKED INTO HIS KITCHEN. HIS HOUSE WAS empty. After the warmth and heady history of Lydia's house, his home seemed even worse—just a box of brick and mortar.

For the first time since his divorce, he felt truly alone. It wasn't the Brownies he missed, or even Dylis. It was the simple pleasure of coming home to someone. Of having someone to care about. He'd walked away from that and never looked back, but Lydia had pulled the blinders off and now he was forced to look at what his life had become. He spent more time with echoes of the past than he did with real people. He hadn't been on a date in eight months. The three dates he'd been on hadn't gone anywhere because the whole time he'd been thinking of the lies he'd have to tell and the things he might see about them, even if he didn't want to. He sighed and fiddled with the broken tea set. The contents hadn't been touched. If he were a Brownie, he wouldn't have touched it either.

He shouldn't have kissed Lydia.

He wanted to kiss her again.

He imagined he could still taste her on his lips, and feel the heat of her body pressed to his. The curve of her hip under his hand and the way her body had shifted closer as the kiss had deepened. After that moment the rest of the evening had been off-kilter. Not awkward, but not comfortable.

Then she'd asked him to stay. Even now he could feel the lingering heat in his blood. It had taken everything he had in him to walk out that door. He craved her touch. But whatever was going on between them, it was a bad idea to act upon it. Not with his heritage. Not if there was a Grey lurking about. He leaned against the kitchen counter and closed his eyes.

Still, there was no doubt his dreams tonight would be full of Lydia.

Something in the air shifted around him and Caspian knew he was no longer alone in the house. He recognized the heady perfume of Court. He cracked open his eyes and saw Dylis; she was what he guessed was her natural height for a change. She had also managed to layer several items of clothing on varying shades of blue to produce an outfit that a fashion designer would be proud of. The longer he looked the more he thought she was wearing enough clothes for three days.

"What are you doing?" she asked him.

"Thinking." Like it mattered to her.

Dylis placed a box on the kitchen counter.

He was tempted to ask about it but decided that he probably wouldn't like the answer. That she came from Court bearing gifts put him on edge.

"Aren't you curious?" She kicked his foot.

"About the box or what you found out about the Window?"

She grinned and bobbed down next to him. "Both."

"Tell me about the Window." But his gaze slid to the box she'd carried in. It came from Annwyn; he could feel the shimmer of magic from here.

Dylis tapped the glass oven door and an image formed

of two polished copper mirrors. Oval hand mirrors—the kind one expected an evil queen to hold as she asked who was the fairest in the land.

Gooseflesh rose down Caspian's arms. He was rapidly coming to dislike mirrors of any type. "What am I looking at?"

"This is the last known appearance of the Window and Counter-Window."

"Why are there two?"

"Together they are a portal to Annwyn. The Counter-Window is somewhere in Annwyn, and the Window is here… we think."

"How could something so valuable be lost in the mortal world?" He should be in bed dreaming of Lydia, not standing in the kitchen talking about fairy-made mirrors.

Dylis gave him a look that had lost its power around the time he'd turned eighteen. "Things get exchanged, misplaced, and forgotten about. You mortals die so fast it's hard to keep track of where things go. Plus it can't be tracked by those with fairy blood."

"So I can't find it anyway." What had she been hoping, that he'd trip over it and realize what it was?

"You will be able to recognize it when you touch it. It's why Shea came to you and not another changeling. It's why I asked you to keep an eye out."

"And I was thinking it was because of my father."

"Ah, no. Most don't know who your father is. Trust me when I say that's the way you want to keep it."

He'd take her word on that. "Why not destroy the Counter-Window and prevent him from getting through?"

Dylis raised her eyebrows as if he'd just suggested

she chew iron filings. "Do you have any idea how hard it is to make something this powerful? The Court would rather it be returned."

Of course they would because they wouldn't be inconvenienced by the search. He would be. "There can't be too many hand mirrors this old lying around. It's probably in a museum."

"No one has seen it for five hundred years. And no one has heard of it in a century. It's probably changed shape a dozen times." Dylis gave a shrug and the image vanished, leaving Caspian staring at himself in the dark glass of the oven, a frown creasing his forehead.

"It changes shape?" Whoever made the portal had gone to a lot of trouble to keep it from falling into the wrong hands.

"I told you that." She crossed her arms. "You don't seem to understand the implications. If Shea uses the Window to get back to Annwyn, the war he starts will cause ripples on the river so big that an outbreak of smallpox will look like a sneeze."

"So how am I supposed to find a mirror that can't be traced and changes shape?"

"I don't know."

Caspian's jaw worked. While usually he didn't discuss his work or his lack of dating with Dylis, Callaway House might be important. He pulled out his camera and scrolled through the pictures he'd taken that evening, stopping on the one of the fairy man. He'd zoomed in and got one of just that picture. "Do you know who he is?"

Dylis frowned. "Where did you get this?"

"I'm doing a valuation at Callaway House. His

picture was up on the wall." He paused, but knew he should tell her about the "ghost." "I think there's also a Grey in the house."

"He is definitely not a Grey."

"You can tell that from a picture?" Caspian looked at the picture again, but still couldn't pick it.

She looked at him like he was an idiot. "Of course I can. Why is a Grey at the house? Did it follow you?"

"No, according to Lydia it's always been there. She thinks it's a ghost."

"Greys don't live forever. Are you sure it wasn't just mice?"

Caspian rolled his eyes. "I know what fairy footsteps sound like. Plus, Greys make me…" there was something about them that warned him they were near, "tingle." And not in a good way.

"Interesting." She took the camera and looked at it again. "Musician?"

The look on her face was far too calculated. "What?"

"Just… the last name connected with the Window was Riobard; he was a Court minstrel who stole some things and left, never to be seen again."

Until now. Cold snaked down his spine. If Riobard was the man in the picture, then the Window could be at Callaway House. It could be why the ghost was there but unable to find it.

"If a fairy touched the Window, would they know what it was?"

"It's a secret portal; you have to know how to activate it."

"So even if a Grey found it, without knowing it was the Window it would be useless."

Dylis nodded. "You can see why it's so valuable."

Oh, he did. He also knew why Shea had come to him, and why the ghost was constantly searching. Without knowing how to activate the Window it was just another mirror. But Shea would know how to use it. Suddenly finding it before Shea did became a whole lot more important. At the moment only he and Dylis knew it was most likely at Callaway House. But if Shea realized it, Lydia could be in danger.

Dylis looked at him, and he knew she'd been thinking the same thing. "You have to get back there and find it."

Finding the Window was going to be like looking for a needle in a haystack, even for him. Callaway House was filled with stuff, then there was the stable and the cabins, and so many places to hide something. For all he knew it was buried, or in the roof. "I need the Counter-Window." It would be his best chance to find it.

He took a breath as he realized what he was doing. Like any fairy he was getting drawn into the twisty world of fairy politics and finding it exciting. No, he was doing it for Lydia. Having a Grey in the house and having something that valuable and dangerous in her possession wasn't good. She knew nothing of fairies and could be tricked into all kinds of trouble.

"I'm working on it. In the meantime, keep looking; we have to find it first." She tapped the box she'd brought with her. "I spoke with your father about Shea. This is from him."

"No, no. I won't be sucked into accepting gifts. You can take it back." Caspian's gaze flicked between the box and Dylis.

"It's from your *father*." She shrunk down to her usual

ten inches to conserve power then leaned an elbow on
the box "I can't take it back."

The box smelled exotic. Sandalwood. It had been
delicately carved so the flowers on the sides looked
like they were swaying in the breeze. He narrowed his
eyes—were they swaying? He reached out his hand to
touch the wood and find out, but stopped millimeters
from the surface. He blinked and broke the spell the box
was weaving.

"What's inside?"

"I don't know. It's a gift."

"What's it for?" If she'd expected him to be delighted
his father had acknowledged him, she was wrong. His
father had never shown any interest in his life, or even in
getting to know him. Biology didn't mean squat.

"I don't know, he didn't say."

In thirty-five years his father had never sent a gift, yet
one mirror needed to be found and one banished fairy
lord appeared on Caspian's doorstep and suddenly presents arrived. He was as suspicious as he was tempted.
He wanted to know what was inside. Even though he
hated his fairy blood, particularly at the moment, he still
wanted to meet his father and ask all the questions he'd
had growing up—even if he didn't like the answers.
As a child he'd always felt that somehow he must be
unworthy of Annwyn since his father was the Prince and
didn't want him. Felan hadn't even waited for him to be
born before casting him off. His mother had said the last
time she'd seen Felan she'd been five months pregnant.
Just talking about Felan had upset her. Another reason
to hate the Prince.

Bloody fairies thinking they could walk in and use

humans for whatever they wanted and leave without a second glance.

"You open it," he said to Dylis. She wasn't here because she liked him. She was here because Felan ordered her to be here. His father thought highly enough of his changeling son to provide a bodyguard and fairy tutor. For that Caspian had to be grateful. Love him or hate him, they would always be tied by blood and Annwyn.

She rolled her eyes and muttered something that could've been about damned souls and rivers, which Caspian chose to ignore.

"You are more like your father every day," she snapped.

Dylis grunted, flicked the catch, and pushed back the lid. She gave a whistle, then glanced at Caspian. "He raided the armory and placed a strategic land mine."

The warning tingle became a tightening of his gut. Despite his better judgment, Caspian leaned over and took a look inside the box. Cradled on a bed of the most delicate green velvet he'd ever seen was a silver tea set. But it wasn't plain silver—that would've been far too simple. Chips of gems were woven into delicate knots that looped around each cup and saucer. The knob on the top of the teapot lid was an emerald the size of a small grape.

Out of habit Caspian immediately tried to place a value on the gift. While he could price the metal and gems, he couldn't begin to cost the craftsmanship. There was nothing like this in the human world.

He swallowed and reached out his hand, knowing it could be a trick and he'd wind up trapped inside or worse. But his father hadn't charged Dylis with his care only to do him harm now. Beneath his fingertips the box was warm as if it had been resting in the sun.

Felan smiled as he held the box, but under the admiration of the work was worry. The tightness around his eyes gave it away. He closed the box and nodded, then he seemed to look directly at Caspian. "Enjoy the gift, son."

Caspian broke the contact and stepped back. They were the first words he'd ever heard his father say. He curled his fingers by his side to stop himself from reaching out just to hear it again.

"Anything?" Dylis leaned forward.

"No. Just Felan holding the box," he lied. He looked at the beautiful tea set; it was obviously meant for his Brownies. "I suppose I should set it up."

For once Dylis said nothing.

Caspian carefully pulled out each piece. The warm metal gave him no impressions of whoever had handled it before Felan. It was odd—there was always a residual something. As he went through the motions of filling the sugar bowl and milk jug, then brewing fresh tea, the silver seemed to glow with life. There was magic in the set. More magic than he liked having around.

"What's it doing?"

"Protecting the house. Shea won't get back in."

"Is that all it's doing?"

"I think so." Dylis walked around the setting as if trying to unlock the secrets of the glowing tea set.

His life was too weird. He could just imagine inviting Lydia over and trying to explain that. *This is my tea set. Why yes, they are real rubies and sapphires, and that's a magic glow, not a radioactive one.*

He rubbed his hand over his eyes. It was too late to be dealing with more fairy crap. He climbed the stairs, ready to give in to the exhaustion and sleep. He was stopped at his bedroom door. A silver dagger with a jeweled hilt had been driven through the wood. Shea had been there. And the message was clear: He wanted the Window, and Caspian was running out of time to find it.

Chapter 8

LAST NIGHT'S FAIRY DRAMA SEEMED SO FAR AWAY. If not for the dagger now on his bedside table and the silver tea set in the kitchen, he could have dreamed it. He showered, his thoughts already on Callaway House and Lydia, and he couldn't stop the smile from forming. It was beginning to feel like a good day. As he dried he tried not to think of the ways it could all go wrong, or that he was going to have to find a way to tell her about his gift.

But he had all day to work that out—that he was actually considering ways to tell her didn't even make him pause.

He opened his wardrobe. None of his clothes were hanging up, none of his clothes were in the wardrobe, instead there was a very large pile of unraveled threads.

He touched the threads and saw Shea.

"How is that possible?" He wrapped the towel back around his waist and glanced around his room half-expecting Shea to be standing in the corner laughing. But he was alone. He opened up his drawers, but everything there was a tangle of strings. Right. He had no clothes. The familiar twitch that only dealing with fairies caused was back.

This was an annoyance, nothing more. And yet it was far more intimate than a dagger through the door. Shea had been in his room and through his things. He suppressed a shudder and tried to be calm. It was only clothes, and if that was the best Shea could do there wasn't anything to worry about.

His gaze landed on yesterday's clothes on the floor where he'd left them before going to bed. Good thing it was jeans and a shirt instead of sweaty running clothes. But he was willing to bet that everything in the laundry basket was still as it should be. Brownies didn't do laundry, and he didn't mind. It gave him a semblance of normality that most people would trade in a heartbeat. There was at least a few days' worth of clothing waiting to be cleaned. None of which he could pack into an overnight bag for his stay at Lydia's.

Dressed in yesterday's castoffs he jogged down the stairs and checked in the laundry. His suspicions were confirmed.

"Screw you, Shea," he muttered as he stuffed the darks into the machine and got them going. A fairy lord wouldn't think of laundry; he'd be used to his clothes getting sorted out by servants.

"Why are you cursing him?" Dylis leaned against the door frame, arms crossed.

"Go look in my closet."

Caspian turned, but she was already gone.

Her high-pitched laughter tinkled through the house like the annoying little bells people put on cat collars.

"Oh my, that is the oldest trick known to fairies." Dylis was still grinning.

"I will have to buy new things right away." Before he went to Lydia's, as he couldn't show up in yesterday's clothes and with nothing clean to put on. He inhaled and forced it out slowly. He didn't need this extra fairy bullshit in his life.

"It's still funny, and it could've been so much worse. He could've done a wear and unravel spell, so you'd be left standing naked in town." She started giggling again.

Caspian gave a snort that almost turned into a laugh. "Point taken."

"It'll be fine." She nodded and smiled. Dylis never said anything would be fine, and her smile was now a little too forced. "You can't stop living just because he could be waiting; if you do he's already taken control and that's what he wants. He wants to make your life so unbearable you agree to whatever deal he offers. Do not let him make the deal. If you have to, you make the deal, you set the terms."

"If I make a deal with a Grey, and word gets back to Court, I'm screwed."

Dylis pressed her lips together but had nothing to say.

Great, just great. He needed to find the damn Window and hand it over to the Court before Shea could do any more damage to his life.

But he didn't see Shea all day. Or any Grey, not even a little one. He collected the new glass for the ex-enchanted mirror, fixed it up, and hung it on display. Got through a pile of paperwork and managed to firm up a few prices on some of Madam Callaway's furniture. He emailed an acquaintance about the books, as he didn't usually deal with them. As well as picking up some new clothes. Nothing fancy, just the basics, and he wasn't even sure he'd be needing the new pajama pants. He didn't want to be using them. But she might have changed her mind in daylight.

He glanced at Dylis lying on a sideboard, arm over her eyes like she was bored out of her walnut-sized head. She'd be dismayed that he'd broken the enchanted mirror and had seemed almost disappointed by the lack of Grey action.

"Give me five minutes to close up and you can come to Lydia's." He hoped he sounded more enthused about that than he felt. At least with Dylis if he was followed by Greys, there would be a measure of protection, plus she could find out more about Lydia's ghost.

That got her moving. She peeled herself up with more grace than anyone he'd ever seen, as if gravity released her for a moment and she floated to standing. "Can't wait to see what *I* find in the house."

Caspian ignored her and set about closing up the shop. When he was ready to leave, Dylis swung onto his arm and held onto his shirtsleeve as he went out the back to where his car was parked. As soon as he crossed the threshold of the shop he knew something wasn't right.

"Do you hear that?"

"A humming?" Dylis climbed higher and stood on his shoulder.

He didn't worry about compensating for her; she'd never once fallen off—even when he'd gone through a phase of riding a motorbike in his twenties. Her balance was unnatural.

"It's not fairy-related. And yet…" She stopped, no doubt because she'd just spotted his car, like he had.

The car was humming. Vibrating. Swarming might have been a better description. The inside of his car was full of black-and-yellow-striped insects. He hoped they were bees and not wasps. But even then he wasn't game enough to walk over, open a door, and let them out.

Dylis jumped down and walked over. Caspian took

a step back. He wasn't allergic to bees, but they didn't seem like happy bees and he was pretty sure that a thousand stings would be fatal.

"Don't open the car."

"I wasn't born last century." She bounced onto the hood as if she were taking a single step and peered through the windscreen.

"He's really gone all out this time. There's a whole hive in there."

"If he thinks this is going to work, he's wrong." He spun, looking for the Grey, as if he could be hiding in any shadow. He had to be nearby. "Hear that, Shea—I will not be bullied by you." He'd been bullied by human children at school and he wasn't going to be press-ganged into finding a very dangerous artifact for the Grey.

Caspian pulled his cell phone out of his pocket and called a cab while his car shook with fury. Shea had done that while he'd been in the shop only yards away and neither Dylis nor he had noticed. Was he getting bolder? What would the next escalation be? He glanced through the shop window and swallowed. While his house might be protected, nothing else was. And Shea had proved he was willing to get close. There was nothing stopping Shea from slowly pulling apart his life the way he had done his clothes.

He couldn't lose everything again. He'd worked too hard to get this far. There was only one way to stop the damage. Find the Window.

———

Lydia heard the car pull up and was at the front door ready to greet Caspian before he knocked. She'd gotten changed after work and had spent a bit of time bringing some of the things out of the stable, now used for storage. There was a lawnmower in there that looked like it hadn't been used in fifty years. But there were also trunks of things that were too heavy for her to lift. It was like Gran had packed up but had never bothered to sort out. The good news was that Caspian would have to keep coming around for a while.

Seeing him was like a break from her real life. A slice of sunshine through stormy clouds. She needed more sunlight in her life.

Caspian walked up the path to her doorstep. "Hi."

"Hi." His gaze slid over her without pausing on any part, but no doubt noticing the dust smudged all over her clothing. "You started without me?"

"I've been unpacking the stable." In the corner of her eyes something moved; she glanced over but there was nothing there. Odd, she thought she'd heard something.

Caspian turned his head and she thought she saw him flinch, but then he turned back to face her. "Let's go in."

A breeze blew a piece of paper down the street and a chill followed. She suppressed a shiver and stepped back. Caspian shut the door after himself and turned the lock. He was security conscious… of course he was; he dealt in antiques and things worth thousands of dollars.

"Did I see a cab pulling away?" She raised one eyebrow.

"My car was making an odd humming sound. I didn't want to risk breaking down."

"It does look like a storm is coming." She glanced at him and smiled. "Good thing you're staying." That he'd turned up with his laptop and an overnight bag was enough to confirm he was sleeping over tonight. In which bed was the real question.

She hadn't been able to get his kiss out of her head. It had been enough to feed her dreams and make her realize it had been too long between boyfriends. Her body bubbled with expectation, lust coiled in her belly.

Caspian nodded and placed his bag and laptop satchel by the wrought-iron hat stand. "Or did you want me to put it in a room?"

"That's fine for the moment. We can sort out the rest later." Why was she so nervous?

"Good idea." He seemed to relax a little. Maybe this was just as odd for him—which was reassuring. If he'd sauntered in confident of his place, she might have changed her mind.

"Before you set up, can you help me get to some of the trunks in the stable? It might save us some time if they are just full of linen."

"Sure. Then I'll do the bedrooms?"

She nodded and tried to ignore the heat creeping over her skin.

"I didn't mean it like that."

"I know." She pushed her hair back. "When I invited you to stay I didn't know if I was inviting you to stay or *sleep*."

"That's okay; I wasn't sure which I wanted."

More like he knew what he wanted but wasn't sure if he wanted to go after it. She'd seen the desire in his eyes and felt the heat of his kiss, but she didn't want to be pushing when he was hesitant.

"And now?"

"I still don't know." His fingers brushed her cheek.

"But not because I don't want you, because I do, but because it's spectacularly bad timing and…" His thumb touched her lip.

For a moment she thought he was going to mention his ex. She held her breath, not wanting to be rebound-girl or cast in the exes shadow.

"It's fast."

"This is our third date." Third meeting was probably more appropriate, but she'd had worse dates. Besides, they were talking and doing the other stuff that happened on dates—today was just as awkward as any *should-we?* type conversation she'd ever had on a date.

He smiled. "True, although we haven't had dinner out yet."

"Is that one of your rules?"

"I don't know anymore." He paused. "Maybe following the rules isn't always the best thing to do." Then he kissed her. Slowly at first as if testing to see if the spark was still there waiting to be fanned.

It was. Heat filled her blood and spread throughout her body. Lust consumed her and for a moment she wanted to forget the work that needed doing and just go upstairs. He pulled away almost reluctantly.

"Stables?" Caspian inhaled and straightened as if readying himself to face something awful. He wasn't kidding when he said he didn't like deceased estates. She reached out her hand to reassure him that she didn't mind him poking around. His hand closed around hers. Warm and firm. She'd stayed up late the night before bagging Gran's clothes and personal belongings. It had been horrible and she'd been glad there'd been no one there to see her. But it was done. The only things left in that room were the jewelry and furniture and a diary that she'd slipped into her purse for safekeeping. There was nothing personal here now, just history. Boxes and trunks and cupboards of history.

She led him out the back. His gaze flickered over the garden that could do with some attention, pruning, weeding, and all the other little tasks that went into making a garden look great instead of scrubby and overgrown. Something rustled to the right and he tensed. His hand gave hers a slight squeeze.

"Are you okay?" She raised her eyebrows. He'd seemed a little jumpy when he'd arrived. Was he just as nervous as her? Maybe they shouldn't even be thinking about it if it was making them both wired... or maybe they should just get it out of their systems. The all-in method as opposed to testing the water with one toe first.

"Yeah, it's just been one of those days."

"The kind where you wished you'd stayed in bed?" Everything out of her mouth was about beds.

"Exactly that kind of day." He nodded as he spoke as if he was reliving the highlights. "But I'd rather be here than at home alone."

"Me too." It was nice to have someone to spend the evening with. Someone who didn't care if she was in old jeans and a T-shirt and covered in dust. She yanked open the shed door, which squealed like it was dying. The sound set her teeth on edge. It hadn't made that noise last time. She swung the door again, but it was silent.

"Old hinges; must have been a flake of rust caught in there." He put his hand on the door and had a look just to be sure.

Lydia pulled a flashlight off the shelves and flicked it on. Something moved in the shadows, and glass smashed. Her heart bounced hard in her chest. "What the hell?"

Caspian muttered something, then spoke up. "Mice?"

"I haven't seen any." She cast the beam of light around the shed with a shaky hand, but this time nothing moved.

Very strange. And now she was alert to every rustle as if she was the one who'd drunk too many espressos. Whatever twitches Caspian had tonight were catchy.

"These two trunks." She indicated two black trunks with metal corners, both padlocked closed. "Once they are out, I can start pulling out the smaller things."

He stood next to her, close enough that their arms bushed. Deliberate or accidental? A shiver of heat ran under her skin. Then he touched the top trunk and gave it a test nudge. "It looks frequently used."

"How can you tell?" She turned to face him.

His lips opened, and this close all she could think about was kissing him again. Was she really that desperate? She glanced at him and the way the torchlight caught his features. He looked otherworldly. Her heart gave a flip-flop that was somewhere between attraction and warning.

"Less rust on the lock. Do you have the keys?" His words were about work but his gaze was on her mouth; he looked up and met her gaze.

Those green eyes were more dangerous than all the glaciers in the Arctic. Whatever was going on behind them was hidden until it was too late. He wanted her and was trying to do the right thing; because of that she wanted him more. She wouldn't be the only woman.

His eyes combined with his dark curly hair made him the kind of man who'd leave a trail of women staring after him, and Lydia was willing to bet he never even noticed. But he was noticing her. Heat seemed to shimmer between them, but neither of them moved to take what they wanted.

"They were in Gran's room," she murmured, not wanting to break the moment. Her toes curled, hoping he'd close those few inches and place his lips on hers. Should she lean forward and taste his lips one more time?

The kiss was left untaken.

"Shall I walk backward?"

Walk backward? Her mind took a moment to catch up; he was talking about moving the trunk and getting on with the job. She had to blink and break the spell he cast to find her voice and form a coherent thought. How could he have that much effect on her? "I know the house better; I'll walk backward."

With that they picked up the handles and hefted the first trunk out of the stable and across the garden and into the kitchen. The second trunk followed. Once they were out the stable looked, well, still full of stuff. Boxes, tea chests, and what looked like a saddle and tack against one wall, along with tools and a rocking horse that looked straight out of one of those decorating magazines—except for the cobweb.

"There's a lot in here." He nodded to himself as if working out how long it was going to take to assess what was valuable and what was household junk.

Yeah, and she had no idea what she was going to do with it. How much of Gran could she throw out? She didn't have room for everything in her apartment. And yet she couldn't imagine living here. She'd rattle around like Gran had, living in only a few rooms while the rest of the house crumbled around her. But it did seem silly to keep her own place while this one was empty. Gran had suggested so many times that she come back home and save her money, and she'd always refused, wanting her independence and distance from the house. A lump formed in her throat and she had to blink in case tears formed and fell. She wished she'd taken Gran up on her offer. Then they would've had more time together.

"Do you ever look at the size of a job and wonder why you agreed to it?" Because if she was him, working after-hours to fit with her schedule, she'd be regretting ever taking the job, no matter how good the money.

"Not this time. The house is amazing; for its age there have been few renovations and those that have been done don't look tacked on." He looked at her. "It would be a shame to lose it."

She looked away and studied the rear of the house, trying to see it as he must. As a historical treasure. But she could only regard it as her childhood home. She didn't see the craftsmanship of the stonework or intricacy of the trellis that led up to her former bedroom. She saw the escape route she'd used to sneak out of the house when she was fifteen. Gran had caught her and explained that if Lydia wanted to go out all she had to do was ask and Gran would drop her off and pick her up and make sure she was safe. After that she'd always walked out the front door. Her poor Gran, yet she'd never complained about raising a teenager in her seventies and had never once said a bad word about her own daughter, Helen, even though it must have hurt.

Caspian was right. Selling to someone who wanted to profit on the past would be wrong, but she couldn't sell, then stipulate to the buyer how to use the property. There had to be a way to save the house and not send her into debt for the rest of her life.

"I can't make any decisions until everything gets valued and divvied up." That was her excuse and she was sticking to it. Then she grabbed the door and indicated that stable time was over and it was time to work. They had to get something done tonight and she needed to know what was in the trunks. Especially the more frequently used one.

He followed her back into the house. "I'll be upstairs if you need me."

She bit her tongue to keep from saying the obvious. "I'll let you know if I find anything really special."

Caspian nodded, then with a last glance picked up his laptop bag and went upstairs. For half a moment she was tempted to follow. In part because she liked to watch him work, so calm and careful, looking at each piece, logging it and making notes with a faint look of concentration on his face that pinched his eyebrows as if he'd forgotten she was even in the room. She'd love to know what he was thinking as he worked.

Later. She'd find a reason to go and watch him, talk to him. She was sure he wouldn't mind. She pulled the keys out of her pocket. There were a dozen keys on an old fob, a man's, embossed with the name T. Thomas Callaway. Her grandfather. He'd been killed in war, but she'd seen a photo of him in uniform before he left to fight. He'd been so young, only twenty, and a year older than Gran. The choices she made after his death must have been difficult, and yet she'd managed to keep Callaway House in the family. And here she was, seventy years later with more opportunities and options and she was still thinking of selling. No, she had to look at ways of keeping it and fixing it. If Gran could, she could.

Lydia fingered the keys, sure that some belonged to locks that no longer existed. There were three little keys that looked like they'd fit the trunk locks, which probably meant there was a third trunk hidden at the back of the stable. She studied the keys, as if she could guess which one would fit the more frequently used trunk, but she couldn't. She couldn't see a difference between a used key and an unused key.

In fact, to her eye the locks on the trunks looked the same. She shook her head. Caspian obviously saw something she didn't. The second key fit and the lock popped. She took a breath before lifting the lid. The hinges squeaked but didn't resist. Inside were more books.

Lydia groaned. *Really, Gran? Did you never throw anything away?* Then she noticed all of them had plain covers. She picked one up, a dark blue one that didn't look too old, and flicked it open. The first page was dated and filled with shaky script. Gran's neat writing had deteriorated over the last five years. This was a diary from two years ago. She put it down without reading and picked up another. It was older. Then she lifted out a pile and picked up the bottom one. It was black, the pages yellowed but otherwise undamaged. Lydia carefully opened the diary, trying to guess the date as she did. 1970? Older?

Twenty years older. Nineteen forty-nine. Callaway House in its early days as a mistress hotel. She flicked through the pages. It was less of a diary and more of a journal. This one ended after only four months, which meant the rest of 1949 was still in there. That meant... she exhaled slowly. That meant she had the history of the house in one trunk. Every time Gran had finished a book she'd locked it in the trunk and never told anyone she kept a diary.

Her skin came up in gooseflesh as if a cold gust of air had touched her flesh. Gran had never said anything because she knew that people would kill to get ahold of them. She put the books back in and closed the lid, then relocked it. What was she supposed to do with the diaries?

Something scuttled over the kitchen floor. She jumped up expecting to see a spider or roach, but there was nothing there. No doubt it was already hiding somewhere, ready to surprise her. Yuck, God knew what she'd brought out of the shed and into the house.

She wiped her hands on her jeans and ran up the stairs to tell Caspian what she'd found. He wasn't in the first two rooms. In the third room he was standing next to the bed, his hand on the footboard, eyes closed. He didn't seem to have heard her and he didn't move. His lips curved in a small smile.

What was he doing?

Was he imagining what had gone on in the house and having some kind of weird fantasy?

Lydia coughed. It was just too strange to see him standing perfectly still yet obviously thinking something.

Chapter 9

CASPIAN'S EYELIDS FLEW OPEN. LYDIA STOOD IN THE doorway looking like a beautiful thundercloud. His stomach sank. How long had she been standing there? Had she heard him talking to Dylis while sifting through the furniture's past? He hoped she wouldn't notice the tightness of his jeans. The trouble with sifting through impressions in a bedroom was it was like scrolling through a porn video. It didn't matter where he looked, there was flesh, and that's all he was. He couldn't help his body's response. He was sure even a fairy would've been affected by the things he saw.

Her eyes narrowed. "What's going on?"

"I…" The truth rested on the tip of his tongue. Dylis sat on the sideboard, her sword in hand. "Sometimes it helps to put myself at an auction. I remember something similar being on the floor a few years ago."

He was going to trip over his lies and fall into the river of damned souls. Dylis huffed and rolled her eyes.

Lydia raised an eyebrow and crossed her arms. She didn't believe him. Ah well, it had been nice to see that look of desire in her eye while it had lasted.

"Right. I never saw you doing that before."

"I did look pretty stupid standing there, and I make a point of trying not to look stupid in public." He'd done that too many times growing up. Tripping over fairies no one else could see, touching something and getting caught in the vision. He changed the subject and hoped she'd let it drop. "Some of this furniture is really old. It predates the notorious years."

Some of it he suspected was as old as the house.

"Really?"

He tapped the wood. "Guest bed. The one down the hall, an old master suit. Do you have photos? It's like a museum, as if your grandmother was trying her best to keep it as it was even as she earned a living."

"How do you know this stuff?"

Because I'm psychometric and half fairy didn't seem like an appropriate response. "I don't know. I'm making educated guesses," he said instead.

Her face softened a little. He was off the hook but not out of trouble. The tension in his muscles eased. Dylis should've warned him Lydia was coming up, but they'd been discussing the sudden increase in Grey activity. It was no longer just the ghost—which Dylis hadn't found. Maybe it was hiding from the interlopers because it was tiny and weak. That made sense if it had been here for as long as Lydia claimed. The ghost was probably close to death.

Tonight there'd also been imps in the garden, hanging around the stable as they'd pulled out the trunks and trying to trip him up, and Dylis had scared off a boggart that had been creeping around the house. While he knew this was part of Shea's campaign to annoy him into making a deal and he needed to ignore it, it was wearing him down. Which was the whole idea. Shea could keep up this low-level annoyance for a very long time. If Shea were using stronger magic, he'd be killing himself faster, so this was much more effective. Had Lydia noticed anything strange about the house yet—aside from him spending quality time with the furniture?

"I think I've found something that could confirm your theories." She turned and went down the hallway.

Caspian followed. In the kitchen Lydia opened one of the trunks. He knew exactly what he was looking at—diaries.

"Are they your grandmother's?"

She nodded. "They go back to World War Two. Well, that's the oldest I've found. And I only had a quick look."

Caspian rubbed his hand over his jaw. The diaries complicated things. "They have a value I can't begin to estimate, and not just in monetary sense."

"I know. What if she listed mistresses and the men? Some of the same families would still have weight in the community. And then there were the deals done at the parties. And then there were the other parties. It only closed twenty-eight years ago…"

She was thinking exactly what he was; there could be very sensitive information in there wrapped up with the real history of the house. Had Gran kept the diaries as a who's who in case there was trouble, or were they simply diaries of her life?

"What are you going to do?"

"I don't know. What can I do? This is her life. I can't burn them."

"No, no. You can't do that, but you need to keep them safe." They were part of the estate. Most times a person's personal diary didn't matter. But this was different. Madam Callaway was a well-known person from a well-known family and her diaries went back. Her diaries had historical significance as well as social significance. "I think you should read some of them, get a feel for what's in there. If it's names, we're going to have to handle things differently."

How desperate would people be to keep their association with Callaway House quiet? The artists probably not much, judges and lawyers and politicians, very much so. And if they were making backroom deals here, he was willing to bet they had the pull to make the diaries disappear.

Lydia slumped down onto the lid of the other trunk, resting her elbows on her knees and her head in her hands. Her gaze glued to the floor. "I can't do it. There's too much here. I can't keep everything and I don't want to get rid of anything. I don't want to sell and I don't know what to do."

Then she began to cry. The kind of half-smothered sob as if she didn't want him to notice. But how could he not notice? Her hiccupping breaths cut at his heart. In that moment he knew it was more than simple attraction. He wanted more of Lydia than just the time at the house. He wanted to see where what they had was going. For a moment he hesitated, not sure what to do, or what she would want him to do. Would she rather be left alone to pull herself together? He didn't know her well enough to answer that yet. However, he couldn't walk away when she was so upset. He sat next to her and put his arm around her, drawing her close. She let herself be pulled into his embrace.

"It's okay to feel overwhelmed. You don't have to decide anything now." His hand stroked her hair. He wanted to kiss her tears away, but after the look she'd given him when she'd caught him feeling the bed, that probably wasn't a good idea. So he let her cry.

He closed his eyes. He didn't know what it was like to lose someone close, but he could imagine the hole that would be left when his parents died. It wasn't just her grandmother; this was the woman who'd raised her.

After a few moments Lydia sniffed. Her head was still resting on his chest as if she was reluctant to pull away. Her breathing steadied. "God, you must think me pathetic for falling apart like that."

"No. Everyone is entitled to grieve."

She eased up to sitting, a few tears still on her cheek.

Caspian lifted his hand and wiped them away. The moment he did he knew he'd gone too far. That simple gesture was more intimate than anything else they'd shared. For a heartbeat neither of them moved. His fingers lingered against her skin as if he was unable to pull away.

Slowly she moved closer, her lips brushing his in the lightest of kisses, yet it was far more intense than anything he'd seen in the memories of the furniture upstairs. The hunger woke, reminding him that it had been a long time since he'd held a woman in his arms. He swept his tongue over her lips and was surprised when her mouth opened and she responded. He imme-diately wanted more, but knew that was impossible. He couldn't fall in love with someone he had to keep lying to. It wasn't fair to Lydia, and he couldn't go through that heartbreak again. He drew away, missing the taste of her lips.

"Thank you for understanding." She placed one hand

on his thigh, a soft kiss on his cheek, and made no effort to move away, her head resting on his shoulder. "Sorry my family is so messed up."

Most men were nothing like him. He understood the weight of family secrets; the only difference was he could never talk about his. "Every family has its secrets and skeletons."

"Even yours?"

"Especially mine." The heat of her palm on his leg sank into his blood. He didn't care how odd her family was, he would always win that competition hands down. How much did he dare to tell her and how much would she believe?

She drew back enough to look him in the eye. "Like what?" Her brown eyes were still glittery from the tears. She was trying to find more common ground. Did she realize what she was asking? Could he even come close to telling her the truth?

"If I told you, it wouldn't be a secret." He tried to make light of it but knew he'd have to tell her something close to the truth.

She tilted her chin and held his gaze. "That's not fair; you know all about my scandalous family."

It was probably a good thing she didn't know exactly how much he knew. Caspian chewed over the truths he could drag out and in the end went with the safest one. "There's the pirate in the family tree."

"So you said."

And he was going to have to do better. He wanted to do better so she knew more about him. He glanced at her before speaking. "My father isn't my father." It was much easier to say than he'd expected. Probably because he'd lived with the knowledge for so long it no longer mattered to him.

Her forehead furrowed. "Your mother had an affair?"

"She did, and to this day I don't think she's told my dad about it—my dad who raised me, I mean."

"But she told you."

He'd stuck his foot in that one. "When I was older she did. My younger brother had been teasing me about how I looked different from him and saying I was adopted. She promised me that I was loved and wanted, even though I had been an accident, but she also made me promise not to tell." And he'd never told anyone until today.

"That's rough." She gave his thigh a gentle squeeze that went straight to his heart.

"That's the way things are. If I changed them, I wouldn't exist. But my brother was right. We both have dark hair but that's where the similarity ends. My mother told me I have my father's eyes."

"Have you met him?"

"No, but I know who he is, and I know it's better I never meet him." It was really nice to tell someone. He'd never shared the details with Natalie because he'd been afraid what she'd think, and what she'd say. With Lydia it was different. She knew what it felt like to have a family scandal and she knew that some things were best not discussed in public. However, telling her his father was the Crown Prince of Annwyn, what she would know as heaven, hell, and the afterlife all rolled into one, might be too much.

She raised her eyebrows. "You're not going to tell me who he is?"

"He's a powerful man who seduced my mother with sweet-talk. That's all I need to know. That's all you need to know." Telling Lydia anything more would be unwise. Even among fairies most didn't know who his father was, according to Dylis.

"So when you told me your father was a mechanic you weren't being entirely truthful."

"I was." In his mind he only had one father; the other one had just contributed DNA and magic. "He's the man who raised me, who taught me to ride a bike, drive a car, and do an oil change. Aside from genetics he's my father, and I'm sure in his heart he considers me his son." Caspian stood, bringing Lydia with him.

Their hands linked without thought. He knew the time for walking away before he got in too deep was gone, and he was quite happy to sink if it meant spending more time with Lydia.

She slid easily into his embrace, her head on his shoulder. He wrapped one arm around her waist, the other was still holding her hand. Against his chest she took a few deep breaths as if she wasn't ready to let him go. Every small movement made his skin crave more. He wanted to feel her hands on him. It wasn't just talking easily to someone that he missed; it was the skin-to-skin contact. And yet he knew that everything he shared with Lydia was still only a half-formed shadow that wouldn't become real until she knew the truth. *One piece at a time*. He'd never been a rip-the-bandage-off-fast kind of person when small steps and caution worked just as well.

For the moment what they'd shared was enough. She knew more about him than anyone.

Dylis peered around the corner, glanced at him, then backed away just as fast.

Lydia looked up at him as if sensing a change. He took that moment to kiss her and pretend that fairies didn't exist and weren't trying to mess with his life for the next thirty seconds. Her hand swept over his chest until her fingers brushed the curls at the nape of his neck. As the kiss deepened he let himself fall into the fantasy that everything would be fine. His hand cupped her butt and she moved against him in a way that tempted him to do more than kiss. And he was sure she noticed the hardness that had formed between them.

But she didn't pull back. Her tongue traced his lip, and danced with his. Her body molded closer.

Then they heard a sharp screech and heavy thump.

<center>~~~</center>

"What was that?" Lydia whispered, glancing over her shoulder. Her ears strained, trying to listen for another bump or strange noise.

"The ghost?" he asked.

Lydia shook her head and listened again, but all she could hear was the pounding of her heart. Her pulse had been accelerating before being startled. Caspian had that effect on her. She was glad she had an effect on him. His arm was wrapped around her as if he would protect her, his hand on her butt, but his shoulder was tense beneath her hand. She looked up at him and was caught in his gaze. His eyes were mesmerizing. He lowered his lips to hers once more, but it was just a last taste.

"Want me to have a look?"

She should say yes, but she didn't want to move.

Not when she'd chipped through his defenses and had learned a little bit more about him. And in exchange he'd seen her crumble and unable to cope. She let her fingers trail down his chest, enjoying the hint of muscle beneath his shirt.

"I'll do it, you… you can get back to cataloguing in the bedroom." Even as she said it she knew that was the wrong thing. The warmth of the embrace faded and the moment fractured as Caspian released her. As his fingers slid away she caught his hand. "Your secret is safe with me."

He looked at her and for a moment she had the feeling that what he'd told was just the tip of the iceberg. "I wouldn't have told you if I didn't trust you. However, I think I should go and see what's banging around."

"I'm sure it's nothing." But as something else went bang she jumped. "I'll wait here."

She watched him walk out of the kitchen. As soon as he was out of the room, she made sure the outside door was locked. Then she peeked out the window, but in the dark garden she couldn't be sure what was shrubs and shadows and what was her imagination getting the better of her. This behavior wasn't normal for the ghost.

A few minutes later Caspian came back. "I didn't see anyone, and I didn't find anything broken."

That should have been reassuring, but it wasn't. The house was still making odd sounds that couldn't be blamed on the approaching storm or the age of the house.

"Good." She tried to look relieved but suspected she failed when Caspian didn't immediately go. "I'm sure it was just the ghost acting up."

"Yeah." Now he didn't look convinced.

"I might go check all the locks."

"Did you want me to come with you?"

"You just said you didn't see anything." The more they talked about the strange noises the more she was sure she heard. Never had being in the house rattled her so much.

"I didn't."

Scuffling footsteps on the second floor made her look up. That sounded more like the ghost.

Caspian pointed to the ceiling. "I'll go check upstairs."

"Okay... I'll check those locks. Call out if you see the ghost or something." It was the or something that was making her stomach tight and her heart bounce high in her chest.

She waited a moment until he'd gone upstairs. Then she walked around and checked all the locks, making sure that the house was closed up properly. She saw nothing out of place and yet she'd never felt so uneasy. She was glad she wasn't going to be staying here alone.

The house creaked and groaned as if complaining of an ache no one could understand. And while nothing seemed amiss, she jumped with every shudder and bump. For a moment she stood in the entrance looking up at the stairs and the landing that overlooked and then led to the bedrooms where Caspian would be. How easy would it be to just turn off the lights and join him?

She pressed her lips together and forced herself to go back to the kitchen. She would not run upstairs because she was afraid of the noises an old house made. Instead she threw herself into looking through the trunks and seeing what she could learn from the diaries.

While she was curious about Gran's life and about

the details of Callaway House, it felt wrong to be looking. But then if Gran hadn't wanted them read why keep them? Why write them in the first place?

She skipped over the recent ones but paused at the diaries from twenty-eight years ago. Her teeth worried her lip. What had been written about her birth? She'd always been told that her mother had left soon after because she was scared of the responsibility of looking after a baby... but she'd never come back, never sent a card or a birthday present. As Lydia had gotten older she'd thought it was to escape the Callaway name. Maybe it was both.

Either way she'd stopped worrying about it years ago. If her mother didn't want to know her, that was fine. She'd had plenty of love from Gran and her aunts. She put the diaries aside and went back a bit further to Callaway House at its peak in the fifties and sixties. Then she took a breath and opened to a random page.

A shopping trip to buy new gloves with a couple of the other women.

That wasn't what Lydia was expecting. She flicked a few more pages, but there was just more chat about life, including that one of the women was expecting and they didn't think the man would want her for much longer. He didn't want a second family, just fun.

Something upstairs crashed.

Lydia jumped up and dropped the diary. *Caspian?*

Her heart pounded hard while the rest of her was frozen in position. She strained her ears listening for footsteps but heard nothing. And he didn't call out. The lights flickered twice then settled. In that moment of fear she wished Caspian was down here with her. Shadows danced at the edges of her vision, but when she looked there was nothing there.

Get a grip.

But she couldn't; panic had taken hold and was ruling her body. Something very odd was going on tonight.

On the floor above something rolled, the sound filled the house, and the hair along her arms spiked. Lydia snatched up the half-dozen books that were on the floor and shoved them back into the trunk, then she slammed the lid closed and turned the key. She grabbed her handbag off the kitchen counter and forced herself to calmly turn off the lights and walk upstairs even though she wanted to run. Her pulse pounded in her ears.

Had Caspian heard the noises? Was he not concerned?

Of course not; it was an old house, making old house noises. It might have been him dropping something. Halfway up the stairs she began to feel more than a little silly.

Then Caspian appeared on the landing. "I was coming down to check on you."

"I was…" Coming to check on him? Running and hiding? "Just packing away."

A rumble reverberated through the house. The storm was about to start. She heard the first few drops of rain hit, then it just became a steady drumming.

She walked up the last few stairs. "How'd you get on?"

"Good." He gave no indication of seeing or hearing anything odd.

"You still up for sleeping in a haunted house?" She tried to make light of it, but part of her wanted to jump in her car and drive to her nice modern apartment.

He grinned. "Ghosts don't scare me."

"What does?"

"Fairies."

She glanced at him, but he looked deadly serious. Okay, no weirder than people who were afraid of clowns, although probably less common. "The ghost never used to worry me, just, I don't know. It feels strange being here."

"We don't have to stay."

"You're supposed to tell me everything is fine and to tell me you've picked a room."

"Would you believe me?"

"No. You can feel it, right?" *I'm not going crazy.*

He nodded, then looked at her and smiled. "The room with the blue and white floral quilt," he said as he walked past and went downstairs to pick up his overnight bag.

She turned to watch as he walked away. He had picked a room. Her lips curved. Well, what else was he going to be thinking about while going through the bedrooms? She remembered the way he'd stood with one hand on the bed, thinking. Thinking of the auction like he'd said, or thinking of something else?

The room he'd suggested wasn't the one she'd seen him in. She turned on the light and tried to work out why he'd picked this room. The bed was just a plain wrought-iron four-post bed that didn't even look antique. She was a little disappointed. She'd thought he'd go for the obvious antique. The big old bed that still had sheer curtains hanging from the top—it's what she would've picked. For a moment she considered suggesting somewhere else, but when she turned he was in the doorway with his bag in his hand. His eyes shimmered with desire. She glanced back at the bed. Heat crept up her cheeks and down her throat. Was she really going to do this?

Yes.

Without breaking eye contact she flicked the quilt back.

Chapter 10

HE WOULD NOT GIVE HIMSELF THE CHANCE TO WALK away. Not this time. Lydia was different; her family was just as screwed up as his. She'd understand. He was sure he was telling himself lies to cover the fact that he was lying to her by not telling her what he was. Maybe afterwards, maybe in the morning over coffee. He'd find the right time to tell her what he was. Would there ever be a right time? He knew there was a wrong time and that was now when all he wanted to do was feel human in her arms and forget about fairies.

Rain hammered against the roof, dulling the sounds of Greys scampering through the house. He'd picked this room because of the iron, but Lydia made it inviting. A surge of desire raced through his body. Was it Lydia or the room? Or was the house making them both crazy?

He walked in and closed the door behind him, then dropped his bag at the foot of the bed. He couldn't deny he'd been thinking about the possibility of having her all day. Maybe he'd forgotten how awkward the first time with someone new could be. It was like a game where neither side was entirely sure of the rules even though they both wanted to play.

Her teeth raked her lip as she watched him. He needed to make a move or this was going to get weird and uncomfortable. He took off his shoes and socks and walked toward her. Beneath his feet the carpet was soft and worn and had been used by couples who'd never made it to the bed or just preferred it. His shaft ached to be touched. He had to get the memories of other people out of his head and focus on Lydia.

He cupped her cheek and placed a soft kiss on her lips, still half-expecting her to change her mind at any moment, or for a fairy to burst in and interrupt. Dylis had muttered something about his last days in the mortal world before standing guard. If it was true he was going to die because of Shea, he wanted to enjoy what was left of his life.

Lydia's hands slid up his chest. Her touch burned away all other thought. Her tongue flicked against his, inviting him to take more as she pressed herself against him. His fingers splayed over her butt and drew her closer. In a step the backs of his legs were against the bed and he was pulling her with him; he braced for the flood of impressions, but the sheets had nothing more than laundry day imprinted on them.

She pushed herself up to straddle his hips, her hair free so it hung loose around her shoulders, the ends curling on the swell of her breasts. He caught a tendril and used it to bring her close. Her lips were a whisper away from his, but she didn't kiss him.

"I just want you to know I don't usually do this."

He knew exactly what she meant. "Neither do I."

He leaned up and sealed her lips before she could say anything else. He didn't want to think because if he did he might stop and realize what a bad idea this was.

Her fingers opened his shirt buttons, then glided over his chest. He was glad he made the effort to run around the block a few times a week. He was in good shape—though that may also be because of his unnatural parentage. The touch of her hands sent shivers of heat running through his skin. No one since his ex-wife had touched him this intimately.

But the pain Natalie had caused him was vanquished by Lydia's caress. Her hips moved over his. There was far too much denim between them. Through her shirt he cupped her breast, felt the weight in his palm as his thumbs circled her nipples. They peaked, pressing against the fabric. She gave a little moan and rolled her hips in a way that made his shaft harden further.

With a few flicks of his fingers he opened her shirt and pushed it off her shoulders, she sat up and shrugged out of it, then went to undo her bra. Her gaze locked with his for a heartbeat, then she was taking off the flesh-colored scrap and letting it fall on the floor. Her pale pink nipples were tight and hard. He sat up and like a man in dream took what he wanted before he could wake.

His tongue circled one nipple before taking it into his mouth. She gasped as his teeth raked the surface, but her back arched, offering him more. He switched to the other side, taking his time to taste her skin and draw the little sighs from her. With his free hand he opened the top of her jeans and traced the line of her panties.

He twisted and lay her down on her back, unzipping and pulling off her jeans. She lifted her legs, kicking free of the fabric. His fingers hooked around her floral print panties, then he hesitated. He was going too fast. But she lifted her hips and pushed them down, not waiting for him. He drew them down her legs and tossed them on the floor with the rest of the clothing.

She was perfect. All curves and creamy skin. At the junction of her thighs her curls had been trimmed enough to offer a glimpse and tease.

He kissed her ankle. She watched. He kissed the inside of her knee. His hand slid up her inner thigh stopping short of her pussy. The tips of his fingers grazed the curls, her legs moved farther apart in silent invitation, her gaze never leaving him as if she was daring him to go further. Would he? But his hand was already moving, his fingers sliding over her slick skin, teasing her clit before dipping into her core.

Her eyelids fluttered but didn't close. "You have too many clothes on." The last word was more of a groan as he stroked her sensitive flesh.

Caspian smiled. He stood and shrugged out of his shirt, then undid his jeans, acutely aware she was watching, propped up on her elbow. It was her turn to look and assess. His pushed his jeans and underwear down in one move—much better to get these things over with than drag them out. Her gaze skimmed down his body. His cock twitched in response.

The impressions held by the carpet of lovers decades ago swelled around him until he could almost hear the sound of skin on skin. He could get lost in the memories. He wanted to give the room new memories to hold on to.

Lydia beckoned him back to bed. There was nothing coy in her gestures, so he responded in kind. He moved over her, one knee dropping between her thighs, his lips taking a kiss. Her tongue sought his before he broke away and kissed down her neck, tasting the sweetness of her skin. Feeling the heat between them. He didn't usually get impressions off people, but with Lydia he felt her lust as if it were his own. Strong like a riptide waiting to drag him under. And he didn't care. If he was going to get hurt in the end, he might as well enjoy the beginning. She pushed him back before he could reach her breast. She glanced over at the bedside table and grasped the foil packet that had been next to her hand-bag. He expected her to hand it to him. She didn't.

Instead she sat up and opened the packet. Then took his shaft in her hand. The touch was a jolt like electric-ity coursing through him. Her fingers feathered over his hard flesh, taking her time as she traced the ridge and circled the head. She glanced up, her dark eyes full of molten heat. And he wanted to sink and drown. With a couple of deft movements she rolled the rubber on and as she lay back down she drew him with her, one leg hooking over his hip as if to stop him from pulling away.

Like he would.

He shifted his hips and used his hand to guide his shaft to her entrance, but didn't enter, not yet. He moved, teasing her and himself. She rolled her hips and arched her back as if that would bring him closer.

"Come on," she whispered against his lips.

"There's no rush." It nearly killed him to say that when all he wanted to do was thrust in.

"I want to feel you." Her nails trailed over his ribs.

He hissed in a breath, then pushed in a little more. This time when she moved he slid in deeper. He gave up the illusion of control. She didn't want it. She met him thrust for thrust, not afraid to grip his hips and adjust for what she wanted. Tension tightened in his balls. He wanted to spill. With a wrench of will he slowed and slid his hand between their bodies, finding and caressing her clit. She covered his hand with hers, changing the movement ever so slightly. It was so much easier to be shown rather than guessing. Her breathing shortened to gasps and her eyes closed. Her sheath tightened around him as she came.

Her half-silenced moans and the grip of her core were too much for him to take. He gave another couple of strokes before giving in and letting the release flood him.

Lydia's hands smoothed down his back. Her eyes remained closed as if she were concentrating on slowing down her breathing or holding on to the moment. He wasn't sure which, but he was trying to do both. He placed a soft kiss on her mouth, which she responded to, but the urgency was gone and it was more of a last caress.

He eased away and dealt with the rubbish. He glanced back at her laying sprawled on the bed as if she were too boneless to move. That was a good thing; it meant he hadn't forgotten how to please a woman—even if she knew what she needed. He padded over to the light switch and turned it off, then joined her in bed, but he was sure he wouldn't be sleeping much as she curled up against him.

Strange beds always harbored too many details of the previous occupants. And while the sheets offered a little protection there was still enough history to give a restless sleep as it filtered into his dreams.

When he woke it was dark, and for a moment he had no idea who he was or where he was. It took a couple of heartbeats for the confusion to fade and for him to realize he was alone and the house was silent. He eased out of bed and pulled on his jeans and went downstairs.

—✺—

Lydia drew her legs up on the loveseat in the parlor. She couldn't use the front room without thinking of Gran. The muscles on her inner thighs twinged and the memory brought a flush to her cheeks. It had seemed like a good idea at the time and Caspian hadn't said no. What man would? He was spending a night at Callaway House. And enjoying the hospitality the way rich, married men once would have.

Except Caspian was neither rich, nor married.

She turned the page of the diary and scanned the pages, reading without absorbing the details, hoping she'd get sleepy again. She'd woken up and after lying awake and listening to him sleep had gotten up even though she'd wanted to remain in bed. His body was warm, and firm, and when he looped his arm over her waist it had seemed so natural. There was a grace to his movements that she'd noticed even when he was working. The way he touched, the way he moved. But it was his eyes, the green ice had been burning when he'd looked at her.

And like the gentleman he was he'd made sure she came first. Too perfect. Yet there was still the morning after to get through, and that would decide if it had been a one-time thing or something that might last a little longer—she didn't expect forever. But she wouldn't mind a few more weeks, or months, of having him in her bed before he learned how hard the Callaway name was to be around.

She hoped he wouldn't care; after all, it wasn't as if his family name could be tainted by association. To stop herself thinking of the end before they'd really begun she made herself concentrate on the diary. Gran had been writing about a singer with the voice of an angel and the looks to match—the too pretty man in the photo? He was very popular apparently and also cash poor.

He gave me a gift tonight, said I'd been most kind but that it was time to move on. I didn't open it until after closing. For a man who never had a dollar on him he gave me a silver compact. Pretty little thing.

Lydia stopped and re-read. She'd seen that silver makeup mirror in Gran's personal things. It had been wrapped up in a piece of tissue paper and tucked in the drawer with her makeup. It was now at her apartment in a box in the spare room. Had she and the singer been lovers? Is that why Gran had kept it safe for so long? Then she shook her head; Gran hadn't thrown anything out. No doubt she'd kept it because it was pretty. She should get Caspian to take a look at it; she'd drop into his shop—plus it would be an excuse to see him again, outside of the house.

"You couldn't sleep?"

She yelped and dropped the diary she'd been reading. Caspian stood in the doorway, half-dressed in jeans.

"Sorry, I didn't mean to startle you."

She picked up the book and tried not to glance over, but her memory filled in the details. Fit without being muscle-bound, just enough hair on his chest to make him a man. A narrow line of hair led from his naval and dipped into his jeans.

"I'm not used to sharing a bed." That was the truth, but she could get used to seeing Caspian in hers. "Did I wake you?"

He was leaning in the doorway, looking far too attractive for the middle of the night—or was this that morning after talk? "No, I never sleep well in strange beds."

She raised her eyebrows—how many strange beds did he sleep in?

"When I travel, for work. I don't..." He looked away, his gaze falling on his left hand resting on the door frame. An unconscious gesture, but she was sure he was thinking of his ex-wife.

This was the awkwardness she hadn't wanted in the morning. Too late now, they were both up. She patted the cushion next to her. "Want to join me?"

He didn't answer; he just sat, without touching her. It took a moment for her to realize that she wanted him to put his hand on her leg or at least acknowledge what they'd done. But they weren't together. It had been an itch that needed scratching. If this didn't go well, maybe she wouldn't bother showing him Gran's mirror. Just cut ties and walk away. One little mirror wouldn't matter to the estate; besides, Gran had never put it on the insurance, or even spoken about it, so it probably wasn't worth much money.

She turned to face him and asked the obvious. "Why don't you sleep well in strange beds?"

She expected a response like too soft or too hard, or fear of bedbugs or something else innocuous. He looked at his laced fingers as if thinking hard. Too hard for the question. A chill brushed over her skin and drew the fine hairs on her arm up in gooseflesh. Around her the house was silent. It was then she realized that was what had woken her. She'd gone to sleep listening to the noise of the storm and the creaking and rattling of the house.

Now it was deathly still. As if the ghost was waiting for something.

Caspian drew in a breath. "Do you believe in psychics?"

That wasn't what she was expecting. "Like fortune tellers?"

"No, like real psychic powers. People who can do things others can't." He glanced over. "Like psychometry."

She wasn't even sure what the word meant. "What is it?"

Again he paused and swallowed. "If someone is psychometric they get impressions off objects. I don't sleep well because I *know* what has gone on in the strange beds."

Lydia didn't know whether to laugh or be stunned into silence. Was he saying he could see the past? Impossible. Yet she remembered the way he'd touched the furniture. The way she'd caught him holding on to the bedpost. He hadn't been thinking of an auction; he'd been looking into the past.

He'd been seeing the past of Callaway House the whole time he was here.

"Are you telling me you can walk up to something and know who has touched it?"

"It's not like that. I get a feeling, some images— particularly of strong emotions—I can sift through to when it was made and get a feel for the age."

"That must be useful in your line of work." What the hell had he seen? Had he just wanted her because of what was going on in his mind? Oh my God, what was she even thinking? She was ready to believe him instantly. Because it fitted. The few comments he'd made about something were like he knew it. *The recently used trunk.* She hadn't been able to tell the difference because there wasn't one to her eye. He'd known that because he must have felt it or seen it or something.

"That's why I do this job. It means I get to use it instead of hiding from it. I still have to prove authenticity and go by the book, but it is a valuable shortcut that has saved me from buying a good fake."

She nodded. Then shook her head. "You know how this sounds, right?"

He looked back at his hands. His finger touched where a wedding ring would have once sat. "I never told Natalie. When I said I caught her cheating, I meant I got an impression of her in our bed with another man. She'd brought him to our house. If she hadn't, I'd have never found out."

Lydia's mind scrambled to process what he was saying. "You left your wife because of something you thought you saw when you touched the bed?"

"I know what I saw. I've had this, this talent since I was a child. She admitted the affair when I asked her about it, said it had been going on for months and then she apologized because she never meant for it to happen. As upset as I was at her for cheating, I share the blame. I never fully let her in. I could never be totally honest with her, and she had to feel that distance between us."

Lydia had no idea how she was supposed to react to this revelation. But she did know that it was a big deal to share such a secret. For him to tell her meant he wanted to be with her—and not just for tonight. Her heart seemed to stutter before steadying.

Did she even believe in the abilities he claimed to

have? Well, only one way to find out. "What does this
tell you?"

She handed him her grandmother's diary.

He took it without question, as if expecting a test.
He held the book as though weighing it and considering its worth, but she knew he wasn't seeing the leather
and pages.

"She enjoyed writing at the end of the day," he began.
"It helped her unwind even if she was tired of smiling
and pretending to be happy." He tilted his head. "She
seemed mostly happy. There was a lover, or someone
she was fond of but could never talk about. She was sad
when he left. But she had to keep up the illusion that
everything was all right even if she was worried about
money." Caspian offered her the diary back. "From
what I've picked up she was an amazing woman. You
were lucky to have someone like that in your life."

"Thank you." That he could appreciate Gran's life and
look beyond the scandal meant a lot. She took the diary
back, but she wasn't sure she believed him about the psychometry. He could've made that stuff up. But he didn't
know what year the diary was from and there was no
way he could know about the mysterious singer—unless
he was just guessing because of the picture. Maybe she
should ask him something about something else. She bit
her lip and her gaze landed on the old love seat.

Caspian shook his head. "Trust me, you don't want
to know."

"How do you live with it? Do you see the history of
everything?"

"I can block out a lot of it, now. It used to cause me
a lot of problems."

"I can imagine." There'd be a lot of things he wouldn't want to see. "You probably know Callaway House much better than me."

"I doubt that. I saw bits of the past, that's all."

"And they didn't affect you at all?"

He gave her a rueful smile. "I never said that. Many of the things I see affect me. I've seen some awful things. I've seen murders I can't report or that happened a hundred years ago. They are no less real than if they were happening in front of me. Things with strong emotions last longer than the day-to-day grind. I nearly turned down this job because I was worried about seeing too much." He put his hand over hers. "I'm glad I didn't."

She turned her hand over and wrapped her fingers around his, the heat of his skin seeping into her and warming her. She searched his face, but his expression was carefully neutral as if he was expecting the realization to slowly sink in and for her to pull away. She wasn't quite sure what to say, only that she needed to say something. "I'm glad you didn't, too."

Her body tingled at the memory. Did he know what she was thinking? Would she be forever wondering what he was seeing? There'd be no privacy, ever. He'd know if she'd shaved her legs in the shower. However, he'd told her, so she could make that decision. It was up to her what happened next.

"So now that you know I'm weird, I'll go back upstairs and leave you to get back to reading." He went to get up but she kept hold of his hand.

He glanced at her, his eyebrows pinched together and his lips parted as if he were going to speak.

She couldn't let him just walk away. After everything

he'd seen he'd been nothing but polite. There was no smug glee or crude comments. Men like Caspian didn't come along very often. There were worse things than being psychometric, right? And he'd found a use for the talent. She was going to have to look it up and find out more. Or trust him. She looked into his eyes. Once she'd thought he was hiding behind them, now she knew he saw everything, more than anyone should. He was protecting himself… and his heart.

And she wouldn't be the one to break it. "I don't think you're weird and I don't regret what happened." She leaned over and kissed him, and what was meant to be a simple kiss deepened quickly as if the lust in her blood wasn't yet sated.

His fingers brushed her cheek. "Neither do I. Are you coming back to bed?"

Yes, she'd be a fool to hide down here while he was up there. But she wanted a moment to herself to catch her breath and work out what she needed to know about him. Not to ask tonight, but soon. And she'd expect him to have questions too.

"I'll be up in a minute." She let his fingers slide free and watched him walk out of the parlor. She knew in that heartbeat she couldn't let him walk out of her life, no matter what he could see.

Chapter 11

"Psst. Wake up."

Someone pinched his face. Caspian opened one eye and saw Dylis standing on his pillow. He blinked a couple of times to pull himself out of the strange dreams of other people's lives and orientate himself in the strange room. He opened his mouth, but Dylis placed her finger to her lips and pointed at Lydia.

Lydia was sleeping with her back to him. It would be much nicer to ignore the fairy and move closer to Lydia and drift back to sleep. He closed his eyes and Dylis tapped his cheek.

Then her voice was in his ear. "Get up. We have a problem."

The last remnants of sleep slid away. This wasn't her being annoyed because they didn't go home. This was something else. Icy panic got his blood pumping and he slid out of bed. He wasn't stupid. He knew when Dylis meant business.

He pulled on his jeans and slipped on his shirt against the cool morning before padding quietly out of the bedroom and closing the door.

He didn't speak to Dylis until they reached the bottom of the stairs. She stood on the bannister and waited.

"What is it?" he whispered. Maybe this would be a short conversation and he could go back to bed, but instinct told him otherwise. The hair down the back of his neck prickled and he almost tasted the fairy magic in the air.

"Come with me."

Dylis led him to the kitchen and pointed out a window.

"What the hell?" he muttered.

Across the lawn, crammed into every inch of space, were mirrors. Hundreds of them.

"It's Shea," Dylis said. "He's trying to force you to find the Window."

He glared at Dylis. "Thank you. I'd worked that out." He'd also worked out that Shea knew where he was—and that left Lydia vulnerable. Everywhere he turned Shea was reminding him that he couldn't escape. He was running out of options far quicker than he liked. He gritted his teeth and stared outside. He shouldn't have stayed here. That wouldn't have mattered; the Greys had followed him and tried to make trouble last night. It was only a matter of time until Shea involved Lydia. "Dammit."

"You knew he'd push."

"I didn't expect him to push this hard." This was hardly in the same category as unraveling clothes and filling his car with bees. He needed to gain the upper hand somehow. "Do you have the Counter-Window yet?"

Her tiny tongue traced her lip. She was about to tell him something he really wasn't going to like. What could be worse than hundreds of mirrors in Lydia's yard? "Does Shea have it?"

"No. I know where the Counter-Window is, but I don't have it yet. It's being acquired for me."

"Meaning?"

"Your father will have it very soon."

That wasn't too bad. "Do you think Shea suspects the Window is here?"

Dylis shook her head. "We can't even find it."

True, and he and Dylis had tried yesterday evening. While he'd worked, she'd poked around in boxes, the stable, and cabins between trying to get rid of the troublesome Greys. She'd brought him a couple of mirrors but they were nothing special. He was beginning to doubt it was here. "Maybe it was once, but it's moved on."

She rolled her eyes. "Don't go there. If it's moved on, we've got nothing to go on."

He raked his fingers through his hair. If the mirror had moved on it could be anywhere in the world. "I need the—"

"I know."

"So all I can do is ignore Shea and hope everything will fall into place." And get rid of all the mirrors before Lydia woke up and looked out of a window and asked what was going on. *Simple*.

"About that. Have you noticed something about those mirrors?"

Caspian walked up to the window and actually looked at them. They were all antique. He moved to another window, and around the house until he'd seen as much as he could without going outside. Every one of them was old and valuable. The bad feeling worked its way to his toes which curled against the wood floor as if they could find somewhere to hide.

"Tell me they aren't stolen." But they were, they had to be. They'd been taken from museums, art galleries, and private houses overnight. This morning people would be waking up and wondering where the mirror worth thousands was and calling the police. And who knew what Shea had left—probably a note with his name and number on it. "Bastard son of a…" Whatever. Shea must have had a human mother or father once, but there was nothing remotely human about him. He was one hundred percent calculating fairy.

He was never going to be able to explain them away when, not if, the cops came to Callaway House. Because of him Lydia was now involved. He wished he'd just gone home instead of staying. At least then it would just be him in trouble. Now Shea knew where she lived. This was getting worse with every passing minute. He looked at Dylis. "Can you get rid of them?"

"I could, but I don't know where they came from, and I'm guessing he'll just bring more."

How many mirrors were in Charleston? How long could this go on? "How long until you get the Counter-Window?"

"Not fast enough. And I can't hide every mirror he brings."

She was right. Shea had boxed him into a corner with cunning and theft. He'd underestimated the Grey and was now going to have to pay the price.

"You're going to have to go out and reason with him."

By reason she meant cut a deal that wasn't going to cost more than he could afford. It was times like this Caspian wished he'd studied law. Legalese would've given him a great background in tangling fairies in clauses. Although to be fair lawyers only came about because of fairies trying to trick humans out of unborn children and souls.

"It's too early to be giving up my soul. I try not to do that before nine."

"Ha ha." Dylis crossed her arms. "Not funny."

"I'm not laughing. Isn't this one of those moments where having my father intervene would be a good thing?" While not the best time to meet his father, now was as good a time as any.

"What would you have the Prince of Annwyn do? Return the mirrors? Kill a banished lord, his mother's lover, no less? Think, Caspian. This isn't about you."

Strangely it felt all about him. He boiled the kettle and made a cup of extra strong coffee. He needed to be thinking as clearly as possible. At the moment all he could come up with was *I'm so screwed*.

How long until Lydia woke up and saw that all was not right with the world? How was he going to explain the mirrors?

"Okay. My father won't step in because it wouldn't go well politically. You're here in his place and you're telling me to cut a deal to my terms. However, there are penalties for dealing with Greys and because I'm half-fairy I still have to bear those penalties... which means my father thinks I'm a liability and wants to see me in the river."

"You are exceedingly dense. I've given you a lifetime of education in all things Court." She spun and walked away. "Your father doesn't want to see you dead or drowned in the river of damned souls. However, he can't intervene without revealing your identity. You think one Grey is a problem?" She threw her hands in the air. "Imagine all the banished on your doorstep, knowing who your father is. Plus, he's also got a lot more to deal with right now because of his mother's affair with Shea."

Caspian put his cup down and looked at her. "So I'm the sacrifice."

"You're mortal. Get used to it," Dylis snapped. She could be mouthy, but she never usually cracked. Whatever was happening was putting her under pressure too. But it still wasn't a good enough reason for him to give up and die.

"I don't want to die today, or next week. Or whenever the Hunter of Annwyn comes to exact payment for dealing with Shea." He wrapped his hands around his coffee cup, but the heat didn't warm him. His blood was running cold with adrenaline and more than a little fear.

"If you find the Window for your father, I'm sure he'd let you off with just a warning." She smiled, that peculiar cold grin that only a fairy could manage. Too many teeth and with a glint in the eye usually only seen by people about to be devoured by something wild and untamed.

The coffee turned tasteless in his mouth. She wanted him to deal to be free of him and get back to her life at Court. Sneaky. He glanced out the window, but there was still the problem of the mirrors. Maybe he could talk to Shea without cutting a deal.

Unfortunately the sky was clear of flying pigs.

"Were you talking to someone?"

Caspian's head snapped up at the sound of Lydia's voice. She'd put on the pajamas that she'd never managed to get into last night. The hot pink and black spots weren't what he'd have expected her to wear. He didn't know what to expect anymore. And he didn't know what to say.

"This just got worse," Dylis muttered.

He resisted the urge to glance at Dylis. How many seconds until Lydia realized it was far too bright in the kitchen and that her yard was full of mirrors? How many heartbeats until she demanded answers he wasn't ready to give and that she wouldn't believe?

Her gaze flickered from to the window. "What's going on?" She frowned and took a couple of paces forward. "Are they... How..." She turned to look at him and he wished he could shrink and vanish like Dylis did. "There are mirrors outside."

"I know."

She looked outside again as if to be sure that was what she was seeing. Then she opened the back door and stood in the doorway. The morning sun caught in the reflective surfaces and threw the light back at her so she was surrounded by a white glow.

Shea had planned that well. Angled them all to catch the sunrise.

"Shit." She lifted her hand to shield her eyes. "How did this happen?" Lydia turned to face him, her eyes narrowing. "You know. Who were you talking to? What's going on?"

Caspian swallowed. He should have told her about fairies last night. Told her the truth about the weird bumps and the *ghost* in the house. Now it was going to be much, much worse. He glanced at Dylis then back at Lydia. Saying nothing wouldn't help either and he'd miss an opportunity to tell her the truth. He'd never told anyone the whole truth—the idea hurt. She'd laugh, or call him crazy, kick him out... all things he'd expected to happen last night, but none had eventuated.

Last night she'd accepted him as he was. He'd had

hope that one day he'd be able to tell her everything and not have her look at him with fear or horror. Now that was gone. It took a moment for him to realize that he cared about what she thought, that he didn't want this to be just one night or even a few days. He wanted more. He'd already told her more about himself than anyone else knew. And because of that she could crush him. Although if he made a deal with Shea, he wouldn't have to suffer a broken heart for long, as he'd be dead.

"You know how I said I'm afraid of fairies?"

Lydia raised one eyebrow and crossed her arms. She and Dylis would get on great. Both of them watching him, neither of them looking impressed. If only they could see each other.

"They are around us, but most people can't see them."

"Uh-huh, but you can."

"I'm psychometric because I'm half-fairy. My biological father, the dangerous man, he is the fairy I've never met."

She pressed her lips together, disbelief hardening her features. He was losing her already, but he had to press on.

"The mirrors were put there by a fairy that wants me to help him find a…" Why stop at fairies? He might as well start talking magic. "A magic mirror."

Lydia glanced outside then back at him. She shook her head. "Fairies aren't real. I don't know how you got the mirrors here or why, but it wasn't fairies."

She was really watching him now, as if he was a dangerous psychopath who'd let go of reality. He knew that was how it sounded, but the look in her eyes was why he'd never told anyone. Disbelief and a whole lot of distrust. He tried to ignore the ache that threatened to tear open his heart. Maybe he wasn't ready for this. Yet he remembered how it had been last night. How she'd believed him about the psychometry. He had to give her a chance to believe in fairies. He needed that chance.

He took a breath and tried logic. "Why would I fill your garden with mirrors?"

"I don't know."

"How would I when I was in bed with you?"

"I don't know." He could see the doubt begin to take hold as her gaze flicked between him and the window.

"All those odd bumps and crashes last night? They were banished fairies, Greys we call them, looking to cause trouble because I have refused to help the other one find the mirror he wants."

"*Right.*" She nodded, but the desire that had filled her eyes last night was totally gone. She'd slept with him and was now regretting every second of the time they'd been intimate, while he was holding onto those same moments as if they were the only lifeline he had.

He only had one thing he could do and Dylis would make him pay for it later. "Dylis, show yourself please."

"No. This is your problem."

"It's yours as well. I'm not moving. I'm not doing anything until you show yourself." And to Lydia it looked as if he was talking to himself. *This was getting better and better.*

"Okay, I think you should go. I'll give you a head start before I call the police about the mirrors." Lydia edged around the kitchen as far from him as she could get.

He didn't move. "Dylis. I swear if you do not do this for me I will do everything in my power to ensure you suffer for the rest of your very long life." His words vibrated with power he'd never felt before. He'd tapped into a magic that he hadn't known he possessed. He knew a fairy's word had power, but the desperation he was feeling must have given his words enough weight for his fairy blood to shine. *Great*. He'd spent years suppressing it, only to have it surface now.

"Damn you." She shimmered for a moment but nothing else changed to his eye.

Lydia gasped. Her hand covered her mouth as she pressed herself against a wall. Her gaze was on the ten-inch woman standing on her kitchen counter.

Dylis gave a bow that bordered on surly. "I'm Caspian's guardian, fairy godmother, or angel on his shoulder—whatever you like to think of me as."

Lydia closed her eyes, and after a couple of seconds she opened them. "You're still there."

"I've been here all night, keeping the imps away from you two," Dylis snapped. "This was not a good idea." She pointed her finger at Caspian.

Dylis wasn't going to forgive him for a while. Generally fairies weren't supposed to reveal themselves unless they were blending into human society. Dylis couldn't do that as she was supposed to be his guardian in secret. No one was supposed to know he was important enough to have a guardian. Now Lydia did, even if she didn't understand what he was telling her.

"You were talking to her?" Lydia took a step forward.

"She woke me to tell me about the mirrors in the hope that I could reason with the Grey that put them there and get rid of them before you got up." He really needed a second cup of coffee for this conversation.

"But I got up too early. You weren't going to tell me." Her gaze lifted from Dylis to him, her dark eyes full of suspicion instead of heat and longing.

"I thought about telling you I was fairy last night, but it's not easy to say and even harder to hear. If not for Dylis, would you have believed me?"

She bit her lower lip, her gaze sliding around the kitchen as if she were looking for more fairies.

"There's no one else here at the moment." He hoped that sounded reassuring.

"But last night..." Her eyes widened as she began putting together what she'd heard last night and what he'd just told her about there being Greys in the house.

"There were two imps and a boggart making trouble. Nothing I couldn't handle." Dylis tapped her sword. "They weren't here to hurt you."

"They were here because of you." Lydia looked at him, still wary.

"Yes. The Grey is trying to force me to find a powerful mirror for him."

"With your psychometry." She paused. "So why not just find it and be done with it?"

That was why it was best that humans didn't know about fairies. They'd make deals without understanding the consequences. If Shea turned up, he'd trick Lydia out of her soul and then use it as a bargaining tool—it's what he'd do if he were in Shea's place. And he knew in that moment he'd do whatever Shea asked to keep her safe.

He had to make the deal to protect Lydia from Shea and his band of Greys, even if Lydia wasn't sure about accepting the fact that he was half-fairy. She didn't deserve to be drawn into his drama any more than she already was.

"I'm going to."

"Caspian, be careful." Dylis actually looked like she cared.

"Wait." Lydia put her hand on his arm. "These Greys are bad news?"

"They are dangerous and will do anything to get back to Annwyn… back home." He knew it was too much strange information, but at least she knew who he was.

"Is this your home?"

"I'm mortal. I was born here." And he hoped to die here when he was old, but the odds of that happening were reducing. "But I am half-fairy so bound by their laws. Making deals with a Grey carries a penalty."

Her grip tightened a fraction. "Then don't do it."

"He has to. Shea won't stop until he does. It is better he makes it on his terms than being backed farther into a corner." Dylis gave Lydia a look that indicated that she thought Lydia was a complication.

"Is that true?"

"Yes." Maybe the deal he made wouldn't be that bad. Maybe his father wouldn't kill him for treason. Maybe Lydia would still want him to stay over after this.

He leaned in and placed a kiss on her cheek. She didn't pull away, but she didn't turn her head and place her lips against his either. Lydia released his arm and he walked over to the back door.

"Dylis, protect Lydia. Please." He didn't wait for an answer before he stepped onto the verandah.

The light was less bright now that the sun had moved, but it made the scene more chilling. It wasn't just mirrors. The garden had been torn up. Pavers and grass had been upturned. Plants had been ripped from the ground and were scattered around. He walked down the stairs—even if he got rid of the mirrors there was still damage that needed fixing. And this was just the backyard.

He took a couple more paces and entered the forest of mirrors. His hand brushed the edges as he walked. Most were mundane. People checking hair, a house getting painted, children playing. His hand jerked back as blood splattered and someone died.

"Was that it?" Shea said from behind Caspian.

"No. The mirror witnessed a murder. A recent one." And there was no one he could tell about it. Sometimes his gift sucked like that.

This time he noticed a half-dozen smaller banished fairies loitering like a gang waiting to be told to start something. Shea's little band of helpers. What had he promised them in return?

He ignored them and took a deep breath, then kept going, letting the images wash over him instead of taking over. He got fleeting glimpses of a hundred different lives. They spun around and made him dizzy. He wasn't used to filtering this much information at a time. Usually it was a couple of items, and spending time with each. He stopped and shivered, momentarily disoriented, and he still had the front yard to go. His stomach clenched on the coffee. He should've eaten breakfast. He needed to ground himself back in the mortal world instead of the past.

"Well?" Shea demanded like a passive-aggressive shadow that wouldn't let up.

"None of these." Caspian pushed the words through gritted teeth. He was cold, like he was standing in iced water. "Return them."

Shea didn't move. He looked shorter in the morning light and less ethereal. The magic was costing him. Caspian bit back the smile. *Burn through it and shrink so you're nothing more than an ugly, little, powerless troll.* As soon as he thought it Caspian realized Shea probably had help gathering all the mirrors. He was a lord not used to doing anything for himself.

"I won't do more if you don't return them."

"You agree to help?"

"I agree to nothing." The sun on his back helped warm Caspian while looking at Shea froze whatever hope he had of pulling this off. Even if he touched all of the ones Shea had brought, there'd be more tomorrow and the next day and the next. Until he had the Counter-Window, then the location of the Window would be revealed.

Could he hold out and still protect Lydia? He knew the answer and didn't like it. The longer he waited, the less advantage he had. But he wasn't ready.

He walked on; again he trailed his fingers over the mirrors, but this time he tried to focus on the grass and dirt beneath his bare feet and the breeze on his skin, the simple things that would keep him in the present. When he'd finished all the ones in the backyard, he shook his head and began to walk around the house to where more mirrors waited in the front yard.

Shea snarled and stalked after him. "You seem to like blondes. It would be a shame if something were to happen to her; she is so mortal."

Caspian turned slowly. "Leave her alone. She isn't part of this."

"But she is. The time you spend with her is time not spent finding the Window. And I have just begun to realize how many mirrors there are in the world now. Last time I spent any time in the mortal world they were a novelty of the rich. Now everyone has them."

"I'm not here for Lydia. I'm here for a job. This is my livelihood," Caspian said.

"That is not my concern. There are bigger things at stake than your livelihood. Or life."

"My job is important to me." And so was his life and Lydia. He was going to have to deal to stop the hostilities and stop Shea from ruining his life. No matter where he went Shea would follow. He didn't want the Greys making more trouble for Lydia.

"Help me and I'll leave her alone," Shea said.

Caspian shook his head. He didn't want to be in a deal that said he was helping a Grey. The wording of a deal was everything. If he botched even one word, he wouldn't live too long to regret it. It had to sound like he wanted to help, but without promising to hand the mirror over... and even then he was counting on Shea not adding clause after clause and binding him up so tight he had no wriggle room.

He found the words he wanted then spoke clearly and slowly so there could be no mistake. "I will find the Window." Give the Grey what he wanted first. "In exchange call off your Greys and cease the petty pestering."

Shea blinked, his pale eyes assessing. "I will stop harassing as long as you are helping. You will check every mirror I bring to you."

"You will return them to where you found them—except the Window, should I find it." Caspian waited for Shea to tighten the terms.

"You swear not to lie?"

That was a bit vague; he might need to lie to Shea at some point... actually, he could see himself definitely lying to Shea. An honesty clause was a bad idea. "I will tell you if I find a fairy-made mirror."

His heart was beating a little too fast. He wanted this over. Already the deal was getting more complex than he wanted.

Shea grinned, cold and victorious. "If you fail to find the Window, Lydia's soul is mine."

There wasn't a chance in hell he was agreeing to that. "I have a year and a day to find the mirror. Then you get *my* soul." Assuming of course he lived that long.

"No. One turn of the moon. Then your soul is mine."

One month. Was that long enough? He hoped Dylis was as close as she claimed to getting the Counter-Window. That was a clever clause. Even if he failed to find the Window, Shea could use his soul to bribe his way back to Annwyn—assuming his father the Prince cared enough to let that happen. That was a gamble they were both taking.

"I accept."

"A bargain is struck." Shea inclined his head.

For a moment Caspian didn't move. That was it.

There was no peal of thunder or flash of lightning. Just the cold surety that he'd made a deal with a banished fairy. If that didn't get the attention of the Court, nothing he did would. He knew in his near future he would be called upon to attend. At least the deal had been reasonably favorable, while there was a time limit he hadn't actually offered to hand the Window over to Shea once found. Before he could sigh with relief while in view of Shea, he turned and walked toward the house.

Chapter 12

CASPIAN APPEARED TO BE TALKING TO SOMEONE OUT in the yard, but Lydia couldn't see the other person or hear the conversation. This was just too weird. If not for the fairy peeking out of the window with her, she would have discounted everything Caspian had said. She almost had. That awful feeling that she'd slept with a stranger, a man she didn't really know, and that he was delusional had filled her with dread.

That he was actually half-fairy and could see things she didn't wasn't much better. It was too far-fetched. And yet how else did she explain the mirrors, and the noises… even Caspian's psychometry?

She glanced at Dylis, wanting to reach out and touch her to make sure she was there and not some kind of shared hallucination.

"You don't have wings."

Dylis turned her head and gave her a glare that was far more threatening than it should've been from someone her size. "Fairies don't have wings; that was some dumb human's idea."

"Sorry."

"Just because Caspian made me reveal myself doesn't mean we are friends. I have a job to do. And so does he. If he screws up, we're all in the river."

"What river?"

Dylis hissed. "One problem at a time. I'm watching Shea to make sure he doesn't do something shifty."

They both went back to watching Caspian. Dylis stiffened next to her but said nothing. Then Caspian turned and walked toward the house, his lips pressed into a thin line. He walked into the kitchen and closed the door.

"I need something to eat." He closed his eyes and kept his hands by his side, his fingers flexing and curling.

Lydia watched him for a moment.

Dylis snapped her fingers. "Food. He needs to ground himself after using all that magic."

That got Lydia moving. Food she could do. In the freezer was a half-loaf of bread. She pulled out a couple of slices and shoved them into the toaster. While she was waiting she made two cups of coffee, then she remembered the fairy.

"Coffee, Dylis?"

"Tea, since you asked."

What was she going to put that in? She looked through the cupboard and settled on a smallish teacup that was still far too big.

"A good deal?" Caspian asked, but he wasn't speaking to her. He was talking to his fairy.

"Brilliant. I couldn't have done better. Except for your soul you could be fairy." Dylis sounded like a proud mother. Except she wasn't Caspian's mother. No, his father was fairy… which meant his mother was human. She looked at Dylis's tiny size. How did that work?

"That probably won't be a problem for long."

"Don't be like that. You'll like Court."

Caspian snorted.

Lydia handed him the coffee. "How much trouble are you in?"

"It's hard to say; it depends on how things play out." He looked at her, his eyes full of things he wasn't saying.

She wasn't sure she wanted to ask. How much did she want to get involved? Or was it too late for that?

The toast popped and she put butter and honey on it before giving the plate to Caspian. "Is there anything I can do to help?"

He finished his mouthful of toast and took a drink of coffee before answering. As he ate he looked better, less like he was struggling to focus. "No. Shea will leave you alone now. A fairy's word is good."

"So what do I do?" Her yard was full of mirrors, there had been invisible fairies scampering through her house last night, and she couldn't do anything even though she knew they were there.

"The best thing you can do is pretend that you know nothing about fairies," Dylis said. "That way you won't engage with them and accidentally make a deal that will undo what Caspian has done."

"Right…" She was going to ask why bother telling her about them, but then she realized Caspian really had no other choice; she'd been ready to throw him out and call the cops. "But Shea will know that I know. Won't he?"

Caspian finished his toast and coffee. "Let's hope not." He glanced out the window then back at her. "All my life I've had to pretend I don't see them, that I'm no different than any other human. It's hard and I didn't want to place that burden on you. You have the luxury of not being able to see them or hear their voices unless they choose. It will be easier. I'm sorry." He shook his head and looked at the floor. "Maybe it was a mistake getting involved with you."

"No. You would've told me eventually, wouldn't you?" But she already knew he'd never told his ex, not even about the psychometry.

"I have more mirrors to check out front. Shea will return them once I am done."

"Caspian," she waited until he turned back to face her, "would you have told me what you are if this hadn't happened?" If he said no, could she still trust him when he was hiding such big secrets? What else could he be hiding?

"I got halfway there last night. That's more than I've ever told anyone. I wanted to tell you, so you would know me, but now I feel selfish. Now you have to live with the burden of that knowledge."

"I won't tell anyone."

He gave her a halfhearted smile. "I know you won't. Who are you going to tell? Who would believe you?" He shrugged and she had an inkling of what his life was like. No one knew about his magic, no one knew he was seeing things they couldn't. No one knew him. Not even his ex-wife.

Her heart ached for him, so alone, half in another world and half here and belonging nowhere. And yet he'd used what he had and made a good life for himself. He'd begun to let her in, and she had to live up to that.

"Can I do anything to help?" She forced a smile and tried to feel more confident than she did. The world she knew had just taken on another shadow.

Caspian shook his head.

"I'll give her a basic education." Dylis walked to the edge of the counter, leaving her tea behind.

"Thank you." Then Caspian walked out of the kitchen. She heard the front door open but not close.

Lydia turned her attention to Dylis. "So, what do I need to know?"

Dylis grinned, a feral toothy smile that made her light blue eyes seem as cold as hail. Then she grew and didn't stop until she was the height of a human. She leaned on the counter and looked Lydia in the eye. Lydia stepped back, her skin cold and plucking up in gooseflesh.

"Number one, looks can be deceiving." Dylis picked up the teacup and took a sip.

Lydia began to feel like she was out of her depth already.

Chapter 13

CASPIAN CAME BACK INSIDE AFTER CHECKING THE mirrors out front. All he wanted to do was sit down and close his eyes for a few minutes. Images were still flickering in his mind in a confusing array of pasts, but when he walked into the kitchen he knew that wasn't going to happen. Lydia looked pale, Dylis looked peeved. God knew what they'd discussed.

"The mirrors out back are going." Dylis pointed out the window.

"Great." At least he wouldn't be accused of theft. Caspian glanced at Lydia, but she wouldn't meet his gaze. "I'll help you get your garden straightened out."

She closed her eyes and took a breath before looking at him. "You have to go to work and so do I."

"I don't want to leave you alone."

"You said he'd back off now."

That was true, but that wasn't the reason he didn't want to leave her alone. He couldn't drop all of this on her and then stroll out the door as if nothing had changed. He looked at the set of her lips and realized what she wasn't saying. She wanted to be by herself to process.

Caspian nodded. "He won't hassle you."

"Okay then." She pressed her lips together for a moment and looked at him as if she didn't know what to say. "So, fairies…"

"Yeah." He didn't really want to talk more about his family in case Lydia changed her mind and decided it was all too much. This was all untried ice and he expected it to crack at any moment. "You know what to do if you see one?"

"Dylis gave me some rules."

Of course she had. Dylis loved to hand out rules and tell people what to do. But what she'd taught him had saved his butt more than once. He hoped it would again. However, it still didn't feel right to leave Lydia.

"If you have any trouble—"

"I'll call."

"I'll give you a call during the day."

She smiled. "You're still worried."

"Anytime fairies start making trouble I get concerned." And Shea had already proven that no part of his life would be spared. Now that he'd made the deal, things were only going to get worse—only with the Court this time.

"We can get through this." Her hand brushed his, then she kissed his cheek. Her touch was different from how it had been last night, more cautious.

He wanted to believe that was true. That at some point in the future Lydia wouldn't think twice about what he was and the odd things that happened around him. "I hope so." But right now she wanted time alone, and he did need to go to work; lingering wouldn't help either of them. "I'll get my things and get going."

"I'll call you a cab."

"Thank you." He left the kitchen and went up to the bedroom. Last night seemed so far away. He should have told her everything last night in the parlor. Maybe then this morning's madness wouldn't have been such a shock. Not that it mattered now. She knew about fairies, for better or worse.

When he came downstairs she was waiting for him. This was not good-bye, although it kind of felt that way. There was something in the air, an uncertainty. But she didn't act like it was over.

He placed a quick kiss on her lips. "I'll see you this evening."

"Yes you will." Her fingers touched his jaw for just a moment before she pulled away.

She was looking at him differently; she was looking for the fairy blood. While she hadn't rejected him outright, she was thinking it through. Carefully. What else did he expect from her?

Who would willingly involve themselves in fairy drama? He hoped Lydia would.

He glanced at her one last time, then walked down the steps and picked his way along what had once been a footpath. Already there were fewer mirrors out front.

Dylis was back to her usual tiny self. She jumped onto his bag as he walked away. "That went pretty good, all things considered."

"Shea could come back. You should stay here."

"My duty is to protect you."

"That's not what I meant." It was what he'd meant, but Dylis wouldn't agree to looking after Lydia. She would, however, agree to staying and continuing her search for the Window.

"Hmm. You have a point. But I think it's best I go to Court."

She was right. She needed to get the Counter-Window.

They waited in silence for the cab. When it arrived he got in and took a last look at Callaway House, knowing he'd be back tonight, but not knowing what to expect.

<center>~~~</center>

After sending Caspian on his way and getting dressed, Lydia rang work and said she was sick. She wasn't scared of being alone; in fact, having the space was what she needed.

Caspian was part fairy. While he and his fairy godmother had been with her she thought she'd done a pretty good job of keeping calm; in truth, part of her wished that she never learned the truth. The other part of her wanted the facts and wanted to know who she was getting involved with. Did knowing this about Caspian change the way she felt about him? That was the question she was hoping to find the answer to.

She'd seen the disappointment on his face when she'd asked him to leave even though he'd masked it quickly. She'd almost changed her mind. But she couldn't work through everything that was in her mind if he was looking over her shoulder. No, a little space would do her good... but already she was looking forward to seeing him tonight.

With all the mirrors gone, she walked around the house to assess the damage. It wasn't good. The Callaway House gardens were ruined. Not that they'd been anything special lately, but with a bit of attention they would have been okay. Now it was like a mini cyclone had swept through and upended everything. The only things untouched were the three cabins at the edge of the block and the oaks.

A shiver scraped down her spine. She'd slept through it all… or maybe she'd been awake reading in the parlor? If she'd looked what would she have seen? Not the Greys, as Caspian and Dylis called them. She would have seen floating mirrors and plants and pavers. She drew in a deep breath. Even the ghost of Callaway House wasn't a ghost, but a Grey.

She shook her head understanding why Caspian hadn't wanted to tell her and yet at the same time being miffed that he wanted to keep secrets. She didn't like secrets. She liked answers and the truth. A mockingbird singing in the tree above her made her jump. Now every noise made her twitchy. Maybe she should have gone to work.

Yeah, but the garden wasn't going to clean itself and she couldn't afford to pay someone. So instead of sitting in the house, she started putting the garden back together. Once she got started, the damage seemed to be mostly cosmetic. As she put the plants back into the dirt and placed the weeds in a pile, it didn't look so bad. Given some time it would look the way it once had—only with fewer weeds. She gathered up another handful of flowers, something that had been budding, and shoved them back in the ground, hoping that they'd re-root. Replacing all of the plants with new ones would cost too much.

The grass and the pavers were a disaster she was trying to avoid. There was too much to do. Her vision blurred and she blinked back tears. She didn't need this, and yet she didn't have a choice. What would Gran do? Just get on with it, one bit at a time the way she always had.

Her cell phone rang in her pocket. She took off her gloves and checked the number. She didn't recognize it so she ignored it. She'd already fended off the press who wanted a statement about the upcoming memorial. Now that she'd stopped she realized how thirsty and hungry she was. Her arms and back ached from the unaccustomed exercise. *Break time*.

In the shade she gulped down some water from her drink bottle and looked at what had once been the front garden. If she stacked the pavers up, she could eventually get someone to relay them. The grass should recover if she relaid the ripped up pieces, stomped on the raised bits, and filled in the holes. In six months' time she and Caspian would look back and laugh.

That made her pause. Despite everything she was still picturing him in her life. Maybe it was true—like the garden in six months' time, it wouldn't matter that he was half-fairy and saw things she never would. What mattered was that he was a good guy who'd done his best to protect her despite the situation. He'd made a deal with a Grey.

She bit her lip and looked at the yard. At least she hoped they'd get the chance to sit back and laugh. From what Dylis had told her the risks were more than what he'd let on. Protecting her or hiding the truth? At this stage she rather know what was going on, but then she couldn't go back to not knowing anyway. She huffed out a breath. It was getting warm and her clothes were sticking. She glanced up at the sun and decided it was time for lunch and a little more reading. At least any salvageable plants were back in the ground.

She left the mess and went inside, washed her hands,

and made a cheese sandwich from fridge and freezer leftovers. If she and Caspian were going to be staying here, she needed to buy some more food. Gran seemed to exist on apples, bread, cheese, and wine. She sat at the kitchen table and picked up the diary she'd been reading last night. It was fascinating. A little piece of history and heartbreak, but she wanted to know what happened to Pearl, the young woman who'd accidentally gotten pregnant and found herself suddenly abandoned. But she'd followed Caspian back to bed before she could find out if it was a boy or a girl.

Each page gave her a greater understanding of the life Gran had lived. The baby was a girl, but the birth didn't go well. After two days Pearl had died and the man had refused to acknowledge the child. Lydia brushed at a tear that traced down her cheek. When Gran held the baby she saw the daughter she'd lost to whooping cough at just two months old. It was Gran who'd named the baby, Helen.

Lydia felt her heart stop for a moment. She re-read the page to be sure.

Helen Callaway.

"Oh my God." Gran wasn't her grandmother. Her grandmother was Pearl, a young and pretty party girl who'd been cast off once she became pregnant and had stayed at Callaway House because she had nowhere else to go. She didn't even know Pearl's last name. She didn't even know if Pearl was her real name.

Her breathing hitched in her chest and she let the book fall closed as if she could lock the secret back up. There was a reason diaries shouldn't be read. How different would her life have been if Pearl hadn't died and Gran hadn't claimed the baby and raised her? Helen hadn't been a late life surprise for Gran. Gran had lied. Why would she do that?

Her whole life was a lie.

Her eyes burned afresh as she lost her grandmother for the second time. She wished she'd never opened the stupid trunk and started reading.

Her phone rang again. Caspian. She couldn't talk to him now. She didn't know what to say. She cradled her head in her hands. Everything she knew was unraveling; soon she'd be left with nothing.

———

The phone rang out and went to voice mail. "This is Lydia. Leave a message."

"It's Caspian. I wanted to see how you are doing." He paused—what was he saying? Of course she wasn't going to be all right. Fairies had come in and shaken her life up. He'd shaken her life up and put her in danger. Was that why she wasn't answering?

He was tempted to drive out there now and make sure, but he made himself take a breath. He couldn't give away that she knew, not with an imp creeping around his shop, listening to every word. "If you need me to come around early and help let me know." He hung up. Would she get back to him?

When he'd left this morning she'd seemed fine, but daylight had a way of altering perceptions. He looked at the phone in his hands. For the moment he'd done everything he could, but he was waiting. Waiting for Lydia to realize it was all too much. Waiting for Dylis to get the Counter-Window. Waiting for the Court summons. Every time someone entered his shop he expected to see the Hunter of Annwyn ready to take him across the veil. It made thinking about work difficult. If these were his last few days he didn't want to be spending them with an imp in his shop. He wanted to be with Lydia, but she'd made it clear she wanted to be alone.

He didn't blame her. If the situation had been reversed he'd have wanted space from the person talking about fairies and magic mirrors too. Last night he'd been hopeful when he'd seen the trunks and the boxes in the stable, but now, after he and Dylis had failed to find the Window, he was becoming more certain it was no longer at the house. The idea that it could be anywhere and that he only had one month to find it was more than a little terrifying. If he did manage to find it, he still had to work out a way not to give it to Shea—and not get killed in the process. It was exactly the reason he spent his life trying to stay clear of all things fairy. If he hadn't bought the enchanted mirror from the garage sale, then maybe Shea would have left him alone.

To distract himself from thinking about fairies he flicked through a couple of news sites, reading the headlines. He noticed the memorial for Nanette Callaway was the day after tomorrow and that there was a large outbreak of golden staph at a couple of hospitals.

That made him pause. While small outbreaks happened, this was more widespread. This time it was because of the ripples on the river. He didn't really want to think about it, but Dylis's warning about plague wasn't something he could shrug off.

Instead of looking up antiques he started searching for disease outbreaks, half hoping the golden staph was an isolated anomaly.

It wasn't. Measles was making a comeback. The health authorities blamed low immunization rates. On the other side of the world in Africa a rapid-spreading, drug-resistant tuberculosis was causing problems. That was where he stopped looking. The trouble with the Internet was it was very easy to find a positive answer to anything. Of course there were going to be outbreaks; there were seven billion people on the planet, a percentage of which would get sick.

But several different outbreaks at once?

He needed to find the Window. That would stop Shea, but Caspian knew enough about Court that finding the Window wouldn't stop the ripples caused by the King and Queen's fighting. They wouldn't really damn the mortal world over a feud?

But the Black Death was proof they would and had before, more than once.

Bloody fairies. He couldn't escape them at the moment. When he was with Lydia he felt normal and could forget for a little while what he was… or he had been able to. Now she knew and was busy deciding if she wanted to see him again. If it were him, he'd probably be running the other direction. Maybe he was asking too much for someone to know him and still accept him. Natalie would never have. And while he'd told Lydia, having Greys show up and destroy her yard wasn't going to help his case. He tried to ignore the ache in his heart and pretend it was better she found out early before they got serious. The trouble was he didn't believe it. For a moment last night he'd thought he'd been on the way to having what he wanted in a relationship.

The imp who thought he was doing a good job of

hiding peeked around the table. Caspian threw a pen at it. The pen bounced harmlessly off the table leg.

Shea's minions were still stalking him even though they were no longer trying to annoy him. "What were you banished for?"

The imp peeked back around. "Me?"

"Are there any other imps here?"

It shook its head. Imps had a bit of magic, but they'd given up stature and gradually looks to keep it. Trolls, on the other hand, gave up looks and magic first. Boggarts gave up looks and stature for magic—they were probably the most dangerous. What would Shea do?

"I tricked a woman into coming to Court." The imp grinned as if proud of what he'd done.

"Is she still there?"

"She was set free and I was banished."

"Why did you do it?"

"Why not?" The imp shrugged.

"Do you regret it?"

The imp regarded Caspian with eyes of the palest blue. "I regret being caught. The child I'd created became a changeling," he spat the word.

"Have you seen the child?"

The imp laughed. "I'm not your daddy. If you're lucky, you'll never meet him. Most view changelings with scorn."

Caspian knew that. But he also knew his situation was more complicated. He was sure the Crown Prince would hear about his deal sooner rather than later and he'd get to meet his father for the first time in a less than favorable situation.

He looked at the imp. He preferred Dylis's company;

at least she was pretty and could kind of be trusted. The imp on the other hand was only looking out for Shea. Caspian didn't need to ask what the imp had been promised. There was only one thing banished fairies wanted—a return to Court.

———※———

Felan walked through the Court's hall of mirrors. They were embedded in the bark or hanging from the branches that arched overhead, their limbs forming the vaulted ceiling. With every breeze they spun and caught the light glittering like stars. Most were no bigger than the palm of a hand. It was beautiful.

In the main hall there were bigger mirrors so the dancers could see themselves. And the occasional changeling who risked glancing at the Court. He'd seen Caspian and heard his thought for just a moment.

Dylis walked toward him looking like a flower in bloom. She swept him a curtsy that was more formal than anything she'd done recently. He was guessing this was the end of their private relationship. A pity because it had suited both of them while they were between lovers.

"My Prince. I bring you a gift." She placed a small mirror on a silver chain in his hand, but didn't release it. "I could deliver it for you."

She could, but he wanted to do that in person. It had been a long time since he'd seen his son. "No. I will attend to that myself."

She hesitated. "He didn't really have a choice."

"The reason doesn't matter." Caspian had broken the rules of the Court and would pay the penalty. While the thought was unpleasant, he couldn't let it go

unnoticed, otherwise questions would be asked about
Caspian's lineage.

She lifted her chin, all brittle, beautiful fairy. "I wish
to thank you for our time together, but I feel it is time
for me to move on now that you have what you want."

They were being watched. He saw a flicker in the
mirrors as they spun but couldn't see who was watching.
There'd be time for that later.

He lifted her hand and pressed it to his lips. Such a
delicate thing for the work she'd been doing. "My bed
shall be much colder without you."

She'd done everything he'd asked, and more. Now it
was time to hold up his end of the bargain and free her
lover. His mother would be furious when she realized
one of her trees was missing.

"May I still dance with you on occasion?" He didn't
want to release her entirely; being seen with her pre-
vented others he didn't trust from trying to be in his bed.
It would also help protect Dylis if they carried on as if
everything were normal.

"As long as it is merely a dance." Her voice was firm.

He understood. With Bramwel about to be freed,
their arrangement was over. He nodded. Dylis and her
lover would be allies, and he'd need them.

She bobbed her head again. "It has been a pleasure,
my Prince."

"And mine. Thank you." He released her hand and
watched her walk away. Without looking at the Counter-
Window he tucked it into his waistcoat, then continued
his walk through the hall.

He paused to glance in some of the mirrors catching glimpses of the world; there was one he couldn't

bring himself to look in. He hadn't been able to look at her face in seven mortal years without feeling his heart breaking. But as he walked past he felt her presence and knew she was alive.

"How is it you walk without a woman on your arm?" Eyra slid her arm into his.

His mother smiled at him. Her eyes were dark blue; they looked human but she'd lost her humanity centuries ago. All that glittered there now was hate, not love. If he made the wrong choice, this was his future. A queen bound to him by magic and hate, love long forgotten.

"My lover has other things to do," he lied. He wasn't going to tell his mother that he was about to turn his attention to the mortal world and finding a queen. Just hinting at that would be fatal. She wouldn't give up the throne and the power that went with it... his father might, just to be free of her.

"I'm sure one of my ladies-in-waiting would be delighted to dally a while with you." She smiled, but it was cold. He doubted she loved him anymore. No, she would see him as a threat and little else.

"A most gracious offer I will have to take full advantage of." He freed himself from her long-nailed grip and swept her a bow. She still thought him shallow and uninterested in anything but dancing, drinking, gambling, and women. That was exactly how he wanted to be seen. It was much easier to get on with stabilizing Annwyn if no one thought him of any account.

"I look forward to seeing you in my chambers." She spun and walked away, looking not a day over eighteen, yet she was millennia old.

He touched his pocket. The Counter-Window was

still there. He drew it out and gazed into the surface, his image rippled and faded, then he saw only black. Not very helpful in finding the Window, but then for what he had planned it didn't matter.

He needed to find Verden, Lord of Hunt. It was time Caspian came to Court and met his father. Caspian needed to remember there were rules in place for a reason. He looked at his mother's back and smiled. With Caspian here he might be able to accomplish several tasks quite simply.

Chapter 14

CASPIAN'S CELL PHONE RANG AND JOLTED HIM OUT of his morbid thoughts. He'd ignored the imp, and managed to pretend today was no different from any other even as he kept checking over his shoulder for a messenger from Court. By lunchtime he'd almost convinced himself he'd gotten away with it. As deals went it was very loose, one could almost say less of a deal and more of a mutual agreement.

Lydia's number flashed on the screen. He answered instead of ignoring it. "Hello."

"I'm sorry I missed your call. I've been working in the garden."

Caspian winced. "I can imagine." He should have been there to help with the cleanup. "Are you okay?"

There was a pause before she answered and his heart jumped. "Lydia?"

"Can you come around early? I'll get some takeout for dinner."

He didn't need bribing with takeout to spend time with her. "In an hour?"

"That would be great. See you soon." She hung up.

Caspian put down his phone. She hadn't sounded right; there'd been an edge to her voice like she was close to breaking. Had Shea done something? His heart clenched. No, she would have said. This was something else… the inevitable breakup? But why invite him over for dinner if she didn't want to see him again? He didn't want to let himself hope, and yet that was all he seemed to have.

His life was making less and less sense with every passing day. The only piece he wanted to hang on to was Lydia. She'd made him remember what it was like to be with someone—the accidental contacts that sent shimmers of heat over his skin, the glances and half-smiles. He hadn't realized how much he'd missed that until meeting her. He didn't want to be alone, but he needed someone who understood what his life was really like. Maybe after all of this had shaken down Lydia would still want to be part of his life… if he still had one to worry about.

Guess he'd find out when he got to Callaway House, by taxi since his car was now full of dead bees and a large hive had grown out of the backseat. He didn't know how to report that to insurance. It was one of those problems that could wait. The imp watched, half-hidden by the wastepaper basket. He was about to shoo it away then stopped.

Caspian looked at the imp again and a smile turned the corners of his lips. He pulled a chocolate bar out his satchel, then walked out the back and got a glass of water and put it and the chocolate bar on the workbench. The imp followed, curious now.

"You want to hang around me and soak up some of the Court energy?" This had to be a sweet job that Shea had given the imp. Like a fairy, Caspian decided that keeping his enemies close was the way to keep ahead of Shea. If that meant bribing, so be it.

The imp's gaze flicked between the water and

chocolate; it was a poor approximation of the tea and cookies Caspian would leave for Brownies, but then an imp wasn't a Brownie. The imp grasped the significance of the layout and nodded slowly.

"My car. And we shall never speak of this again."

"You will put out a spread?"

"I might leave food out. If it were to vanish, I wouldn't know who had taken it." Because agreeing to leave a spread for a banished fairy was almost as bad as the agreement he'd made with Shea.

The imp's eyes were narrowed as if he were calculating how much trouble he'd be in with Shea. "If your car were to be cleaned, and your shop too, I couldn't say who had done such a thing. I'm merely here to watch you."

"Exactly." Caspian pressed his lips together to keep from smiling. The imp had been banished from Court, but he'd do anything to stay close to its power to keep from dying. Dylis would have a fit. But things had changed, and if the imp began to trust him maybe he'd trust Shea less. Without looking back, Caspian went back into the store and began to close up.

Caspian walked slowly up to the house, carrying a potted plant. It was a lame offering considering the damage. But Lydia had been busy today. This morning the garden had looked like a bunch of fairies had vented their anger on everything they touched. This afternoon the yard looked roughed up but otherwise ordered. The plants were in the garden beds and while they looked bedraggled and droopy, in a few days' time with a bit of water and sun they would come back. Even the lawn would come in well.

He knocked and waited, but not for long.

Lydia had her hair pulled back in a messy bun, she looked tired, but her eyes lit up with warmth when she saw him. Then she threw her arms around his neck like he was the lifeline she'd been praying for. It had been so long since anyone had held him like that, he almost couldn't breathe. He slid his free arm around her waist and for a moment just held her. He'd thought she'd slipped through his fingers, but she was still welcoming him with open arms. He closed his eyes, aware of how lucky he was. She was his link to all that was human as he was being surrounded by fairies. But more than that, she understood that he had a foot on both sides of the veil.

He breathed in the delicate scent of her skin and placed a kiss on her cheek. "You're okay? Shea hasn't been back?"

She shook her head, still pressed against him. "I haven't heard anything strange. Whatever deal you made I think they have all gone."

He wanted to believe that Shea had gone for good, but he knew that wouldn't be the case. However, at least he wasn't terrorizing Lydia anymore. "I'm glad. The garden looks better."

She sighed against his neck and her breath tickled his skin like a lover's caress. "It looked worse than it was."

"I bought you a gardenia… and I will pay to get the paving relaid."

Lydia pulled back. "You didn't have to." But she smiled as she took the pot.

"It was my fault it all happened."

"You can't help what you are." She paused and looked at him. "It won't happen again, right?"

The easy lie was to say no. "I can't guarantee that. But I hope not."

She nodded. "I hope so too." She raked her teeth over her lip. "I didn't call you to talk about your family—I think I've had all the fairies I can handle for today. I ah… I read some more of the diaries. I wish I hadn't. I don't know what to do."

People's diaries were private, but he understood her curiosity. Unfortunately some things should remain private. And he still had no idea what the best thing to do with them was. "There are names?"

"No, but I'm not a Callaway."

Caspian blinked. How could she not be a Callaway? "What do you mean?"

"Gran wasn't my grandmother; a woman died after giving birth and Gran raised the baby as her own. She lied to me. Said my mother was a late life surprise."

"Hang on." He shut the door. This didn't seem like a conversation that should happen on the doorstep.

Her eyebrows were pinched and she was looking at him like he should have the answers… maybe he did. He wasn't raised by his biological father. He put his satchel down by the hat stand. The iron should keep any curious fairy away. But he hadn't seen one in the cab or any around the house.

"You said I should flick through and see if they named names. Well, I started flicking and caught up in the drama of a young woman who had partied here and then stayed when she became pregnant. She had the baby and then died." She looked at him like he should be making connections. "That baby was my mother."

"How do you know that for sure?"

"Gran named the baby Helen. Then I read a few of the later ones—that baby was definitely my mother. My mother had me at seventeen and ran to escape the Callaway name and house. She didn't want to be trapped by history like Gran. Helen wasn't even a Callaway."

Caspian cupped her face. He couldn't tell if she was angry, frustrated, upset, or all of the three. "I know it's a shock, but take a breath and think about who put Band-Aids on your grazed knees and read you a bedtime story. Blood means nothing."

She looked up at him. "But I'm not a Callaway. I don't know who I am. Gran lied to me."

"You are a Callaway. You're tough and smart, just like your grandmother taught you. She loved you like a daughter, raised you. You owe her that respect. If she said nothing, it was to protect you. If she hadn't claimed your mother, what would've happened? Would the child have been sent to an orphanage, placed in state care? Would that have been better?" He cupped her face, his thumbs brushing her cheeks.

She bit her lip and shook her head. "Maybe things would've been different."

"You'd trade the love your grandmother gave you?" He couldn't imagine doing that, but then he'd known since he could speak that he was different. But Lydia needed to see that it didn't matter who her grandmother was. It was the woman she called Gran who was important. "The important people are the ones who love and care about you."

And Dylis had been there his whole life, protecting

him from Greys and telling him about his real father. The scheming she was part of probably ran deeper than he could ever know or want to understand and she wouldn't sell him out to Shea. Dylis was part of his family.

"You really believe that?"

"With all my heart."

"I feel like I've lost everything again."

"You've gained. Your gran would've had to fight to keep your mother, and then she'd have battled again to keep you. She would have been an amazing woman. You're lucky to have known her." He placed a kiss on her forehead. "Come with me." He led her into the living room. On the shelf was a plaster child's handprint. He'd seen it and touched it out of curiosity.

As he picked it up Lydia looked at him as if he was a little crazy. "I made that for Mother's Day when I was in kindergarten."

"I know." He nodded. "And she loved it. She loved you. When I pick this up that is the only impression I get. This boundless love. She'd have done anything for you. She wanted to do better than she had with Helen—I got a sense of failure and loss off the picture of the toddler." He pointed to the wall of photos.

"Maybe you know her better than me." Her face crumpled like she was going to cry.

"No. I get fragments of her life. You have the whole story in the diaries. Maybe some of it you weren't supposed to read, but if you read on I'm sure you will see just how much she loved you." He placed the handprint down. "It's always a shock to find out not everything is as it seems." And Lydia had found out more than the average person today.

"You're not just talking about Gran."

He shook his head. "I'm sorry you've got mixed up in my stuff."

She gave him a halfhearted smile. "It's what happens when you get to know someone." She paused and met his gaze. "Please don't tell anyone about Helen."

"Does Helen know the truth?"

"No."

"Are you going to tell her?"

She shrugged. "I've never spoken to her."

Helen probably deserved to know about her parentage, but then what would it change? It wouldn't bring Helen back into Lydia's life and Lydia didn't seem to want to know her. Whereas he wanted to at least meet his fairy father, or he had until this morning.

She covered his hands with hers. "Thank you for listening and sharing what you know. I knew you'd understand. But I still don't know what to do with the diaries."

"If there are no names, you don't have to decide yet. They have no scandal value, only historical. Have you read the early ones?"

She shook her head. "I should."

"It would be nice to know what happened. Callaway was once a respected name."

"You don't know? I thought you would have been able to see."

"It doesn't work that way. I get impressions, not the detailed history."

"I know there was a gambling debt, and I know Gran's husband died in World War Two. I don't know why she opened Callaway House as mistress hotel. I'm sure her husband must have rolled in his grave."

Caspian glanced at the fancy ceiling and the old-fashioned light fitting that had been converted to electricity. "Something went wrong. And I'm sure it wasn't an easy choice."

Lydia followed his gaze. "You don't see what I do. I grew up here and took it all for granted. I thought all houses were like this, full of art and chandeliers."

He laughed before he could help himself. "My brother and I shared a room. We had linoleum on the kitchen floor and green kitchen counters. Our house would've fit in here three times."

She raised one eyebrow. "You weren't that poor."

"I never thought we were. Everyone I knew lived the same way. When I was in high school we moved to a bigger house. My parents still live there."

"You see them often?"

"Not as often as I should." He wanted to see them in case all the fairy stuff went pear-shaped, but on the other hand he didn't want to bring Shea to their door. That would be a shock his mother wouldn't forgive him for.

His mother had a fear of all things fairy so he'd stopped mentioning anything he saw after she'd been horrified by his gift. For a while he'd tried to suppress and ignore it. But he couldn't. It had been easier to learn how to manage it and mold it than pretend it didn't exist. He was sure his mom knew that he used it daily in his business but she never said anything. She'd been there during the divorce. His dad had put his hand on Caspian's shoulder and told him, *Son, bad things happen to good people. Don't be scared to try again.*

He'd never managed to follow that piece of advice. And until now he hadn't wanted to. But Lydia was tempting him to walk the paths he'd sworn never to take again. In her arms he believed he could love again. He brushed a strand of hair off her face, unable to resist touching her and yet knowing that if he didn't step away soon he'd get nothing done. And as much as he enjoyed being here, it would be simpler if he wasn't working here.

"I should get to work. A bit left in the stable, and then I'll have a look in the attic."

"Then that's it except for the cabins." She sounded disappointed, as if she wasn't sure she'd ever see him again once he'd finished the job.

They looked at each other for several heartbeats. Then he stepped forward and kissed her. She didn't have any idea what this meant to him. She knew what he was and wasn't afraid. He wasn't about to give her up. Her lips moved against his, tempting and teasing, but if he stopped to play now he wouldn't get any work done. Slowly he broke the kiss and they drew apart.

Her tongue traced her lower lip as if considering the same thing he was thinking. Forget working and dinner—there were other things to do. And he wondered how long it had been since she'd had a boyfriend. There were so many things he didn't know about her.

She gave a little sigh as if reluctant to do the right thing. "Okay then, I'll let you get on with it."

"What are you going to do?"

"Find out how the mistress hotel started."

He picked up his satchel ready to go out the back. "Will you tell me over dinner?"

"Maybe." She grinned, then walked away. He watched her hips sway then followed her down the corridor wishing he didn't have to spend a few hours working before relaxing upstairs with Lydia.

Fortunately much of the stable was filled with junk, the same as most people's basements. Just because it was old didn't make it valuable junk—a lot of people came to his shop thinking old equaled valuable. They often thought he was trying to rip them off.

He locked the stable door, knowing if Lydia sold she was going to have to make the decision about whether to keep or discard. Just because it wasn't valuable didn't mean there wasn't sentimental value. There were old dolls in a box that had probably belonged to Lydia's mother. While he'd found a brush with a tarnished mirrored back, it wasn't the Window. It would have been much easier to find if he could sense it... but then all fairies would have been able to and it would have fallen into a Grey's hands long ago.

Lydia stuck her head out the back door. "Pizza is here."

"Okay, I'm done." He went in and washed his hands.

They ate at the table that had seen many morning afters and a few rendezvous. He tried not to think about what people had done on the table as he ate. Across from him Lydia concentrated on her food.

"I opened the second trunk. You might want to log the crystal, plates, and silver candle holders."

He glanced at the trunk, now closed, hopefully. "What else was in there?"

"A wedding dress."

"She packed away her dress and wedding presents?"

Lydia nodded and picked up a photo she'd hidden on the seat. It was beautifully framed. The couple smiled surrounded by the bridal party. She handed it to him and he braced for the flood of memories. The stronger the emotion the greater the residual impression. The first ones were of great sadness and tears as everything was packed away, anger lingered underneath, but beneath that there was great joy.

He put the picture on the table so they could both see Nanette Callaway. "Have you solved the mystery?"

She nodded and swallowed what she'd been eating. "While most people know that Callaway House was making liquor during Prohibition, that isn't the full story. The reason Mr. Callaway Senior got involved in liquor was because he liked to gamble. The debt was huge apparently and his son inherited it with the house. Apparently old Charleston blood doesn't forgive and forget some debts. Which was fine while he was alive and earning an officer's salary."

"But once he died—"

"Gran either had to give up the house to pay the debt or find a way to keep going."

Caspian frowned. "Why didn't she sell?" Surely that was the easy option.

"The house was all she had left of her husband and child. Their little daughter died while he was away fighting. She couldn't give up the only home she'd known, the place that still held their memories."

"The outbuildings had already been sold?" Caspian asked.

Lydia nodded. "Callaway Senior sold them along with some of the land. This used to be a proper farm. What my grandfather inherited was a reduced property and a big debt. Gran was working in a factory to help with the war, barely getting by and someone—she doesn't say who, just calls him the doctor—asked if she'd be willing to let his *friend* stay. Of course she knew what he as asking, but she saw the opportunity. Soon there were half a dozen women here. The men coming out to spend their weekends partying and playing."

"And no one said anything?"

Lydia shook her head. "Rich men had mistresses and stashing them out here away from town made it easy. Gran took board and lodging money and also put on the parties. That was when the poets, painters, and musicians got involved."

"Ah, and then its reputation really took off."

She grinned. "And then some. Apparently they had to turn people away because the house was too full."

"Did she pay the debt off?"

"Yep. By then she had an established business as a mistress hotel and a bit of an exclusive club."

"Until mistresses went out of favor."

"Actually, that didn't seem to dampen things. By then it was the sixties and the parties just kept rolling. I think some of the women who lived here were making money upstairs… but Gran never says that directly." She raised an eyebrow and looked at him for confirmation.

"Yeah. There was a lot of action upstairs but without spending a lot of time digging I wouldn't be able to separate it out—I don't want to do that. That's people's private lives." He grimaced. What he could do wasn't normal and he didn't want to be peering into the raunchy bits of history. "But I'd say your suspicions are correct."

She gave a single nod as if happy to be unraveling her family history. He knew his, both fairy and human, but couldn't be open about it. Or at least hadn't been able to be open until Lydia. He picked up another slice of pizza and waited for her to continue. It was so rare he actually got the full story instead of just the highlights as impressed upon the furniture or as seen by mirrors.

He stopped before taking a bite and realized what had been missing from his visit tonight. The house had been silent. "Where's your ghost gone?"

"What do you mean? I thought you said it wasn't a ghost?" But now she was sitting up listening, the past forgotten.

"It's not. But I haven't heard it all night... in fact, I haven't sensed a single thing."

"That's good, right?"

"No. Your ghost has been here for years. Why leave now?"

They both went silent. All Caspian could hear was the beating of his heart. The Grey that had been in the house was gone. Had Dylis scared it away? Had Shea scared it away or had it found what it was looking for?

"Where's your fairy?"

"She's working, trying to help find the mirror."

"Ah." She glanced around the kitchen. "I'm now creeped out because there isn't a ghost in the house."

He flicked her a smile. "It's odd, that's all." And he didn't like odd as there was usually a reason and it wasn't usually a good reason when it came to fairies. "No reason not to stay." Staying here was more enticing than going back to his house where Shea could be lurking. Although at least his house was protected by the silver tea set. Maybe it would be smarter to go back to his place. He met Lydia's gaze and held it. "Unless you'd rather go back into town, you could always come to my place?"

There was a pause and for a moment he thought he'd crossed a line he shouldn't have. Callaway House was like neutral ground. She didn't live here, so the only impressions he got of her were recent or so old it didn't matter. Knowing his lover had had previous lovers was very different from getting glimpses of them. It happened all through his twenties until he married. It made dating difficult—and dating was hard enough. Or maybe he'd just never been good at it. Fairies didn't seem to date, so maybe there was a bad dating gene he'd inherited.

"As tempting as that is, I'm not going to be chased out of the house because there are no fairies tonight. Last night there were too many, tonight not enough. I feel like Goldilocks."

He laughed.

"Have you always seen fairies?" Lydia asked.

"Yes. I thought it was normal until I was about five. After that I tried to pretend I couldn't see them. Sometimes not very well."

"And the psychometry?"

He frowned. "I was still a child, maybe ten. At first it was small things. But I went through a really bad phase of being sucked into visions and not knowing how to get out. My mother freaked, my father thought I was daydreaming and didn't get it. My brother used to tease me mercilessly. Dylis helped me."

"So your mom knew it was because of the fairy blood?"

"Yeah. That was when she told me the truth about my father, but Dylis had told me years before."

"Do you want to meet him?"

Not now with the deal with Shea hanging over his head. "There was a time when I did. When I wanted to know why he'd left me and when I thought I'd be better off in Annwyn, but not anymore. I have no desire to go to Court and be surrounded by fairies."

She sipped her soft drink and he could see the questions forming in her mind. She wanted to know more about Court. Humans might have forgotten about Annwyn, but when something reopened that door old longing rose up. That was why it was so easy for fairies to trick the unaware into going to Annwyn and giving up their souls, or firstborns while still in the womb.

"So why are you human, not fairy?"

"Dylis didn't explain?"

She shook her head. "No, she made me memorize a bunch of rules."

That sounded like Dylis. "Those rules could save your life. Did she tell you about iron and water?"

"Yes." She reached into her pocket and pulled out an iron bolt.

Caspian put his hand out and she placed it in his palm. There was a jolt of pain as he fisted his hand around it for a few heartbeats. He could feel his skin heating. Then he handed it back and showed her the red burn marks. They would heal overnight, but it would prove his point.

"I am fairy. Iron burns me. But I don't have a fear of running water like they do."

"You said you were human."

"No, I said I was mortal. There is a difference. I was born here; I am a changeling. If my father had taken Mom back to Annwyn to give birth, I'd have been a soulless fairy. Fairies need humans to breed."

"You make it sound so... cold."

"Fairies aren't like you. They have different morals, different ethics, their world is based on power and deals. Their word is their bond. The King's word is law. They deal in death. The Victorians did every human a great disservice in reducing fairies to humanoid butterflies."

"You speak as though you are one of them."

"I am, and yet I'm not. I have to stop myself some days from being too much like them. The curiosity is always there. I make deals for a living. I'm not excusing it, but you need to realize I'm not simply human with a bonus touch of magic. I am a mortal fairy."

She leaned back in the chair and looked at him. He was pretty sure he'd just put the iron nail in the coffin of their relationship. He probably shouldn't have pushed so hard, but it was nice to be honest for a change and he didn't want to trick her into thinking he was human when he wasn't—no matter how hard he pretended.

"So what will your children be?"

That wasn't the question he'd been expecting. But he'd asked Dylis once, not that Natalie had ever suggested they have kids. "Human—with a touch of magic. They won't be able to see fairies, and they won't be bound by Annwyn's laws."

Lydia nodded as if happy with the answer. She was weighing him as a prospective partner. Already. The idea was far too tempting. He didn't want to think that far ahead and risk it all falling apart. He desperately wanted to lock his heart away again but it was already too late. He'd offered it to her when he'd started telling her the truth. The kitchen became warm. He could feel the pull between them, thickening with each breath. One of them had to move to break the spell. He needed to. He needed to step away before he fell in too deep.

"Just the attic to go." He hoped there wasn't much in there, as he was done for the day. Checking all the mirrors in the morning had left him tired, and while he hoped Shea wouldn't bring mirrors every morning, he knew it was a wasted wish.

She nodded, but he saw the flicker of disappointment in her eyes. Had she expected him to sit and answer every question tonight? He couldn't be what she expected him to be because he wasn't and never would be, but at the same time he didn't want to spend all their time together talking about fairies.

"I know this is all new and exciting to you, but for me fairies have always meant problems."

"You sound like you are trying to put me off."

"I'm trying to be honest." *For a change*. And he wasn't sure if it was simplifying or complicating things.

Lydia ate another piece of nearly cold pizza but her mind was on Caspian. He was staying, again. She pressed her thighs together but the ache in her belly intensified along with the butterflies trapped in her chest where her heart should be. She wanted him; she'd wanted him since the moment he'd appeared on the doorstep. She wanted him regardless of who his parents were or what he was. She glanced at the kitchen doorway.

Should she go after him?

And then what? Was he right that she should be afraid of fairies? The Greys, yes, she could see that. But Caspian? No, he was more human than he thought he was.

She cleaned up dinner and put the diaries away. It was too easy to get caught in the past. What had happened thirty years ago, or fifty years ago, didn't change who she was. In that respect Caspian was right. It didn't matter who her grandmother was, it didn't change the love she had for Gran, or her love of the house. Before she went upstairs, she checked that the doors were locked, then she ventured up into the attic. Caspian had turned on the light but was still holding the flashlight to poke around the dark corners.

"What did you find?"

He flinched as if startled. "Baby clothes and toys. Things she couldn't get rid of." *Things she couldn't fit in the stable, more like*. He pointed the flashlight to a corner. "You have a leak in the roof. There's a lot of mildew. It's probably a good idea to move the boxes in case they go through the ceiling. What's below?"

"A bathroom, I think." Or a bedroom. Was it really that bad? Her heart sank a little at the thought of all the repairs that would need to be done if she kept the house, on top of the fairy garden damage.

"Is there water damage on the ceiling below?"

"I'll have a look." She went back down the ladder and checked the ceilings. There were marks on the ceiling that weren't just age-related. She didn't want Caspian moving boxes and risking going through the ceiling.

She scampered back up before he could do anything.

"I think so. I'll call the insurance people and see what they say."

"If it's poor maintenance, I don't like your chances."

Damn. He was probably right. And it would be due to lack of care. "What do I do?"

"Clean the gutters and get a quote for repairs… if you aren't selling. If you are selling don't worry about it. The house won't come down around you in the next few months. It's probably been like this for years."

How was she going to pay to get the roof fixed?

She smoothed her hair back from her face. "I can't make any decision until the valuation is in."

"I'm working on it. I think all of this stuff is either ruined or of personal significance only." He walked back over, carefully ducking the beams in the very low roof space.

"So you're done?"

"Yeah, there's a few outstanding prices, but I'll have it back to the company in a few days and they can inform the lawyer."

Lydia forced a breath out between her teeth. "I may not have any option but to sell."

"There're always options. If your grandmother could turn it into a profitable business, I'm sure there's something you could do." A frown creased his brow. "I didn't mean—"

"I know." She nodded and smiled. From another man those words would have had entirely the wrong meaning, but not Caspian.

"What's the split of the estate?"

"My mother gets the cash accounts. I get the house and whatever is left. Without cash I can't keep the house."

"It's mortgage free?"

"Yes. But it needs work. A lot of work. I have my own mortgage and car payments. I can't afford an empty house."

"You could sell and live here."

And rattle around like a lonely pea in a pod like Gran? But she didn't say that living here alone held no appeal. She'd known this place when it was full of life and that was how she wanted to remember it.

"And lose money on my place?" It wasn't a sellers' market at the moment. She shrugged. "I know you're trying help, but I've thought of everything."

"At least get quotes so you know exactly how much you need to fix the place up." He smiled, the white of his teeth catching in the light. "Quotes, at least, are free."

"True." She could do that. Maybe if she'd been more attentive while Gran was alive the house wouldn't have gotten so shabby. But she hadn't wanted to see that Gran wasn't coping. Gran had always been strong and capable; to see her as anything else would mean acknowledging she was getting old.

"Hey. It'll be fine." The back of his fingers brushed her cheek.

"And you know this how?" He saw the past, not the future.

"Because I have faith in you." He kissed her, not chaste or even curious. His mouth claimed hers as if he were starving for contact and needed everything she had. When his tongue swept over her lips she opened her mouth to taste him.

Lydia pressed her body closer, needing to feel him against her. Without words getting in the way there was no doubt about what he wanted. Her hand slid up his neck and her fingers threaded into his dark curls. The need that had been simmering in her belly broke free. She wanted him like she'd never wanted anyone. She wanted to sink into his touch and forget everything. A moan escaped her lips as his hand gripped her hip, and the length of his shaft pressed against her in a tempting promise of things to come.

"Not up here," he murmured against her lips. "There are spiders."

She opened her eyes and realized he was being serious. A moldering attic was not the best place to pick for a tryst. She took his hand and led him toward the ladder, an idea forming. He followed her down, which gave her a moment to check out his butt.

Caspian followed as she went down a flight of stairs, but instead of going to the room they were using she walked past to the landing that overlooked the entrance. She wanted a glimpse into the house's past. She wanted a glimpse into what he saw, to understand him better. Asking him to do that in the bedroom wouldn't be right, he'd already said he didn't want to pry into those parts of history. But out here? Would he agree or brush her off? She saw his raised eyebrows and wondered if she was asking too much.

"I want to see what you see and be a part of the house." What would she be saving by keeping the place?

"I can't do that."

"But you could tell me what you see."

He looked at the wooden railing but didn't touch it. "It's not a party trick. I can't be in the past and with you at the same time. Too long and reality and the past blur. It's why I needed to eat and ground myself this morning." He lifted his gaze to her. "You don't want to recreate what has already happened."

"Not recreate, but I want to know what it is you see when you are in the house." She took his hand in hers. "Just let me into your world for a few minutes. I won't ask again."

She could see the possibilities spinning in his mind. He wasn't used to talking about it let alone sharing anything about it.

"You could have asked me over dinner about the table."

"It's just a dining table. I was thinking something more... intriguing."

He smiled and it hid a thousand secrets. "There's no such thing as just a dining table."

Eww. But then she remembered she'd been eating breakfast at that table since she was old enough to sit in a chair. What he was talking about was decades old.

"Are you sure you want to get a taste of what I see? Because you'll never be able to look at it the same again."

"Then how do you live with it?"

"I buy new furniture. The antiques I sell so I don't have to live with the history. I try not to buy things that have been present during a murder. I don't like the vibe."

"Okay." That wasn't the direction she'd been hoping to take. "How about one object, your choice."

He looked at her as if trying to work out what it was she wanted. Then he pushed her against the railing, his hands on either side of her. She put her arms around his neck and risked a glance over her shoulder.

"I won't let you fall," he murmured in her ear. "But now you are part of it as she was."

And she realized this was it. This is what she'd asked for. He'd picked the railing and had pushed her against it the way someone else had been years before. Caspian's cheek was against hers, his breath on her skin, and while she couldn't see his face she could feel the tension in his shoulders beneath her hands.

"She leaned back as far as she could, not caring of the danger. His arm around her waist as he kissed her neck and slowly moved lower. The risk of getting caught, but neither cared." He swallowed. "Lust is the overriding emotion. The longer I tap into the past the more real it becomes. Music drifts up from downstairs. Laughter."

Her breathing quickened as he moved against her, hard against her stomach. But as his hand slid around her waist she realized he wasn't actually with her. He was in the past. And she understood what he meant and why he'd been reluctant to do this.

She slid her hands down his chest then pushed him back, breaking the connection.

He took a couple of steps back and blinked. "I thought you wanted to know."

"I do… I did. You got lost." Was he back?

"Not lost; when I'm lost it's very hard to get free. That hasn't happened in a very long time."

"You weren't here either."

"The impression was close to what I want, so it was easy to tap in and easy for it to take over."

"Close to what you want?" She took a couple of steps, until she was toe to toe with him.

"Mmm." He cupped her cheek and kissed her. His other hand snaked around her waist and drew her closer.

She untucked his shirt and slid her hands under, needing to feel his skin. He must have had the same idea as he worked open the buttons on her shirt and pushed it off her shoulders while she tried to do the same to him. Her fingers skimmed the muscles of his stomach down to the button on his jeans, then she flicked it open.

"And what is it that you want?" She needed to make sure he was here with her, now.

"You, in the room down the corridor." He tugged on the waistband of her jeans as he walked backward toward the room they were sharing.

Chapter 15

NEITHER OF THEM HAD BOUGHT GROCERIES SO IT WAS bread from the freezer again for breakfast. It was so boring and normal. He hadn't had breakfast with any-one in… well, in four years, since he'd walked out on Natalie. Lydia knew what he could do and she'd still come back to bed for more.

After several days of being surrounded by Greys and a twitchy Dylis, he felt good. He smiled at Lydia as she sat opposite him at the table. The shop was closed, so he had nowhere to be and nothing pressing to do. And there were no mirrors in the yard—which probably meant Shea was pacing his front yard, but Shea could wait.

A movement on the windowsill caught his eye. A fairy wren hopped along, stopping and turning, its feathers flashing brilliant blue in the morning sun. Caspian watched, willing it to vanish, or to be attracted to him and not a herald for the Court. Not today, not here. Not now.

Three knocks at the front door shattered the hope he'd had. He'd been lulled into an obviously false sense of security. The wren flapped away, its job done. Whoever was waiting out front was associated with Court.

Lydia looked at Caspian. "I'm not expecting anyone."

He was, but he'd thought he'd gotten away with it when they'd taken so long to come. "I'll go have a look." He finished his coffee.

The fairy knocked again. This time the sound reverberated with power and Caspian felt a stirring in his blood as the fairy in him responded to the call of the Court. He stood, then paused to make sure he'd stood of his own accord. He had—a fairy wouldn't go so far as to control a person; they much preferred to muck around with the limits of free will.

On one hand he could pretend to ignore the knock, on the other he knew he had to answer or the results would be worse. So he would do what any normal person would do—answer the door and then decide what to do with the person on the other side.

He walked barefoot through the house, the echoes of parties long since finished humming around him. Memories of last night lingered but offered no warmth. He wished he could go back and not make the deal, anything to buy himself more time with Lydia.

The fairy on the doorstep was dressed in green and brown. Almost plain by fairy standards. But it was the cut and finish of the clothes that tugged at an unconscious memory. The fairy's green waistcoat was delicately embroidered with silver deer around the edge, his white shirt was untied at the cuff in elegant untidiness, and his brown leather boots were embossed with oak leaves. A long sword of fairy silver hung from his waist. Everything about him said carefully restrained power. This was no low-level messenger.

Caspian met the fairy's cool gaze. His eyes were pale like smoky quartz.

"Caspian ap Felan ap Gwynn ap Nudd." The fairy inclined his head with more than token respect.

Caspian didn't admit it was his name even though the

power of the words spoken by one of the Court cloaked around him. "And you are?"

"Verden ap Hollis, Hunter of Annwyn." There was a glint in Verden's eyes that chilled Caspian to the core.

The Court, possibly his father, had sent the Lord of the Hunt after him. That was either a sign of respect or he was in far deeper trouble than he'd imagined.

"The Crown Prince of Annwyn and guardian of the veil cordially invites you to attend Court at your earliest convenience."

"My father wants to see me."

"To put it coarsely." Verden's expression didn't change.

"Is everything all right?" Lydia walked up behind Caspian. Verden shimmered and as Caspian turned to Lydia he glimpsed what she'd see. A man in a dark suit, wearing sunglasses, his dark brown hair pulled into a messy, but somehow stylish ponytail with a very obvious bulge under one side of his jacket. To her eyes it would be a gun.

"Oh." Her gaze flicked between Caspian and the now glamoured fairy.

"Good morning." Verden smiled with all the charm of a fairy. No mortal could resist. He half-expected Lydia to fall into Verden's arms.

She didn't; she moved further behind Caspian. "What's going on? What does he want?" Then she lowered her voice. "Is he fairy?"

"Caspian's father needs to speak with him," Verden answered before Caspian could even form a word.

"Your father, the mechanic?" she said hopefully.

Caspian half-turned so he could keep one eye on Verden and the other on Lydia. "No, the other one." He gave her a look which he hoped conveyed that yes, this man was a fairy and she should go back to the kitchen. It obviously failed.

"Ohhh." She looked at the Hunter of Annwyn again as if realizing that he wasn't human. "I thought you didn't know your biological father?"

Verden smiled without warmth. He was here to collect and was enjoying watching Caspian squirm as his two worlds collided.

"I don't, but that doesn't mean he doesn't know me."

Lydia glanced at the fairy again. "I thought fairies would look less gangster."

"She knows?" Verden crossed his arms.

Caspian shrugged. "I don't keep secrets from my lover."

Verden shimmered again. Lydia gasped as she saw him how he really looked, all sharp-edged beauty and elegant clothes. This time he expected her to swoon.

She stepped back as if fully appreciating the danger. "This is about the mirrors. How did he know to find you here?"

"Caspian's father keeps track of him," Verden added unhelpfully.

Caspian turned to the fairy. "That's really very creepy."

"Very." Added Lydia. "Just how powerful is your fairy father?" she added in a lower voice, as if hoping the man at the door wouldn't hear.

He paused for a moment. Now probably wasn't the best time to mention his father was actually the Prince of Death. "Let's say extremely and that he's sent his most powerful messenger."

"Forgive me for not introducing myself. I am Verden,

Lord of the Hunt. I've come to escort Caspian to Court. I would have been more upfront had I known you knew about Annwyn." He gave a small bow.

"Shit," she said and then glanced at the fairy. "Sorry." She turned back to Caspian. "You can't go to Annwyn. I thought that is heaven and hell and all that. Won't you die?"

"Hopefully not." He really hoped that he would make it back.

"You knew this would happen."

"I suspected. But I did what I had to. It will be okay." He took her hand. "I'm sorry I brought this to your door."

"Is there anything I can do?" She squeezed his hand, and her brown eyes filled with concern.

Caspian shook his head. "Just be safe, follow the rules."

She nodded but looked uncertain.

"Are you coming with me or do I have to set the dogs?" Verden's hand flicked to his side and two large black dogs appeared.

Their heads were hip height and their eyes glowed with a red light most people mistook for demonic, but it was simply pure hunger and bloodlust. These were the bad kind of fairy dogs. The ones used for dragging unwilling souls to Annwyn for judgment. He really was in trouble if the Hunter had brought the shucks and not the white hunting hounds.

Lydia hadn't said anything about the shuck's magical appearance, which meant she couldn't see them, or hear them. That low rumble could be distant traffic—or wishful thinking.

"I'll come, just give me a moment." Caspian pulled

Lydia farther down the hallway. Not out of earshot of the fairy, but Lydia didn't know that. "I can't refuse the invitation. This is what I meant when I said I'm bound by Annwyn's rules. Making that deal I broke them. I knew that. I had no other choice."

"You shouldn't have done it."

"Shea would have torn this house down. He'd have tricked you out of your soul just to get me to obey. That would have been far, far worse."

"Will your father protect you?"

He didn't have an answer for that.

"Caspian?"

He looked at Lydia. For two nights he'd tasted the kind of life he'd like, one where his lover knew the truth. One where he could happily wake up in her bed and eat toast at the kitchen table. He was imagining a life with Lydia in it and just as fast it was snatched away.

"You're scaring me."

"I am scared. I'm just trying not to show it." He tried to smile but was pretty certain it wasn't reassuring.

"You're doing a good job." She put her arms around his neck and whispered in his ear. "You'd better come back. I don't invite just anyone into my bed." Her lips pressed against his for a moment before she drew back.

He gripped her hands, an idea forming. He could make a deal with her, one that would hopefully guarantee his return from Annwyn. "If I'm not back in three days, panic."

Her eyes widened. "Three days? Don't most people get killed in the first twenty-four hours?" He must have looked shocked because she immediately apologized.

"Oh my God, I'm sorry. I didn't mean your father was going to kill you."

"If he was going to, he would have done so already." He almost believed that. He touched her cheek and let the strands of her blond hair trail through his fingers. "I'll be back. I want to be back. I want to come back to you. So if this hasn't freaked you out totally, kiss me good-bye and keep me in your prayers. I understand if you'd rather walk away."

Lydia looked at him—was he serious? "I'm not walking away, and you're coming back to me."

"I will come back, I swear."

For a moment she felt the force of his words. She had to believe that was true. But when she glanced at the fairy on the doorstep she wasn't sure. At first glance Verden looked melt-at-the-knees hot. The face, the casual disheveled look like he was too cool to care, and those pale gray eyes. Women could get whiplash if they passed him on the street. But after that first glance, when she looked a little closer, that was when warning raked icy fingernails down her back. He smiled and she saw the restrained power, and the hunger as if he could never be satisfied. His eyes weren't cold and empty, but whatever he wanted out of life had eluded him. The Hunter of Annwyn, but what was he really hunting?

She stepped back as he leveled his gaze at her.

Caspian stepped between them. "Leave her out of it."

Verden inclined his head and tapped the sword at his side. "My patience is wearing thin."

Caspian turned as if to go, but she wasn't ready

for him to leave with Verden. What if she never saw him again?

"Wait, you need your shoes and wallet."

"I won't need them. Look after them for me." He glanced up at the ceiling and drew in a breath. He was trying to remain calm. "Why don't you get those quotes while I'm away so we can make plans to save the house when I return."

He was thinking about quotes now? No, he was trying to keep things normal. He was trying to think of the mundane and not the fairies. He was giving her something to do and something else to think about instead of where he had gone.

She stepped forward and gave him another hug. "Be safe."

"You too." He returned her embrace and held onto her. "I will do everything I can to come back."

"You will get him back. Debts must be settled. Reparation made. You don't want to be late, so come along." Verden smiled, but there was nothing friendly in it.

She swallowed and released Caspian. She didn't want him to be in any more trouble with the fairies. Especially this fairy.

Caspian took a step back, gave her a single nod, and then turned away. He closed the door. For a moment Lydia stood in the entrance, not sure what to do. Was there anything she could do? Praying that she hadn't seen the last of Caspian seemed like the only option.

Chapter 16

CASPIAN CLOSED THE DOOR BEHIND HIM AND STOOD ON the step with the Hunter of Annwyn. "Is this where you get the dogs to tear me to pieces?"

"Mortals are so melodramatic. Do you have any idea how complicated arranging this meeting has been?" Verden walked down the steps. When Caspian didn't immediately follow, he turned. "If you want to be dragged into Court by the dogs, I can do that, but I thought you'd like to walk in with a bit of pride. Do you really think the Prince would send *me* to kill for him?"

Caspian didn't answer. Keeping his mouth shut around fairies had always worked in the past, and he was still trying to work out what Verden meant about engineering a meeting with his father. He walked through the garden and out on to the road.

"You're here to take me to Court, nothing more?" The asphalt was cold and rough against his bare feet. He knew they were walking toward the old graveyard and church that had once been part of the estate.

"Your safe transit to Court. What happens to you there is not my business, although I will ensure you don't come to harm since you know nothing of the ways of Court. I wouldn't want the Queen getting her claws on you. Your return…" He shrugged. "I'm sure your most recent deal will bear weight."

Bear weight, but not necessarily be enforced. "I had to make the deal with Shea."

"Plead your case with the one who cares." Verden crossed the road and stopped at the gate of the grave-yard. The gap between hallowed ground and regular dirt could be used to cross between the worlds. "Know your actions have had far-reaching effects that you don't understand. Shea ap Greely has tentacles everywhere. While I realize you have loyalty to the Prince, if you move against the King, I will release the hounds." Verden moved his hands as if opening a door. The gap where the gate was shimmered like a heat wave, and the heavy scent of blossoms filled the air. "And I don't care who your father is. After you, changeling." Verden stood aside and indicated for Caspian to go through.

Caspian took a final glance up the road to Callaway House, then crossed his fingers and hoped he wouldn't get trapped in Annwyn forever.

Behind him the gate closed with a snap like a break-ing twig. He turned to look behind him but there was no gate, just two trees that looked no different from any other two trees around him.

He appeared to be in a forest of some kind. But the trees were taller and bigger than was possible and the color was wrong, not brighter, but more vibrant. The magic he'd felt of the silver tea set was nothing com-pared to the power in the air here. He could taste it, almost metallic on his tongue.

"Am I dead?" It sounded like a stupid question, but it was always good to check the technicalities and read the fine print on the ticket.

"Not yet."

"So I'm physically here." Caspian flexed his fingers. He felt real.

"Yes."

On one hand that was good, on the other it meant he'd vanished from the mortal world and given that time moved differently he'd have no idea how long he'd been gone for.

"Three mortal days."

"While I said she'd get you back, I didn't specify in what condition." Verden looked at him, his pale eyes almost amused. "And neither did you."

Caspian gave himself a mental kick. "Why did he send you?" He couldn't bring himself to say the Prince, and Father sounded too personal.

"Security. The hunt is more than a game. The Prince might be able to summon the army, but without me it has no teeth."

That was the fairy way, spread the power so no one could rule alone. The King needed the Queen to keep the magic of Court alive. Duties were divided amongst the loyal. If Verden was loyal to the King, he'd be pretty pissed about Shea and the Queen. But that didn't put him on the Prince's side either. The Prince was a threat, the one person who could overthrow the King and take power.

Annwyn was balancing on a knife waiting to see who'd flinch first.

Verden began walking, crossing the lush green lawn. Caspian followed. He tried not to glance wildly around him, but part of him couldn't contain the glee at being at Court. Part of him, the fairy part obviously, was reveling in the sensation of power. The mortal part, the part he usually listened to, was far more cautious. So he reined in all emotion and tried to ignore the magnificence as the forest began to change and thicken.

Overhead the branches arched to form a roof and the forest became a living building. The walls were the trunks, but embedded in the bark were what looked like gems. From the roof vines and flowers tumbled, the colored petals danced in the breeze. Shadows flickered along the edges, but they didn't belong to Verden or Caspian. Shadow servants. They looked human, but they didn't speak and kept their gaze on the grass at their feet.

The doubt and fear rose to the surface, smothering any wonder he felt about being in Annwyn. This place was unnatural. He shouldn't be here. He didn't want to end up like the shadow servants, bound to serve to pay a debt. "Where are we going?"

"Hall of Judgment. You made a deal with a Grey and a hearing has been called."

Caspian stopped walking. "I thought you said my father wants to see me?"

"He does. How do you think he was ever going to manage that?" Verden tilted his head. "You needed a reason to come here, the same way he needed a reason to call you here. I think it's all tied together quite well." Verden considered for a moment. "Very well."

Cold tumbled through his blood and lodged in his heart. "What do you mean?"

"You're going to miss your hearing and that would look really bad. Not a good first impression. Bow to the King and *Queen*." The word Queen was loaded with something close to disgust. "Acknowledge the Prince but not for too long—don't want to give away that he's your father. Then shut up and let them work out what to do with you."

As Verden walked toward what looked like a solid wall of trees, giant double doors swung open. What Caspian glimpsed in the mirror had been a reflection of the true beauty of the Court.

The fairies were beautiful. Sharp cheekbones, pale eyes of every shade from blue to yellow to green and pink. Their clothing was cut in styles no human hand could replicate, like haute couture had taken nature as inspiration and blended it with styles straight out of history but without the modesty.

Skin and silks.

He looked away before he could be drawn in, his gaze dropping to just a few yards in front of him as he followed Verden. In his bare feet, jeans, and shirt he drew curious gazes as he walked forward. Some hissed and drew back as if mortality was catching. In the mortal world being a changeling gave him status above the banished; here it meant he was at the bottom of the pile, slightly above shadow servants.

Verden stopped and swept a low bow. "As requested, the changeling has been brought forward. He came of his own volition, aware of the serious nature of the crime."

"Thank you, Lord Verden." The King's voice rolled around the chamber. His hand lifted off the arm of the throne and Verden moved to stand beside the King.

Caspian was left standing alone in the center of the Court. Those dreams where you show up to work naked... nothing like this. This was like showing up to your own funeral naked and alive but not being able to tell anyone because they thought you were dead.

He gave an awkward bow and risked a glance at the King and Queen. His grandparents. They didn't look a day over twenty-five, and yet they were centuries old. The Queen looked annoyed like she was going to yell *off with his head* at any moment. The King looked concerned, as well he might. His kingdom would crumble if he did nothing. The only thing he could do was abdicate, and he could only do that if the Prince had a wife.

Caspian nodded in the direction of the Prince. The same pale green eyes and dark hair, but that was where the similarities ended between father and son. His father barely glanced at him; he spoke to someone standing at his side. Caspian let any hope go that his father actually gave a damn. He felt like he was a child again, learning that his father was different. He'd entertained hopes of one day meeting him before getting wiser. But it still bit that his father looked at him with something akin to pity, not love. He was an inconvenience who served no purpose.

All of Dylis's chatter about Court and how much fun it was still didn't make sense. Every fairy in the room looked like a fresh-faced twenty-something, but most would be centuries old. All would quite happily trick him out of his soul and firstborn before lunch. A trickle of sweat formed between his shoulder blades and rolled down his spine. He was half fairy yet he wanted to get out of Annwyn and back to the mortal world. He should have stayed in bed with Lydia.

Even as he thought it he knew the Hunter would've dragged him out of bed regardless. Would he get to see Lydia again? *Would he be alive when he saw Lydia again?* was probably the better question.

"You made a deal with a banished fairy. Do you deny?"

"No." How did he address the King of Death again? "Sire." All of Dylis's lessons about Annwyn that he swore he'd never use might save his ass and hopefully his soul as well.

"The nature of the deal?"

"I was to find the Window."

There was a collective gasp. Spots of color appeared on the Queen's cheeks. She looked like Snow White, if Snow White had become a heartless immortal Queen. Her years of living at Court had given her features the sharp beauty of the fairies—and also taken her humanity if what Dylis had told him was half-true.

The King lifted his hand and silence fell. "And once you have the Window?"

"Not specified." Caspian swallowed but noticed most of the fairies weren't looking at him anymore. They were watching the King and Queen. It wasn't him on trial. It was the Queen, but she couldn't be tried. The King couldn't act against her without bringing down the veil between the worlds.

Verden's comments made sense. Bringing Caspian here meant there could be a meeting between father and son, but also the Queen would be publicly told off without her losing face and doing more damage to the fragile magical balance. Caspian didn't know whether to sigh in relief or be more worried. The Queen was a powerful enemy, and her lover was in the mortal world with Lydia.

"In exchange what did you get?"

"That he would stop harassing me and mine. I have one month then my soul is forfeit."

There were some more mutterings. And spoken aloud he had to agree it was a dumb deal, but better than Lydia handing her soul over. It was the best he'd been able to do at the time. The King nodded. He turned to his son and conferred, then to another fairy who stood behind the throne.

He turned back to Caspian. There was a weariness in his eyes despite his apparent youth. "In this instance there has been no harm done. If you make another deal with a banished fairy, you may not be so lucky. You may have a mortal soul by virtue of your birth, but you are bound by the same laws as the rest of us. Think well, child of woman, before you deal again."

Caspian bowed. No one had mentioned the potential loss of his soul or a punishment. He took a step back, hoping to get out of the hall before someone realized.

The King raised one finger. Caspian paused. *Damn it*.

"You may not break the deal. A fairy's word has weight, even in the mortal world." The King almost smiled. "Enjoy the hospitality of the Court before you leave."

Caspian took another step back then turned and walked toward the large doors. They swung open and once again he was in the hallway of the living castle. For a moment he just breathed, sucking in gulps of air laden with scents that made his head spin. He wanted to run back to the gateway and leave.

A shadow drifted over and beckoned him into an antechamber. There was no furniture as such. The tree roots had arched out of the ground to form bench seats that were now littered with a rainbow of cushions in delicate fabrics and bold shades. A large slab of pale

rock had pushed through the grass and was acting as a
table. The shadow placed a pitcher and cup on the table.
Both were elegant and made of tinted glass.

Do not drink. Do not eat. Do not dance.

Three simple rules for surviving Annwyn.

He ignored the pitcher, even though he was suddenly
thirsty, and concentrated on the trees forming the room.
He put his hand on the trunk. The bark was smooth and
cool beneath his palm and he got nothing. No impressions, no memories, no past. It was like losing his sight
and being blind. Had he really come to depend on the
psychometry? He tried another tree, but the result was
the same.

"The gift your fairy blood gave you is null here. Our
magic works in the mortal world, not here. Annwyn has
its own magic. While you are here you are one of us, not
bound by the laws of mortality." His father, the Crown
Prince of Annwyn, closed the door.

———

Felan looked at his son. The son looked older than the
father. It pained him in a way he couldn't easily express.

"Why am I here?" Caspian asked.

"You made a deal. The hearing was a necessary
formality." Felan flicked his hand. The hearing had
been an excuse to meet his son, and take a shot at the
Queen. Everyone knew what was going on and they
were all waiting for him to do something. "I have
waited years for this meeting. The opportunity couldn't
be ignored."

Caspian shook his head. "Why wait so long—if you
cared so much?"

"Few know of you for your own safety. I have enemies who wouldn't hesitate to kill a child of mine."

"You had Dylis look after me."

"Shh." Felan shook his head. "Names have power here. While the Lord of the Hunt could use your name freely in the mortal world, saying it here could bind you in all manner of ways. The same for you speaking another's name. The more names you know the more power you have. Another reason to keep your birth secret."

Caspian had grown into a fine man. For a heartbeat Felan was filled with regret for not seeing him grow up. "You made a good deal, one any fairy would be proud of. Now you must keep it."

"Keep it?"

"Your word is like law, binding." He reached into his waistcoat and pulled out the mirror on a chain. "This will help you."

In the mirror a woman ran her finger under her eye and removed a smudge of makeup. Felan smiled. "There's someone in it today." He held it still for Caspian.

Caspian frowned, a flicker of something in his eyes. Then he took the Counter-Window without a word and slid the chain over his head. "You want me to return it to you. But then what will stop the Grey from killing me?"

"I wouldn't let harm come to you. I have done my utmost to protect you always." Everything he'd done over the last three mortal decades had been to protect Caspian. It was why he'd been such a poor father.

Caspian wouldn't look him in the eye. "Why did you let me be born in the mortal world where you knew I wouldn't fit in?" He spoke softly as if unsure he should even be asking.

Felan had expected the question. He'd imagined having it from a much younger Caspian, but he'd never been able to construct a meeting that wouldn't arouse suspicion.

"It was both an easy choice and one I have doubted every day over the years. Particularly now. I met your mother by chance. I was checking a doorway that had been tampered with by a Grey and she was walking through the cemetery. She was so beautiful I had to stop and talk to her. Over the next few weeks one thing led to another and I began thinking I'd found someone to sit by my side when she conceived. Even then Annwyn was in trouble."

Felan grimaced. The old hurt was like a wound that didn't heal. But compared to the newer one it was but a scrape. Now he had no one and needed someone to help save Annwyn. "Then I saw her with the human she'd married. His hand was on her stomach and there was something in her eye that wasn't there when she was with me. With me it was lust and desire, but with him it was love. If I'd brought her here I'd be on the throne looking like my father in five hundred years' time with a cold queen full of hate by my side."

"You knew she was married?"

"She knew I was fairy." Felan shrugged. "In hind-sight maybe you should have been born here. I would have taken the throne, my father would have stepped down, and all of the current nastiness could've been avoided. I guess I was too selfish." He wanted too much, he wanted everything.

Caspian shook his head, still frowning. "You must have loved her enough to realize she would be happier with my father. The man who raised me," he corrected.

"I know you view him as your father, but I wanted you to know your birthright. You are my only child."

Felan looked at Caspian. He wasn't ready to send him home to die. Whether in ten years or fifty it didn't matter. This was why he didn't want a gaggle of changeling children. It was too painful, knowing he'd outlive them all. "Stay a while. Enjoy the pleasures of Court."

"I will get trapped."

"I will care for your soul; you can have it back later and go back to being mortal." He just wanted to spend some time with his son, show him how beautiful Court could be, and maybe Caspian wouldn't want to leave.

"And how many years will have passed while I drink and dine?"

"You are refusing an invitation?" Felan narrowed his eyes. No one refused. No one thought to disobey him. Did Caspian think he could just because he was the only child?

Caspian gave a small bow as if sensing the shift in the air. "No, I wouldn't decline such an honor. But I have my deal to keep and I'm sure you'd like the issue with the Grey finished."

"You promised your lover three mortal days?"

"Yes."

"Then you shall remain for three days and remember that half your blood is fairy and that should you chose to surrender your soul this could be your home." He laid his hand on Caspian's chest and a ring formed around Felan's middle finger—silver with a curious pale green stone split with a red line up the center. "You will get your soul back when you bring me the Window." Taking Caspian's soul would also stop Shea from getting it should Caspian fail to find the Window within the month.

Caspian looked at the ring; he placed his own hand on his chest as if trying to feel the difference.

"You won't miss it. I promise."

"I will in the mortal world. Without it I will be fairy."

"And technically banished. Like any fairy caught making deals with the banished."

"But you said the hearing was a formality."

"It was. I didn't need the hearing to punish you."

"Then all that fatherly crap…"

Felan caught Caspian's chin and forced him to look him in the eye. "Not crap, Caspian ap Felan." The name seemed to echo as Felan ensured Caspian saw the truth, felt it burn in his body. "I haven't lied to you. You are my son, my only child, and a source of great pain and regret. I love you like any father loves a son. But I have a bigger role. Annwyn cannot fall. Its safety is also your responsibility." He released Caspian. "Do you understand?"

Caspian blinked; there were unshed tears in his eyes. For a moment Felan regretted exposing Caspian to what he felt, the fear, the heartache, the responsibility, everything.

"I understand. You will keep your word?"

"My word is law. Three mortal days and you go back to your lover. Your soul in exchange for the Window."

"You don't need my soul."

"No, but I want to hold you close for a little longer."

Felan caressed the stone on the ring. "Besides, three days here without drinking and dancing would be torture, and I'm not cruel."

"You took my soul for my own good?"

"Yes. Now enjoy the party." Felan opened the door. "You may go where you wish except the Queen's chambers."

"What about my shop?"

"You have a new assistant, Bramwel. His specialty is statues."

Caspian opened his mouth, then shut it again.

Felan waited, sure his son had something to say.

"This isn't over, Felan ap Gwyn." The words vibrated in the room.

Felan smiled. Caspian was a quick learner, a sharp thinker, and good-looking. So fairy despite his mortality. His heart swelled with pride. He'd done the right thing letting him be raised in the mortal world. He had to believe that. And he had to make the most of what little time he had with him.

"No, it's not." He touched the ring that held his son's soul. It was warm and fragile and reminded him of holding the delicate newborn over thirty years ago. "Just watch where you throw my name around. It could attract the wrong kind of attention."

Caspian went to walk out of the antechamber, then paused. "How will I know when three days are up?"

"I will escort you to a gate."

"And see me safely through?"

Felan placed his hand over his heart. "My word as Prince, and as a father. I won't let harm come to you while you are here, and I'll do my best in your world."

This time Caspian nodded. "Accepted."

A little shimmer of power ran through the air. If Caspian had been born here, he'd have been a powerful fairy.

Caspian followed a shadow servant through the castle. He wanted to avoid the actual Court where the parties happened. It wasn't that he didn't trust his father, he just didn't trust fairies. He ran his hand over his chest again, but he didn't feel any different. Certainly not dead. Without a soul he should be dead. A human would be dead. The only thing keeping him alive was the fairy blood in his veins. Maybe he felt lighter somehow. Like he'd had a couple of drinks and was feeling taller and less mortal.

He was less mortal. He was immortal. He stopped to consider that and what it meant. If he stayed here, he would never die. It was an odd sensation to realize he could live forever. But that would mean a life surrounded by fairies, not humans, and a life without ever seeing Lydia again. Beneath his feet the grass was soft, and the trees rustled in the breeze. This place was like a gentle dream—one that would keep him from truly living if he fell under its spell.

"Take me to a private room," he ordered the shadow. He almost apologized at the harsh tone of his voice then saw no point. His step faltered as he realized what he'd thought. He'd dismissed the shadow as nothing, not even worth kindness. Was the loss of his soul having an effect already?

The shadow didn't seem to notice and led him up a winding staircase made of branches and carpeted with leaves. Music and the scent of food drifted up, but he refused to be tempted.

In the small room he closed the door and sat down to think.

Somehow he'd become a pawn... maybe more valuable than that, a knight, or bishop, in a fairy game of chess. The trouble was he couldn't determine the players, which boards they played on, or how many games they were each playing.

He pulled out the smooth shard of mirror. The surface was dark no matter which way he turned it. When Felan had shown it to him Caspian had been sure he'd seen Lydia. Impossible; he'd looked at everything in that house, been through boxes and the attic, stables and the run-down cabins. The Window wasn't there. If darkness was all it was going to show him, it wasn't going to be much help. He touched the surface but got nothing. He was as blind as any man. Maybe it would be more use in the mortal world. He kept the shard in his hand and waited, waited for another glimpse of Lydia. Waited for the three days to pass.

He wouldn't join the Court and he wouldn't be lured into lingering. He had to remember the reason why he had to get home and it had nothing to do with fairies and the damn Window or even his soul. His heart was much more important. He'd forgotten that after the divorce. He wouldn't forget again. He wouldn't forget Lydia.

Chapter 17

LYDIA CHECKED HER CELL PHONE AGAIN, IN CASE SHE hadn't heard it ring while it had been in her handbag. There were a couple of missed calls from the media about tomorrow's memorial service, and a few texts from her friends. They wanted to see the latest chick flick—something about a wedding and the wrong guy—but she wasn't in the mood for anything funny.

Caspian hadn't tried to get in contact. Then again, he'd left with no shoes and no wallet. Could he even get in contact from Annwyn? Was he even still alive? She bit her lip and shoved the phone back in her bag.

Her apartment creaked around her as if trying to get her attention, but it was better being here than at the empty Callaway House. There it was much easier to miss Caspian no matter where she sat as he'd been in every room. He'd never been to her place... which hopefully meant the fairies wouldn't know of it either. She was afraid for Caspian and for herself after seeing the Hunter.

Something went bump and she froze. It had sounded like the Callaway ghost, which she knew now was a Grey. She held her breath and listened. Silence. Whatever it was sounded like it had come from the spare room.

Oh God. The box of Gran's personal things. What had she brought home with her? She wanted to run, but she forced herself to take calm, measured steps. There was only one thing of value in there. The compact that Gran had been given by the singer.

In the spare room she opened up the box into which she'd packed Gran's personal things. She carefully pulled out some personal items and the few photos that had been in the bedroom. A half-read novel with a receipt for wine used as the bookmark. She smiled even as her vision blurred with tears, but she kept digging through the box. She knew it was in here. Her fingers touched tissue paper and she pulled it out and unwrapped the mirror.

A compact the size of her palm. The silver case was embellished with leaves. She flicked the catch and the compact opened. Inside the mirror was perfect. No chips or signs of rust. She could see why Gran had kept the mirror, but something like this should be used, not hidden away.

Lydia sniffed and wiped a tear from beneath her eye before her mascara smudged. What would Caspian say about the mirror and the man who'd given it to Gran? What would he see when he touched it? More than just the silver case and mirror. He'd see the history, he'd be able to tell her about the singer and Gran. Did she really want to know?

The hair on the back of her neck prickled as if she was being watched. Maybe she shouldn't have brought the box home, but the idea of fairies rummaging through Gran's things was too much. She looked again at the mirror. It looked like nothing special, just a decorative compact. But what did a fairy-made mirror look like? She hadn't asked, hadn't thought to ask. All the mirrors in her yard had been big—big enough to use as a portal back to Annwyn. This was tiny.

She frowned and rewrapped it. Her grandmother had kept it safe for years, so there was no way she was going to let the Greys get hold of this. It might be nothing. It probably was nothing. It was too small to be anything. When she saw Caspian next she'd show him the mirror. If she saw him again, but she quickly squashed the thought. He'd be back. He'd promised. For a moment she sat on the floor surrounded by Gran's personal items. She tried to imagine boxing up everything in Callaway House and stuffing it into her small house, but she knew it would never fit. If she had to sell Callaway House she was going to have to get rid of some things.

Like Gran, though, she didn't know where to start.

That's when she started laughing. They were more alike than she'd ever realized. If Gran had found a way to keep Callaway House, she could too. Caspian was right—she needed to get quotes for the repairs instead of hoping they'd just go away. Something in her bedroom creaked, as if someone was poking around. She shivered. An evening out with her friends suddenly didn't seem like such a bad idea. She could listen to their news, they'd have a drink for Gran, but she knew none of them would show up for the memorial. That was okay—but she also knew that if Caspian had been here he would've and he wouldn't have cared what people said. Gran would've really gotten a kick out of Caspian and his ability as well as his screwed up family.

Three days until he came home.

Three days had never seemed so long.

—◇◇◇—

Lydia swallowed and forced herself to take a breath as she entered the church on day two of Caspian's time away.

She lifted her chin, ready to face the curious stares of the guests at Gran's memorial service. She nodded to a few older ladies. Had they once partied or lived at Callaway House, or had they met Gran after its closure? Gran's doctor was there. An old man himself, he looked slumped and sad, confirming Lydia's suspicion that there had been more going on.

The priest opened the memorial service. But Lydia tuned out the words. She didn't want to remember Gran as dead and buried. She wanted to remember her alive. This was just a formality and a chance for others to say good-bye.

And for others to stick their noses in.

Still, Gran would have been happy with the turnout.

Lydia stood near the photos of Gran to deliver the eulogy. She'd chosen pictures that represented Gran's life. Her wedding photo, one where she was dressed to the nines and sitting in the garden of Callaway House, another of her much older but with a young Lydia on her lap. She wanted to make the point to everyone listening that Gran was more than just the disgraced Callaway name. She was loved, and loved in return.

As she spoke she was aware of a camera flashing and she knew her words were being recorded, but she didn't care. Maybe the article they wrote would focus less on the past and more on the person. She let her gaze drop to her notes, and paused for a moment before inviting others to come and talk about Nanette Callaway.

She expected no takers. But to her surprise the doctor got up and said a few words about his favorite patient. *A sense of humor that he'd miss*.

Some of the older women also took a turn. Not one of them mentioned the house. They talked about Gran's kind heart, always willing to help another, her donations to charity and her love of book club—especially the opportunity to debate the story over a glass of wine.

The priest kept the memorial moving along. After a final prayer for Gran's soul everyone drifted outside. Lydia glanced down the road at the house. Her house.

What the hell was she going to do with a house that size?

Fix it. Or at least find out if it could be fixed.

Gran had given her the house and she was going to keep it. Whatever it took.

A tingle formed between her shoulder blades and traced down her spine as if she was being watched, but when she glanced behind her she saw no one. She hated cemeteries.

As a child she remembered looking out the front window and watching as dusk settled on the church. While most of the time it was just a building, occasionally she'd get a weird feeling like there was something or someone over there. She suppressed a shiver.

A man stepped in front of her and held out a little voice recorder. "Can I get a few words from you about Nanette Callaway?"

Lydia had no doubt he'd already recorded the whole service and was looking for something more. "She will be greatly missed." Lydia forced a narrow smile. They weren't the words he was after.

"Is the house now yours?"

Lydia nodded.

"What do you intend to do with it? Sell it? I hear there are plans for a bed and breakfast."

"The will is on probate. I can't comment." Where was he finding this stuff?

The man nodded, but there was a glint in his eye. "Is it true Madam Callaway kept diaries?"

Her breathing stopped like she'd been kicked in the stomach. How did he know about them? "I don't know, is it?"

He stared at her, and she stared back, daring him to say something else.

Then he clicked off the voice recorder. "The newspaper would be willing to offer you a decent sum for the first look at the diaries." He handed over a business card.

Lydia took it without looking, her fingers closing mechanically around the card. He thought she was for sale. The money could pay for the repairs.

"Have a think about it, Ms. Callaway." He gave her a nod and then walked away.

Oh God, what kind of story was going to be printed? She glanced down to see which paper he was part of and her stomach sunk a little further. It wasn't even one of the respectable dailies. Would he mention the diaries in the story? Of course he would… and then anyone who'd ever been to Callaway House would start to worry.

"Lydia Callaway?" a man said behind her.

She turned, bracing for more media, but instead an older man in a dark pinstripe suit stood there. A lawyer; he had that look, like he already knew the answers. She studied him for another second. Her mother hadn't had the guts to turn up so she'd sent her lawyer.

"Yes."

"I'm representing Helen Turner, your mother." He pulled out a business card and handed it to her.

Lydia glanced at it, then smiled and she hoped it looked polite. "I'm not sure what you want; you must know my grandmother's will is being handled by her solicitor."

"Mrs. Turner just wanted you to be clear that as long as you don't try to make contact or mention her name she will not contest the will."

"Don't worry, Gran was the only mother I ever needed or wanted. The only reason Gran left her anything was because she never stopped loving her daughter." Lydia bit her tongue before she mentioned Helen wasn't actually a Callaway. No, she'd keep that to herself and let Helen live thinking she was a Callaway. After the way Helen had treated Gran it was the least she could do. After all, Gran had never seen fit to tell Helen the truth so she was merely doing as Gran wanted, right?

"You plan to contest the will?" The lawyer looked surprised.

Lydia had already had this discussion with her lawyer, but she had no desire to change anything Gran had put on paper. A person's last wishes should be respected. "No. I'm happy with the split. I hope she enjoys the cash." *Hope it keeps her warm and fills her with happy memories while I try and save the house.*

God, she sounded bitter. She inhaled and exhaled slowly. "Is there anything else I can help you with?"

"No. I think we have an understanding. I'm sure my client will be relieved."

"Good." Lydia walked away before the man could say anything else. She walked up the road and to what had been the paved path to the familiar red door. Once inside she let herself close her eyes and sag against the wood where no one could see just how much this was taking out of her.

Around her the house was silent as if it paused to remember the woman who'd saved it the first time around. If she was going to save it this time, she needed Caspian's valuation, and she needed the will to be finalized. She needed to make plans, none of which she could do at the moment.

Caspian would be back. He'd promised. He'd been gone one day already and today was half-gone. There wasn't much longer to wait. And if he never came back, what should she do? Report him missing? Would they think she'd killed him? The ground around the house had been torn up, which looked even more suspicious.

Damn fairies.

Her lips curved in a half-smile. How quickly she was getting used to them?

How fast had she gotten used to having Caspian in her life?

While she knew plenty about the fairy side of his life, she actually didn't know that much about his human side. She could organize the quotes, go past his shop, and see what she could find out.

With the afternoon sketched out she peeled herself off the door and smoothed her skirt, ready to put her ideas into action. At least if she was doing something she wouldn't be wasting time on useless worrying about what was happening to him in Annwyn. Maybe she'd look that up on the Internet too.

She'd expected the King Street antique shop to be closed, but the door was open and the lights were on. Her heart gave a lurch. He wouldn't have come home and not rung, would he? She parked around the back and saw his car was parked there. Hadn't he taken it to the garage after it started making noises?

A small blue bird hopped around the asphalt as if looking for crumbs. Its feathers gleamed in the sunlight. The skin on her arms popped up in gooseflesh as she got out of her car. There was something very wrong going on. For a moment she considered just going home, but if he was here she wanted to know why he hadn't called. Lydia rolled her shoulders and walked into the shop, half hoping Caspian was there, half hoping he wasn't— because then she'd have to ask why he'd left her hanging and worrying. Then she hated herself for thinking the worst of him and for wishing he was still being held hostage by his fairy father.

A young man with long sandy hair was behind the counter. He looked up as the bell chimed.

Her heart chose that moment to stop and fumble before finding a beat. He looked like the kind of guy found in underwear ads. All cheekbone and casually tousled hair, his pale blue eyes gave him a wildness that most men would try and hide.

Words dissolved on her tongue. "Er... is Caspian here?"

"He went away for business. Can I help?" His voice was smooth and deep and he was a few years younger than she was. What was he—straight out of college? He walked over with too much grace. And yet... there was something about him that reminded her of Caspian. She just didn't know what it was.

She shook her head as if trying to remember why she'd come here. "He didn't mention an assistant."

"It's temporary." The young man smiled. He was far too pretty.

Temporary—the young man was keeping the store going while Caspian was in Annwyn. This man was fairy.

Her heart bounced in her chest as she slid her hand into her handbag. *It's okay. He doesn't know that you know.*

She swallowed and tried not to panic. That was two fairies in as many days, not including the Greys. This man wasn't a Grey. She was sure of that. He also didn't have that same hungry air that Verden, the Hunter, had worn like a cloak.

Maybe this man knew something that could help. "Has he called, or said when he'll be back?"

"He'll be back before the three days is up." The fairy considered her for a moment, his gaze flicking to her handbag.

Did he sense the iron? Surely not. *Play it dumb. The dumb blonde act usually worked when all else failed.* As much as she hated doing it, people fell for it—who was dumb?

"Oh, I was hoping he'd be back sooner." She faked a smile. "Never mind."

She took a step back. She shouldn't have been so nosy and insisted on checking out his shop. If his car hadn't been there she wouldn't have stopped. Who was she kidding? She totally would have, just to see what he sold in here and what the price tags were.

The bells on the front door chimed again, but there was no one there. Another fairy, one she couldn't see. How nice it was that this one had made himself visible.

"I'll let Caspian know you stopped by. And you are?" He smiled as if inviting her to tell all.

Dylis's warnings echoed in her ears. She had iron, she hadn't agreed to anything, she hadn't eaten or drunk anything he'd offered, and she certainly wasn't going to give her full name. She could do this and get out of here with her soul intact.

"Lydia."

"Lydia." Her name rolled off his tongue like it was made of silver bells. "Bramwel at your service. I shall pass your message on." He gave her a half-bow.

Who did that? Fairies, apparently.

"Thank you." She forced the words out.

"Do not fear, we always keep our word." He flashed her another smile, but this one was more calculating, as if he'd known all along that she knew what he was and held iron in her hand.

Chapter 18

"Caspian ap Felan," Felan intoned, "do you surrender your soul willingly to Annwyn?"

Caspian glanced back at the castle and all the things he hadn't seen, but in that heartbeat he knew he could spend his whole life here and never see everything—that was the trap. "No. I choose to remain in the mortal world and live out my days there."

"Very well, I shall ask you twice more before you die." Felan moved his hand over the gap and the surface shimmered. "You are free to leave Annwyn, but be aware without your soul you are the equivalent of a banished fairy. You will weaken and die."

"How long?" What would it be like to live without a soul? Would he miss it?

"I can't say exactly, one turn of the moon or three? You had less magic in you to begin with and you won't be able to resize like a Grey." Felan touched the mirror hanging under Caspian's shirt. "Find it fast and help me stop the poison corroding Annwyn."

He looked his father in the eye. "Are you commanding or asking?"

"Both. I have no wish to see you die." Felan offered Caspian his hand.

Caspian clasped it, but Felan drew him into an embrace. "Do not fail me, son."

Then Caspian found himself in a cemetery in the rain.

Water trailed down the back of his neck and he tipped his face to the darkened sky. The air wasn't scented with flowers, just the tang of ocean and heavier smell of dirt. The plants were duller. Loss for the beauty of Annwyn cut through him like a knife. He couldn't think past the pain. He wanted to be part of beauty. With each breath the fog that had enveloped his mind thinned. He knew he was in the mortal world for a reason. He touched the sliver of mirror hanging around his neck. Down the road was a house. That was where he needed to be. Beneath his hand his heart beat. It took a moment for him to register what that meant. He was alive, but not human— that part of him was still in Annwyn.

Which meant he didn't have long before he'd start to wither like any other Grey.

Lydia jumped at the knock on the door. She peeked through the front window to see who was arriving so late. Caspian was on her front step, soaked through. She flung open the door and stared at him for a moment, not sure if she should throw her arms around him and never let him go, or tell him to leave because she couldn't go through all that worry again.

She wrapped her arms around him before she could check herself again and behave a little more appropriately. She'd missed him so much. She'd worry about the consequences of falling for a fairy later. He put his arms around her waist and kissed her cheek, then found her lips. He kissed her like he'd been starved and was hungry for everything she had. She let him steal her breath, his tongue slipping past her lips. She melted against him, not caring that the cold and wet seeped into her skin. Relief pushed every other thought aside.

"Oh my God, I was so worried you weren't coming back. I went to your shop but there was some guy there claiming to be your assistant." She kissed him again. "What the hell happened?"

He looked at her, but his pale green eyes seemed different somehow. There was a faraway look.

"Are you okay?" She touched his cheek, rough with stubble. Had he been drugged?

"I'm fine." His arms were still around her as if he couldn't bear to let her go. "What day is it?"

Her breath constricted but she forced her voice to be calm. "It's Monday."

He nodded like the day held great significance. "I missed you."

"Me too. I mean I missed you." She placed her lips against his again. His lips were sweet. Too sweet and too tempting. Yet cold. "Let's get you in; your skin is freezing."

He stepped into the house and Lydia realized he was still in the same clothes. His feet were bare and muddy. How far had he walked like that? Maybe he was just glad to be out of Annwyn. With a last glance outside she closed the door and locked it, knowing she'd be sleeping here again because the idea of letting Caspian out of her sight was unthinkable—what if he disappeared again? A frisson of excitement ran through her at the idea of sleeping with Caspian. Then she glanced at him; he looked like he needed to actually sleep.

"Why don't you have a shower to warm up? I'll put your clothes through the dryer." Water dripped off his jeans and onto the rug. For a moment the wet splotting sound was the only noise.

"Lydia…" He reached for her as if he couldn't live without the contact. His hand was cold. How long had he been standing in the rain?

"It doesn't matter. Tell me later, if you can." She wasn't sure she wanted to know; she already knew far more than any human should.

His shoulders slumped. "I feel like I haven't slept in days." He pushed the fingers of his free hand through his wet hair. "Like I'm not sure what's real." Then he looked at her again as if he didn't know what to say.

"You're in no shape to get home on your own." But aside from looking drained he didn't seem to be hurt, but then she didn't know what kind of damage a fairy could inflict. They probably had much more subtle methods than humans. She suppressed a shiver. They'd let him go, for the moment that had to be enough. "Come on."

Lydia led him upstairs. She fetched clean towels and put on the heater. He fumbled with the buttons on his shirt before shrugging out of it. She eased the sodden fabric away from his skin. Her fingers brushed over his arms, she let them linger on his skin for a moment, unable to pull away. It had been days and all she wanted was to have him in her arms and make sure he was really there.

She turned on the shower, but kept her gaze on him. He turned around and her tongue swept over her lip. Then she saw the necklace hanging against his chest.

A piece of mirror on a silver chain. It was nothing special, and yet… Maybe it was the curved shape or the smooth edges. She was used to seeing sharp shards when mirrors broke but this looked polished. Her face was reflected back at her. He hadn't been wearing it last time, which meant he'd been given it in Annwyn.

"Was that a gift?" She pointed without touching.

He glanced down as if seeing it for the first time. "It's to help me find the mirror."

Lydia nodded slowly. "With your psychometry."

"Yeah."

"How are you going to do that?"

He lifted his gaze and looked at her, his eyes totally unreadable. There was almost an alien quality, like he wasn't really part of the world. While he'd always been attractive enough to make her heart skip a beat, today that beauty was sharper, more defined... there was a hidden edge. He looked more fairy.

Or maybe she was just noticing now that she knew. If he hadn't slept or eaten much over the last three days of course he was going to look edgier and leaner. That was all it was. Still, whenever he looked at her she just wanted to melt.

Her hand trailed up his chest, his skin cool and damp from the rain. Then she stepped closer for a kiss. She brushed her lips over his in a light caress. He lifted his hand and cupped her cheek as he tasted and teased with his tongue.

A moan formed as her blood heated. This wasn't what she'd planned. He was supposed to be having a shower and rest. And yet as he drew her closer, and the hard length of him pressed against her hip, it seemed sleep was the last thing on his mind. He turned her away from the shower so her back was to the wall. He worked her shirt open, kissing down her neck as her fingers threaded into his hair. She'd missed him so much. He opened her jeans and pushed them down her hips, along with her panties.

She pressed her hand against his length, stroking as she fumbled for the zipper. She needed to feel him in her. His jeans opened and she pushed her hand into his briefs, her fingers grazing the smooth head of his shaft. Her breath hitched as his fingers dipped lower and slid over slick skin. Her back arched into his touch. He'd learned her body so fast, his finger using just the right amount of pressure, the right motion. She closed her eyes; she was so close. His lips trailed along her collarbone and lower, his tongue tracing the edge of her bra. Then he stopped.

She opened her eyes and he lifted his head and looked at her with his eyebrows raised as his finger touched the iron nail in her bra.

She swallowed. "In case a Grey comes back."

He drew away, the heat gone. "I'm not good company at the moment."

How could he say that? Now? Her blood was running hot. She needed him. Her fingers curled at her side, but she bit back the frustration. What did she say? What could she say? He didn't want her... and yet thirty seconds ago he'd been as keen as she was.

She took a moment to fix her clothes and gather up as much calm and dignity as she could. "Okay. I'll leave you to it." But she paused in the doorway, waiting for the rest of his clothes.

He stripped off his jeans without a trace of embarrassment and handed them to her. She glanced away not wanting to see him aroused when he'd just turned her away.

Something wasn't right. He seemed different, but she couldn't say how. *Exhaustion, that's all.* Of course he wasn't going to be into sex even if his body was saying something different. "Did you want something to eat or did you want to go straight to sleep?"

"Sleep would be good." He looked at the wet clothes in her arms, then back at her face. "I'm not being a very good guest."

"Don't worry about it. We can talk later." She even tried to sound like she meant it.

He looked at the running water and hesitated before stepping under and closing the door. The glass warped his outline, but she saw him just standing there, head bowed, letting the water drum on his shoulders.

She bit her lip and turned away, shutting the bathroom door behind her to keep the heat in. Was she in over her head? She had more than enough problems of her own, including the relocated ghost. Yet that fairy had been in Callaway House for as long as she could remember without causing problems. She wanted to show Caspian the mirror in her handbag, but now wasn't the time. Maybe in the morning.

She put his clothes in the dryer on low, as jeans had a horrible tendency to shrink. He wouldn't care at the moment he would in the morning.

The sound of water running through the pipes rattled above her reminding her how old the house was. It had never been a silent house. It had always creaked and groaned and sighed and rattled with life; now it was too silent. The ghost hadn't come back yet. She almost wished it would. The pipes shuddered as the taps were turned off.

In her mind she saw him drying off and the heat in her blood rose. She was tempted to go up, but hesitated. She didn't want to intrude and she didn't want to be turned down twice. She knew when she was shattered all she wanted to do was lie down and be left alone. So she left him alone, hoping that when he woke up he was more like himself.

For the next couple of hours she made a list of all the diaries including the dates they spanned and then photographed them the way Caspian had done. This way there was record of them, just in case someone thought to destroy them and act like they never existed. There'd been no mention of the memorial in today's paper, but she was expecting something and she was expecting the reporter to mention the diaries. She'd have to ask Caspian who he'd spoken to about them. But that would have to wait until morning, along with the rest of her questions.

As she thumbed the old pages she wished there was a way she could make a copy of them, but she didn't have the time to photograph every page. There was just too much. Carefully she packed them back into the trunk and locked it. For the moment she'd done all she could.

With a sigh she walked around and turned off the lights, double-checking that the doors were locked as she went. She hadn't planned to stay here tonight, but she wasn't leaving him alone, and she didn't want to wake him to take him home. It was better they were both here. While she wanted to slide into bed next to Caspian, it would be smarter to sleep in the bed she'd used growing up. But she didn't think she could sleep in the same house in a separate room.

She used the little lie of checking on him. The bedroom door was open as if he was leaving an invitation... or he'd been so out of it he hadn't thought to close it. Light from the corridor cut across the bed. He was on his back, his chest rising and falling with each breath. The mirror pendant was still around his neck, but she couldn't see his face as it was in the shadow cast by the door.

"Join me." His voice was soft like he was half-asleep.

She should leave him to rest, but she wanted him and her feet moved as if she couldn't resist the request. Desire still ran through her body, aching and unsatisfied. She pulled her hair free of the grips so it tumbled down her back, still a little damp from washing it that morning. Then she took off her clothes, carefully placing the iron nail on the bedside table, and then slid into bed next to him, glad to feel his skin against her again and know he was safe. Even as she lay there she tried to clamp down on her rising desire. But her body was aware of every move and every breath he took. She was on edge from before. He turned toward her and drew her close, her back against his chest, the hair on his thighs tickling the back of her legs. She let out a shaky breath. Her thoughts were on everything but sleep.

Behind her his skin was cool against hers, even though he'd been in bed. His arm was looped over her waist, his fingers trailing along her stomach. When he placed his lips on the back of her neck she shivered. Then his hand slid higher and traced the curve of the underside of her breast. The simple touch made her stomach tighten. His thumb brushed the swell but never came close to her nipple, which was already peaked and aching to be touched. Yet his touch couldn't be called seductive; it was more intimate than going straight for the erogenous zones where nerve endings made it easy to arouse someone.

He kissed another vertebra in her neck, pausing long enough to taste her skin with a flick of his tongue. Against her butt, part of him warmed up and hardened against her skin. She swallowed and tried not to wiggle her hips closer in invitation. He pressed his palm flat to her belly, the tips of his fingers barely brushing her curls. She wanted his hand to move lower. It did, but he smoothed down her hip to her thigh, his hand never slipping between her legs. Lydia pressed her teeth together to stifle the frustration at having him touch her everywhere but where she needed to feel his hands.

Behind her he moved, placing a kiss on the side of her neck, his teeth raking gently over her skin. His breath raised gooseflesh as he worked his way to her shoulder blade. She moved, separating her legs a little. But still he made no effort to realign his shaft between her thighs, and his fingers stayed away from the wetness slicking her sex. She'd been waiting hours for this and now he was drawing it out.

He cupped her breast, teasing as if he enjoyed driving her to distraction and knew she was enjoying it. Her belly was a tight knot of nerves waiting to unravel. One touch. She bit her lip, not wanting to make a sound in case it broke the moment somehow.

She reached her hand behind her, felt the curve of his waist and the bone of his hip before letting her finger dip lower, seeking him out. He caught her hand before she reached his hardened flesh and laid it across her belly, trapped beneath his. This time she didn't care; she pressed her hips against him and rocked. She thought she felt him pause mid-kiss to smile, then he rolled her onto her stomach. The length of his body was along hers for one glorious moment before he pulled away.

The tearing of foil made her lift her head, but he was just out of view, kneeling between her legs. His thumbs brushed the crease of her butt as his hands slid over her hips. She lifted up, wanting to feel his fingers between her thighs and delving into her core. He leaned over her and she held her breath. But all he did was run his tongue between her shoulder blades.

In response she arched her back, curving her butt into the air. He was there, the heat and hardness against her for a moment.

"Caspian." Was that her voice? All breathy and strung out when he hadn't done anything to her yet?

"Mmm." His hands swept along the sides of her breasts.

"Please."

She gasped as his hand moved under her hip; his fingers were so close that another inch and they'd be on her clit. Her teeth ground together, but she couldn't get him to give her the touch she wanted.

He moved and then he was between her legs. The length of him stroking her slick folds, but never sliding in. His hand on her hip keeping her still. She couldn't take it. Her hand moved to try and find her own release. Again he stopped her, catching her and pressing it to the mattress beneath his.

"Trust me."

"Love me." She ground out the words.

"I do." It was barely a whisper, and the words were almost lost as he thrust into her with one smooth stroke.

Then he remained motionless inside her. That was just as maddening. She whimpered and tried to bow her body to entice more from him. His hand released her hip, his finger lightly brushing the curls at the apex of her thighs. Teasing, never quite touching, but getting closer. She stopped moving and waited. Her breath coming in small pants as expectation consumed her.

His finger circled her clit and the drought was broken. The wave rolled down her spine before crashing into her belly. She clenched around him, unable to do anything but give in to the pleasure washing through her body. He groaned and began to thrust slowly. With every nerve ending awakened she felt every inch. He leaned over her, his strokes becoming less controlled. She tumbled over the edge again, dragging him with her.

Caspian rested over her. She couldn't move even if she wanted to. Her heart was still bouncing around, unable to settle. He placed a kiss on the back of her neck, much like the one that had started this, and pulled away.

She moaned at the loss. She hadn't been ready for it to be over, but he came back to bed and eased in next to her. She turned into his arms and kissed his lips. He returned the kiss, but his eyes were already closed. Within minutes he was asleep. For a few moments she watched him. His dark lashes against fair skin. Whatever worries he had left him while he slept.

Caspian. It was such an old name. No one called their kids Caspian. And yet it suited him. She'd have to ask him in the morning where the name came from. Maybe it was a family name. But which family?

It was daylight when Caspian woke. This time there was none of the disorientation of being lost in the impressions left by other people. He knew where he was, and where he wanted to be, and he could almost forget that he hadn't been forced to relinquish his soul. He closed his eyes again. The sliver of mirror rested against his skin. That something so small and delicate could hold so much power over him… he huffed out a breath.

Best he get moving and stop wasting time.

His jeans and shirt were on the end of the bed along with a note.

Gone to work. Help yourself to food. I'll call you later. XX Lydia.

He touched the piece of paper and a shimmer of concern ran through his fingertips. Her worry about him. She'd been here wondering what was going on while he'd struggled to hold on to her. Last night he couldn't help himself. He'd needed her—even though the iron in her bra had been disconcerting. He still needed her. She had the Window. He couldn't let himself think of anything but finding it, and it had to be here somewhere.

He dressed—thoroughly sick of these clothes, made himself coffee, and took a slow walk through every room. The Counter-Window hanging around his neck revealed nothing, only blackness, so he opened drawers and cupboards, feeling like a thief. His coffee grew cold.

"Damn it. Where is it?" He shut the drawer in old oak dresser too hard. He was having to rein in his magic because every time he used it, it would take a little from him, slowly killing him like any banished fairy.

"Damn the lot of you." A futile curse given they couldn't hear him and even if they could he doubted very much they'd care. He scrubbed his hand over his face. He needed to shave and get clean clothes. His cell phone was dead and needed charging.

Three days in Annwyn had cost him everything. If he didn't find the Window and return it to his father he was going to have to walk away from Lydia. He didn't want her watching him waste away by a disease human doctors couldn't identify or fix.

What was he missing?

He closed his eyes, thinking about what he'd seen; one glimpse of Lydia in the Counter-Window. It had to be somewhere for her to use it. Around him the house seemed hollow for the first time as if all of its past had fled at his intrusion. The ghost was gone. The Window had been here all along. The Grey that lived here hadn't been aware of what it was attracted to because of the magic of the Window. But if the Grey was gone, so was the mirror.

Lydia had taken it.

Which meant it was either at her place or at her work. How was he going to find it without arousing suspicion? Then he caught himself. Was he really thinking of stealing from her? He had to. The Window for his soul.

No. He shook his head. There was another way. He wouldn't raid her house and take what he needed. He had to tell her his father had his soul and that she had the Window. And if she refused to save him? He wanted to believe that she wouldn't, that they had something special… but he'd been wrong before. Been burned.

It was better to go out honestly than like a thief.

However, even as he thought that, part of him disagreed. Stealing and living was better than dying honorably.

The loss of his soul had changed the way he felt inside; he couldn't tell something was missing until he did something that didn't seem quite right. Even last night, there'd been more fairy in his touch than he'd have liked. Sweeping her into his spell like any fairy after a human conquest. And he'd been unable to stop because he'd wanted her so badly; he'd needed her to make him feel alive. It had, he'd never felt closer to anyone, as if her thoughts were pressing into him. He'd meant what he said, he'd fallen for her, but it had taken him too long to remember how to love again after being wounded. Now it was too late, and the moment they'd shared reminded him how un-alive he really was.

Caspian looked at his hands. He couldn't do that again. Glamouring someone into bed drained power and since he now had a finite amount he had to be careful. Very careful. Again he stopped himself. Glamouring someone into bed was wrong because it interfered with free will, not because it would drain power from him. He tried to recall every touch, and while he'd commanded her to bed, she'd been a willing participant with what followed. Did that make it okay?

"Fuck." He dragged his hands through his hair. He was becoming more fairy by the second, willing to split hairs so fine most humans couldn't even see them.

He called a cab on Lydia's landline, and while he waited he put on his shoes and socks, and gathered his useless cell phone and wallet. He was collecting his car, getting changed, finalizing the valuation so Lydia wouldn't be left in the lurch again, and then finding a way to get the Window off Lydia without stealing or lying or glamouring or doing anything vaguely immoral and fairy.

Given that he was no longer human he didn't like his chances.

———

Lydia skimmed through the day's newspapers, and then yesterday's, catching up on the news and making sure there was nothing in the papers that she needed to action. But she was thinking of Caspian. He'd been different somehow. Exhausted. He'd barely spoken to her. And yet when he'd hugged her it had been like he hadn't wanted to let go.

He loved her.

He hadn't exactly said it as much as admit it and that was worth more. An unguarded moment had revealed the truth. And she hadn't responded. She hadn't known what to say. She still didn't know what to say. She'd been so worried and scared while he was gone, and now that he was back she just wanted to be with him and find out what had happened.

She did love him. Not the kind of love where the words are spoken to be kind and return the favor; she'd done that before. But the kind that made her unable to say the words because she was scared if she did it would all fall apart.

Should she call and check on him?

No. He'd been dead to the world when she'd left this morning. She'd considered waking him to show him the mirror, but had decided that a few more hours wouldn't hurt. Besides, if he had to face Shea again it was probably better to do it well-rested.

Her gaze glided over the story about a new drug-resistant strain of malaria that was killing fast. Some were calling it a bioweapon test, others that it was the beginning of the end and listed a whole bunch of other diseases that were springing up. Others dismissed the notion and blamed the new outbreaks on climate change. She shook her head and moved on. There were always people preaching about the end of the world.

Deeper into the paper there was a small heading about the memorial service, nothing salacious just that there'd been a good turnout to farewell Nannette Callaway. Of course the reporter had mentioned the House's past, but it had been balanced by the mention of family and community. She smiled; that was probably as good as it was going to get. But then this was the respectable paper. It was reading the other one she dreaded.

Her cell rang, she checked the number, then let it go through to voice mail. The reporter had already rung once this morning wanting to know if she'd changed her mind about selling the diaries.

Changed her mind?

She'd hardly had time to think. She was still waiting for the repair quotes to be finalized and she hadn't had a chance to mention the offer to Caspian. She hadn't had a chance to talk to him about anything. They'd barely spoken, even though they'd needed each other so badly.

She hadn't spoken to the lawyer yet either. She added that to her to-do list. Was she even allowed to start repairing the house before the will was finalized? Probably not; she was in limbo.

Damn it. She needed that valuation turned in. She hated waiting. She forced herself to take a breath. Once the valuation was in it would settle. Helen wasn't going to contest—unless her name was mentioned. How was she going to keep the media from scrounging that up?

Her stomach gave a quiver as she picked up the other newspaper. It wasn't front page, but then she hadn't expected that. But it was page three. A photo of Gran in her heyday coupled with a headline about secret diaries. Her stomach contracted and for a moment she thought she might be ill.

If that didn't stir up a shit storm, nothing would.

She wasn't afraid of what was in the diaries, but as long as she kept them hidden other people would be. Her mother would be. She could see a fast settlement evaporating. As if on cue her cell phone rang. Blocked number. For a moment she considered leaving it, then answered. She couldn't ignore every call she received.

"Hello?"

"The Callaways will burn for what they've done," a male voice snarled down the line.

Lydia froze and said the first thing that came to mind. "Pardon?"

"You'll be left with nothing but ashes if you go public with those diaries." Then the line went dead.

It was a moment before she lowered the phone from her ear. She put down her cell and took a sip of water. Her hand shook as she placed the glass down. The media outlets chasing a story was to be expected, that kind of venom wasn't. Her heart continued to skip and race.

He must think there were names or mentions of backroom deals in the diaries. There wasn't; going public would be the best way to prove that, right?

Her phone rang again. The reporter this time, the one

who'd mentioned the damn diaries in the first place. She was beginning to wish she'd never found them. She hit ignore and let the reporter talk to her voice mail.

She wouldn't sell the diaries to that paper on principle.

Would Caspian sell the diaries to fund the repairs? Was that the smart thing to do? She was sure it was, but it didn't feel right. The other option was to give them to the historical society and let them take care of them. She worried her lip. Gran had left no instructions and no clue that they even existed in her will.

She pressed her teeth together and forced out a breath. She'd never needed anyone to help her make a decision before, and she wasn't going to start now. She'd work it out on her own, the same as always. She didn't need Caspian... no, it was much worse. He was under her skin and lodged in her heart.

Chapter 19

THE SHOP LOOKED EXACTLY LIKE HE'D LEFT IT, EXCEPT emptier and open. The door chimed as he walked in. A fairy man walked in from out the back. He smiled, that odd smile that offered friendship at a cost. Caspian had seen a lot of that lately. To the average human the man in his shop probably seemed pleasant, friendly, hell, even good-looking. Once again Caspian thought a life without fairies would be so much simpler.

"Caspian ap Felan." The fairy extended his hand. "Gratitude to your father and you." He gave a half-bow that should've made Caspian uncomfortable.

It didn't; instead, there was the growing feeling that he deserved this respect. He didn't like this fairy blood of his rising to the surface so rapidly. It was going to reach a point where he didn't trust himself.

"And you are?"

"Bramwel ap Joria," he said like his name should mean something.

The name meant nothing, but that he'd given it freely did. Bramwel had nothing to hide and was happy to associate with him. This was his new temporary assistant. Who was owing who the bigger favor?

"You were sent by my father."

"I owe him a debt. Since you can't enter your house at the moment I took the liberty of bringing clothes here for your return."

Caspian blinked. "Why can't I go home?"

"The tea set protects against the *banished*." Bramwel said the word like it left a bad taste on his tongue.

"And what has Dylis got to do with this?"

"You don't know? She never mentioned me?" Bramwel's eyes went wide in shock. "I spent three hundred years waiting for her and she never mentioned me once?"

Caspian regarded the fairy for a moment, the little pieces of the puzzle dropping into place. He'd always liked puzzles. It was because of Bramwel that Felan had been able to get Dylis to look after Caspian. Deals were made, and made again to guarantee an outcome.

Bramwel regarded Caspian cautiously. "So, the Prince really took your soul."

"Yes." Really, aside from the threat of death if he didn't get it back, he wasn't really missing it. Maybe he could just get un-banished and remain fairy? That would be the blue blood talking. He wasn't fairy and he didn't like their games. But his father's offer of dwelling in Annwyn permanently lingered in his mind.

"Whatever they are up to must be high stakes. I've never heard of ripping out a changeling's soul before."

"I don't know what Dylis had told you, but I don't have time to stand around filling you in." He glanced around his shop. The big un-enchanted mirror was gone as was a writing desk, several vases, an old typewriter, and one of those old black Singer sewing machines that everyone liked. "You seem to be running the shop well."

"It's quite easy." Bramwel smiled again, and Caspian didn't have the heart to tell him to stop swaying people's opinion with magic.

Fairies couldn't make someone go against their beliefs or personal morals; all they could do was amplify the need. Lydia's response last night had been real. She'd wanted him as much as he'd wanted her; he'd just lowered the barrier that had stopped her from jumping into bed with him straightaway. Again he caught himself justifying behavior that wasn't naturally his. Maybe it was and he'd just done a bloody good job of suppressing it and acting human like he was supposed to.

"Oh, also, you have an imp problem. I chased him out of the shop but he's hiding by your car."

"Ah, enemies closer and all of that. Got any food on you?" Caspian placed his laptop satchel down on the counter next to the cash register.

Bramwel frowned but opened a drawer and revealed a stash of chocolate. If Caspian ever went back to Annwyn, he was taking chocolate with him; he could buy friends by the ounce. Caspian took one and went outside. His car was immaculate. The silver paint gleamed in the sun, and there wasn't a bee or a hive in sight.

The imp stuck his head out from behind a tire.

Caspian squatted down and handed over the chocolate. "You will be allowed back into the shop."

The little imp sniffed the packet and grinned. Since Caspian was technically already banished, making a deal with the imp wouldn't do any further damage.

"I've got a proposition for you."

"I'm listening."

"You want to go back to Court?"

The imp's eyes glittered. "What do you require, banished changeling?" He gave a bow.

"Just bring word of Shea's plans. I'm sure you over-hear things, now and then."

"And in return?"

"I plead your case to Prince Felan."

"Not enough."

Caspian stood. "Fine. Shrink away to nothing. How long have you got at your current size? Months? Weeks? Do you think an offer like this will come along again? Power is shifting; you want to make sure you're sup-porting the right side."

"And you know this, soulless human shell?"

"I've just returned from Annwyn. My lack of soul is temporary, as is the banishment. Is yours?" Caspian's lips curved, and he caught his reflection in the win-dow of the car. Cold and calculating. He'd left his soul behind but picked up a nasty case of fairy mannerisms in exchange. He shivered. Lydia didn't make him feel alive, she made him feel human. He needed to hold onto that or he might as well quit now and give himself up for dead.

"I suppose if I overheard something then I might be able to tell you."

"And I might be able to help you." Not a binding deal, but enough that Caspian might get a heads up should Shea try something. Which he would, especially once he learned Caspian had been to Annwyn; it was just a ques-tion of when and what that Caspian couldn't predict.

In the back of his shop Caspian changed. He looked around for his spare phone charger and found it. Then he sat down to work, letting Bramwel run the front of the shop. Next to him on the desk he placed the Counter-Window, hoping that Lydia would use the Window again and give him a glimpse of where it was, and an idea about how he could persuade her to give it to him. He might love her... but how much did she love him?

———

After lunch Lydia had turned her cell phone to silent. She'd had three threatening calls already and after answering the first one every unknown or blocked number could talk to her voice mail—some had and she wished they hadn't. She didn't want to listen to the hate-filled diatribe. But she couldn't turn it off as she was hoping Caspian would call. When she tried to call his cell phone, it went to voice mail. Was he still sleeping? She could call the shop but she wanted to stay away from the fairy assistant.

Her cell rang again with a blocked number. She was sure it was the man again, he wanted the diaries burned, he wanted her burned. He thought there was something in the diaries that would implicate him or his family. Her blood ran cold as the caller gave up without leaving a message. She had to do something with those diaries fast, before the caller did what he was promising. The idea of Callaway House being razed made her sick. With shaking hands she rang Callaway House, hoping Caspian was there. The call went through to the answering machine. Surely he was up by now? She rang again in case she'd woken him and he hadn't gotten to the phone in time. No answer. She tried his cell, but it still wasn't working. As a last resort she called Caspian's shop—and if he wasn't there?

"Mort Treasures." That too smooth voice again.

Her heart sank; she hoped Caspian would answer.

Still, he might be there, doing stuff other than answering the phone. She hoped he was, otherwise she was all out of ways to contact him. What if he'd been taken back to Annwyn? "Is Caspian there?"

"Lydia, is it? He is. Just a moment." There was silence then a rustle as the handset changed hands.

"Hello?" He sounded normal this afternoon.

A little bit of the worry eased. He'd just needed to rest. Right, after driving her crazy with lust first. She could totally get used to that. "You sound better today."

"I am. Thank you for letting me stay."

She wondered if he remembered what he'd said last night. Then decided that now wasn't the time to bring it up, especially since she hadn't responded, and wasn't sure quite how to respond now. She'd left it too late. "I've a question about the diaries." She had questions about a lot of things, but over the phone wasn't the place to ask them.

"Okay… I don't have a value for them, but the heritage society was most interested. They want to have a look at them and depending on content would like to display some—I did tell them there were no names mentioned, but the man was quite insistent that he needed to see them."

"No, no. I've been getting offers. There are some media outlets who want to buy them. It's a lot of money—"

"Don't do it. The minute you do they'll own you and you won't like what you become." There was an edge to his voice. He knew all about making deals and then having to pay the price and live with the consequences. Again she wondered what his father had asked of him, aside from finding the mirror.

"I wasn't seriously entertaining the idea, but it would pay for the repairs and then some." As she spoke she knew it was a lie. She'd been waiting for Caspian to tell her to sell, to make it alright to take the money. Putting prices on things is what he did.

"Lydia, every minute you spend there will be tainted by the price." Just what kind of deal had he struck in Annwyn?

But he was right about the diaries and the house. As much as it would ease her life now, she'd have to live with the knowledge that she'd sold Gran's life to the highest bidder, reducing her life down to cash. That Caspian understood that made her like him a little more. He wasn't so business-oriented that he didn't understand. She wanted to ask if he thought the paper's offer was a fair one, but if she wasn't going to take it she didn't want to know. None of that helped her immediate problem.

"Well, what do I do with them? I can't keep them at the house anymore. I'm getting odd phone calls."

He was silent for a moment. "What kind of odd phone calls?"

She licked her lip and lowered her voice. "The threatening kind."

"Have you spoken to the police?"

"No, the calls only started this morning after the newspaper article, and the caller says if I go public he'll burn Callaway House to the ground, then he hangs up."

"Don't go home alone. To your place, or Callaway House."

Her blood chilled; where was she supposed to go?

"I think it's just to scare me, not hurt me." She tried to sound more confident than she felt. "I need to get rid of the diaries now, don't I?"

Another weighted pause. She didn't like those.

"Should I give the diaries to the historical society?" Maybe she should just burn them, but the idea of destroying something Gran had put so much time into made her sick.

"Can you live with your family's past on display?"

"Gran never hid anything." Except the diaries and the names of everyone who'd ever visited.

"And your mother?"

Lydia thought for a moment. Maybe the newer, more personal diaries she could keep. After all, the historical society would only be interested in the mistress years. While Helen's first name was mentioned, that was all there was and there were plenty of Helens; would anyone really try to track her down, especially after she'd changed her name and effectively vanished?

She sighed. This was such a mess. "What else am I supposed to do? I won't burn them. I can't sell them and if I keep them someone will try to steal them." And she'd forever be waiting for the worst, for someone to take a match to the house. No, it was better they were public. There was nothing to hide in them. Her mother's new name wasn't mentioned. And once people realized there was no scandal and no names the heat would go away. Next week someone else would fill the tabloids.

"Have you spoken to the lawyer?"

"Yes. He suggested locking them up at a bank. But

that doesn't help; then those who want them will still think there's something in them. And there's not."

"Nothing at all?"

"Nothing." She hated admitting it, but selling them would be a really public way of showing everyone that there was nothing to see, just the daily trivia of sixty-plus years.

He was quiet again. "I can't tell you what to do, but if you sell them I think you'll regret it."

"This from the man who buys and sells things for a living."

He laughed, but there was no joy in it. "Some things shouldn't be sold."

What have you done?

But she couldn't ask over the phone. She wanted him to look her in the eye as he told her. Did she really want to know? She bit her lip and deliberated. She could let him walk away now. They'd both had fun, but it didn't have to continue. Except he wasn't like any other man she'd ever known and she didn't want to throw it away just because he was part fairy. That she even thought that was possible showed how much knowing him had changed her.

She lowered her voice. "Are you coming around tonight?"

"If you're inviting me."

"I am."

"Be careful, and ring the police to let them know about the threats, just in case."

Just in case.

"I will." *You be careful too.* She hung up. The only way she could make this end would be to make her

own statement about why she wouldn't sell the diaries
and that there was nothing in them. There'd be people
who didn't believe her, but that was their problem.
Before she did that, she'd call the historical society
and arrange for them to collect the diaries for vetting
and display. She doubted they'd want the risk of being
burned down because some old well-to-do family got an
unwanted mention.

———⚡———

Caspian leaned back in his chair and stared at the
phone. Lydia had invited him over. On any other day
that would've made him happy. Today it filled him
with a low-level dread. He was going to have to tell her
the truth and ask her for the Counter-Window. He'd
thought about asking about the mirror over the phone,
but Bramwel was listening and no doubt the imp would
be too. He couldn't trust anyone with the knowledge
that he might know where the Window was. Could he
trust Lydia?

Again he pulled himself up for thinking like a fairy.
Lydia knew what he was, she wasn't trying to out-
scheme him. She was human. She was what he wanted
and could only have once he'd taken the Window from
her. Would she sacrifice the mirror for him? Or maybe
the real question was would she want to keep it once she
knew what it was and the power it had? Probably not.

But he knew he'd do what he had to, to keep Shea
from getting it. The only way to do that was to give
it to his father. *Maybe*. He thought over the wording
of the deals he'd made and what his father had asked.
From where he was sitting the most important thing was

getting his soul and stopping Shea; how that all played out wasn't specified.

He could make all the plans he wanted, but he actually needed the Window first. Which meant he had to be sure Lydia had it. He needed to see it. Until then he needed to make sure she was safe from the fairies she couldn't see.

"Bramwel, where's Dylis?" Caspian called out.

"Around," the fairy said as he stuck his head out the back. "Why?"

"I need her to go to Callaway House." Someone needed to keep an eye on the house and Lydia. Since Dylis had been watching Lydia while he was at Court maybe she could watch over her and the house for a little longer.

Bramwel looked at him like he was pond scum. "She doesn't work for you; she works for your father."

And Bramwel was only here until his part of the deal was done. As soon as Felan was crowned the fairies would be out of his life for good. Just like he wanted. Yet now he wasn't so sure. He didn't know what it was like to live without having a fairy watch over him.

"Can you go?" Caspian smiled and hoped that Bramwel wouldn't follow the terms of his deal to the word.

Bramwel raised one eyebrow. "I'm here to look after your place of employment, that is all."

Damn it. "You brought me clothes." For which he was very grateful; he'd never fully appreciated the luxury of having clean clothing every day before.

"No, Dylis did it out of an affection I don't understand. You're an adult, not a child."

But Dylis had known him since he was a baby. Not having her around would be odd—as well as peaceful. His house would be almost his own. "Can I talk to her?"

He'd expected her to be here, or somewhere close by, if not for him then to at least see Bramwel.

"She's at Court at the Prince's command." The longing in Bramwel's voice left no doubt that's where he'd rather be, or maybe he didn't care as long as he was with Dylis after so long apart. He bit down on the curiosity about where Bramwel had been for three hundred years. It probably wasn't pleasant.

Caspian tried a different tack. "I thought you two would be together."

The fairy shook his head and looked at the floor, obviously wishing that they were together. "There is still work to be done."

So Dylis was still helping Felan, no doubt securing ties and cementing a place on his Council for both her and Bramwel. She was no fool. He was on his own. The imp had skived off to do whatever imps do—probably make trouble, but hopefully to follow Shea around. Caspian made himself relax. If Shea was going to move against Lydia, the imp would tell him. Caspian had seen the glint in the imp's pale eyes at the thought of returning to Court. And besides, Shea didn't know where the Window or Counter-Window was.

Lydia could handle human problems. All he had to do was handle the fairy ones and everything would work out. He had to believe that.

"Fine." Caspian flicked his hand and dismissed the fairy as if he'd been doing it all his life. He looked at his hand as if it had just offended him. He didn't care if changelings were looked down on; he'd rather be one of them than fairy. He needed his soul back fast.

Tonight.

Chapter 20

LYDIA DOUBLE-CHECKED THE TRUNK OF DIARIES, THEN put the key to the lock and a copy of the list in an envelope. She'd come around early to meet the representative from the historical society, who was thrilled to be getting his hands on the Callaway diaries—some of them, anyway. The more recent ones Lydia had already separated and put away. Caspian had been right about their interest in the diaries, but also their concern about the contents. One woman's life through a couple of wars and various changes in government and policies was a rare collection. Lydia was glad they'd be valued and hoped something useful would come of them instead of the endless speculation and threats. No wonder Gran had never mentioned them.

A sharp rap on the front door made her jump. While she might be doing the right thing, her stomach was still in knots. What if Mr. Johnson looked at the diaries and decided not to take them? Then she'd have to find a way to take the scandal out of them and make the contents public herself, take the risk herself. Was it right that she was letting someone else shoulder the burden? She let out a slow breath and opened the front door. A thin man of less than average height waited on the step. Not what she'd pictured when talking to him on the phone. He'd sounded older.

"Mr. Johnson?"

"Yes." His pale blue eyes glimmered and she felt herself nodding.

"Come in and I'll show you where the diaries are." She stepped aside and let him into the house. As she did a shiver of warning rolled down her spine. Her gaze tracked him as he walked past the painting in the entrance. His reflection caught in the glass… and it looked nothing like the man she was seeing.

Her throat closed. In the reflection was a gaunt pale face, like life had hollowed him out, and his eyes were as cold and pale as ice. The same menace she'd felt when the fairy had arrived for Caspian now lodged in her gut, only bigger and sharper. This man who was pretending to be Mr. Johnson wasn't here to talk. He was a Grey.

The Grey didn't seem to have noticed that his reflection didn't match or maybe he didn't care. She took a step back. But the door slammed and locked behind her.

"No!" She pulled on the handle and tried to turn it. Lydia spun back to face the Grey.

Her heart thudded, but all he did was look at her and shake his head. "I thought we'd wait for Caspian together. I can't have you running around outside. You might get hurt." *Hurt* was emphasized as if she was safer in here with him.

Her handbag was in the kitchen, along with the landline. But she had iron tucked in her bra, and the hat stand was iron. All she had to do was keep him talking and then what? Whack him with the hat stand? Press it against his skin until he burned? Her stomach tightened. Could she do it?

"What does Caspian have to do with this?" Maybe she should just pretend she didn't know this man was a fairy. Isn't that what Dylis had told her to do first? No, that was ignore and it was too late for that.

She glanced at the man's reflection again and bit her lip at the unsightly visage. How had he tricked her into thinking he was Mr. Johnson when he looked like a walking corpse? The grim reaper come for tea?

"Everything. I asked him to do something for me and he failed."

Her heart hiccupped. "Well he's not here. He's at his shop."

He sneered. "He'll be here soon enough. He'll come to protect you and then he'll give me what I want."

She didn't want to be used in a fairy game, and certainly not as a pawn to force Caspian to do what this Grey wanted.

"I don't think so." She grabbed the hat stand and swung it at the Grey. It connected with a sickening crunch against his face, but she didn't stop to assess the damage as she ran past the howling fairy. Straight for the kitchen for her phone and more iron.

He yelled and cursed and his footsteps pounded after her.

Lydia slid around the dining table. She flicked on the tap. *Running water. Fairies hate running water.* Then she grabbed her cell phone from her handbag and turned to face the Grey. Half his face was blistered and bleeding and he'd dropped the illusion of being human. This was the scary Caspian faced every day. This is what he saw and pretended not to. Being fairy, even part fairy, was so much more than she'd ever thought.

"What do you want?"

He laughed. "So you know what I am." He stalked

toward her, his clothing dull and frayed, his fingers bony claws.

She flicked a handful of water at him and he came no closer.

The Grey narrowed his eyes. His gaze darted from the iron to the tap and back to her as if weighing his options.

"What do you want?" she repeated. Then she remembered she shouldn't be talking to him at all. What if he tricked her out of her soul, or she tripped up and made an accidental deal? Oh God, she was in over her head. Where was Caspian? Where was Dylis? Where was anyone who could help her?

"I want the Window. I want to go home." He watched her but didn't move closer.

"The Window? Which window? You can have whatever window you want." She played dumb, and hoped he'd fall for it.

"Not *a* window, stupid. *The* Window. A doorway back to Annwyn."

"Oh." This was the Grey that had filled her yard with mirrors, the one who had forced Caspian to make a deal that had gotten him hauled off to Annwyn. Shea ap Greely. This wasn't any old Grey.

Was he desperate enough to kill? She suddenly felt very mortal and very insignificant.

The doorbell rang. Mr. Johnson from the historical society. She gasped with relief and opened her mouth to call out, but the words caught in her throat. She tried again, but her throat closed as if she were silently choking.

Shea wagged his finger at her. "You might have iron, but I still have magic." If it was possible he began to look

worse, deep pits hollowed his cheeks and the burn began
to weep. "The man at the door won't bother us again."
Wasted and angular Shea got uglier by the minute.

Lydia swallowed. "What did you do to him?" Her
voice was croaky as if it hadn't been used in too long.
What had he done to her?

"Encouraged him to think no one was home."

"Uh-huh." This was a bit of a stand-off. Behind her
the tap ran on.

Shea pulled out a chair and sat. "Shall we wait?"

No, she'd much rather leave, but that didn't seem like
an option and she was trying to limit what she said. She
leaned against the kitchen counter. "For what?"

"Caspian."

Lydia waved her cell phone. "I could just call him."

Shea tilted his head. "That will bring him?"

Or send him running. She dialed his number and
prayed he'd answer. She didn't know how long Shea
would be willing to wait.

Glass shattered. Caspian looked up. Another window
broke. There was the unmistakable sound of singing silver as Bramwel drew his sword. Caspian bolted for the
shop front. And stopped. He'd been expecting human
kids making trouble, not a bunch of five-foot-high ugly
banished fairies… trolls to a human mind.

They stood outside the shop, rocks in hand. There
wasn't much more glass to break, but the rocks could
still damage the furniture. He looked at Bramwel, his
sword hummed ready for use as he stalked toward the
doorway and the trolls. He may not want to help Caspian

personally, but at least he took his promise of looking after the shop seriously.

The trolls swaggered closer like any overconfident bunch of teens looking for trouble. Except it was broad daylight and no one had been drinking. At least he hoped they hadn't been drinking. There was nothing more bad tempered than a short, ugly fairy fuelled by a bottle of wine.

"Are you glamouring?"

Bramwel gave him a withering glance. "Of course."

At least if people saw anything it would be a bunch of troublemakers, not something best left under a bridge to make trouble for travelers.

"I'm going to call the cops."

"What are they going to do? Arrest them?" Bramwel snorted.

"Unless you have a spare sword, it's the best I've got." The cops arriving would at least scare them off. Caspian was willing to bet Shea was behind this attack, and the imp hadn't said boo—that's what he got for relying on banished fairies.

"Can you even use a sword, banished changeling?"

"I did fencing." Much to his human father's horror and Dylis's delight. He'd also been on the track and field team to balance the scales.

"Not the same. Go and ring your cops."

Yeah, and at least if there was damage it would be covered by insurance. He turned around and heard the stampede of troll feet. When he glanced back Bramwel had already killed one. The rest were staying out of reach. They were just here to destroy.

He snatched up the phone and rang emergency. As he

did, the imp jumped onto his chair. He panted, one hand over his tiny heart. While Caspian spoke to the operator, and listened to the crashing out front, he kept one eye on the imp who was doing a strange pantomime that involved choking and a zombie walk. He'd never been good at charades.

As he gave the details to emergency, no one was hurt, just a burglary in progress, his phone beeped from a missed call and message.

Finally the imp gave up on the dance routine and punched some words out on the laptop in the middle of his document.

Shea is with a woman.

Caspian blinked and hoped he'd read that wrong. He hadn't. Lydia. Shea was with Lydia.

There was a very human cry of pain. The operator was warning him not to be a hero and that the police would arrive shortly. He hung up. Bramwel's arm was bent in the wrong place. But he was still fighting. Furniture was overturned. He wanted to join the fray just to hurt something, but that wouldn't help Lydia. This was a distraction, or a warning, or maybe a parting shot. It didn't matter. He had to get to Lydia.

"I have to leave."

Bramwel threw piece of broken chair at a troll who danced and laughed, which sounded more like the crunching of gravel than anything joyous. "Go, you're no use to me here." He jumped back to avoid the swinging of the other piece of chair as it swept toward his shins. "Finish him, finish this. Don't let the bloodshed be for nothing." The words were gritted out.

The imp scuttled past, tripping a troll as he went.

At least Bramwel had help until the cops arrived. That didn't stop Caspian from feeling like a coward for walking away from the fight. He checked the missed call; it was from Lydia. But he didn't need to hear the message to know what was happening. Shea was at Callaway House, waiting for him.

Caspian picked up his car keys, hoping he didn't have to choose between Lydia and handing over the Window. He couldn't. If he lost the Window he was as good as dead. And if he lost Lydia, he might as well be dead.

Chapter 21

LYDIA KEPT HOLD OF THE PHONE, HER BACK TO THE counter. Beside her the tap ran on. Shea got up and paced, but he held his distance. She expected him to lunge for her at any moment, but the running water seemed to keep him at bay. In her bra she could feel the iron nail pressing into her skin. Dylis had been quite specific about what would work. Compared to the hat stand it seemed so small and yet when she looked at Shea she saw the damage iron could do. She knew exactly how to use the nail. Would she be able to get it out in time?

Shea stopped and stared at her, his eyes cold and dead. "Make me tea."

She bit the inside of her lip to keep from saying anything. She wasn't doing anything that he asked. Obeying a Grey was dangerous.

"You think you can stop me? You're nothing. A soul to steal, bait, or bribe. Your lover is already in trouble. Lost his soul for dealing to me."

Years of practice was all that kept her from looking shocked. No soul, how was that possible? But she remembered the way he'd acted when he'd first come back, the way he'd stopped when he'd found the nail in her bra and the hesitation to shower, the look in his eye and the way he'd avoided talking while still trying to hold onto her. If he had no soul, what did that make him?

The answer was right in front of her. She swallowed. Caspian was a Grey.

Shea paced closer, his gaze flicking between her and the water. Dylis had said afraid of water, not that it would hurt a fairy. She needed the iron nail in her hand. But she couldn't get it out while he watched.

"Used you to get to the Window." Shea grinned. "Your little friend who lived here followed you home, saw you holding a mirror." He rested one hand on the back of a chair. He was far too close for comfort now. "I'm willing to gamble it's the Window—and so was your friend."

The compact in her handbag. *Don't look at your handbag. Keep looking at Shea. I'm going to have nightmares.* "That old thing? That's just my grandmother's makeup mirror."

How long had Caspian known? The whole time he'd been here? Or just since he'd come back with the mirror around his neck?

"Where is it?"

"At home, with the rest of the things I took from here." Her heart was bouncing around and making breathing hard. Could he tell she was lying?

His eyes narrowed. "Don't you want to save your lover?"

"Yes." But if Caspian had lost his soul in Annwyn then it made sense that the only way to get it back would be to give the mirror to his father, not Shea.

"Then give it to me."

"It's at home," she said really slowly. "Want to take a drive?" She didn't want to be in a car with him, but if it kept him away from her handbag for a little longer she'd do it.

"You agree to fetch me the Window?"

She opened her mouth then realized that he was trying to get her talking to trip her into a deal. She shut her mouth and bit her tongue for good measure. Why hadn't Caspian told her all of this?

Because she'd have freaked out because he was a Grey. She'd slept with him while he was missing a soul. Her thoughts swirled around like papers in a breeze. *Take a breath and think.*

He was still Caspian, and he still needed the Window. That she had it made things simpler. Except Shea knew she had it too. He took a step closer. She flicked some water at him. This time he winced but didn't step back.

Shit. She'd seen Caspian shower last night, so maybe a fairy's fear of water wasn't that great unless it was a river or an ocean.

"I wonder what he'd do to save you." He tilted his head and flexed his fingers.

Her phone beeped as a message arrived, but she was almost too scared take her eyes off Shea and look. How far could she run? How many invisible fairies were in the house waiting to grab her or trip her up?

The front door opened and Shea turned. She used that moment to slide the nail out of her bra and into her hand.

Caspian appeared in the doorway. His lips tightened, but that was the only sign of distress. Was he even worried about her or just the damn Window?

"You broke the deal. Your thugs attacked my shop. You came here and invaded her house." Caspian looked at Shea.

"You broke it first. Have you bothered to check a

single mirror I left at your house? No, you were too busy at Court meeting your father and losing your soul. I propose a trade. I keep your lover until you get me the Window."

"That wasn't the deal."

"We make a new one, banished to banished. We can both get what we want." Shea took a couple of steps and grabbed her arm, dragging her away from the water.

"Let go." She smacked him in the face with her phone as she tried to get the nail into her fingers ready to use.

He tightened his grip. "A fear of water is one thing, but it is not enough to stop me from getting what I want and getting home. I need the Window and I will have it."

Caspian stepped forward, then stopped as if unable to move. Shea's face hollowed, his features becoming more drawn and haggard as if was wasting before her eyes. He was using magic. On Caspian.

"Use magic to fight me, darkling," Shea sneered.

"I'm not a darkling. My father is Court." Caspian forced the words out, his gaze on Shea, not her.

"Fight to free yourself. Let's see how fast you wither." Shea's grip on her arm eased a fraction as if he was weakening.

Caspian seemed to be fighting for every breath. She almost dropped the nail as she turned it, then it was ready. She said a quick prayer and then drove it into Shea's thigh.

The scream was like that of a wounded, enraged animal. Shea released her and she moved—but not to Caspian's side. She went to the other doorway, the one that led to the formal dining room. Without iron or water she had nothing but speed and distance. But she couldn't bring herself to leave. Plus her handbag was still on the kitchen counter. *That was dumb*. But neither Grey knew what was in there wrapped up safe with iron.

Shea reared up and snarled, dark blue... blood, she realized... dripped onto the floor. He stepped toward her, but Caspian pulled the necklace out of his shirt. Shea stopped to watch.

"One more step and I destroy the Window." Caspian lifted the chain over his head.

"Don't give it to him," Lydia whispered. Caspian needed his soul back, didn't he? Or did he no longer care? Was he on Shea's side now because he was a Grey? It was all too confusing.

Shea stared at the shard of mirror. "You're lying. She has it."

Caspian shook his head. "I went to Court and saw where it was hidden. Here amongst the jewelry. Clever." That wasn't right; he'd said it was to help him find the Window. Had he lied about that too? Then she realized she was watching him trick another fairy. He was playing the Grey at his own game.

"Prove it's the Window," Shea demanded.

"Prove it's not." Caspian shrugged, and his face remained expressionless. "What are you prepared to risk, Shea ap Greely?" He set the mirror swinging, and the chain moved closer to the ends of his fingers, millimeter by millimeter.

Lydia watched as Caspian prepared to break the mirror. What was he risking by doing that?

Caspian took a step closer and smiled, but there was nothing remotely human about it. Lydia shuddered.

She'd been to bed with him like this. Soulless and hard, and yet at the time he'd seemed more lost than anything.

"I didn't break the deal. The only way I could be free of you was to find the Window. Which I have done. Annwyn took my soul for dealing with you, but you will not take what is left of my life." He inclined his head at Lydia.

"So if you found it why haven't you given it to your father and begged for your soul?"

"I was on my way; there is a doorway at the cemetery. But Lydia rang to tell me you were visiting and I couldn't leave her here with you. I know how a Grey will do anything to get home." The mirror slid a little further down his fingers and Shea drew in a sharp breath.

Shea seemed frozen, as if he didn't know whether to rush for her or Caspian. His gaze darted between her and her lover. She couldn't move and didn't dare say anything in case she damaged whatever Caspian was trying to do.

"Let's make this more fun. How about I call my father?" Before Shea could answer he drew a breath. "Let it be known I have found the Window. The deal is complete."

Caspian didn't raise his voice but his words echoed with power. She felt in her blood something ancient and powerful stirring—the same way she'd felt his invitation to bed last night. He really wasn't anything close to human at the moment and yet she couldn't take her eyes off him as the silver chain slid down his fingers. To his fingertips. She held her breath.

Then the mirror began to fall.

Shea leaped for the mirror, his belly hitting the

floor, his hand outstretched as he muttered some kind of incantation.

"I never promised it would be whole," Caspian said.

Chapter 22

CASPIAN JUMPED TO THE SIDE AS SHEA LANDED ON HIS stomach on the floor, stretched out his hand, and then vanished in a flash of light into the mirror just as Caspian had expected him to. It had been a gamble but the only one he'd been able to make and now the Counter-Window was in three pieces on the kitchen floor. For several heartbeats he waited for Shea to reappear through the Window that was somewhere in this house—hopefully. He didn't want to have claimed to have completed the deal when in actual fact the Window was still lost and he'd broken the Counter-Window.

When there was no enraged snarl, no cursing, and no sign of the banished fairy lord, he let himself breathe for a moment even though he didn't have long to find the Window before his father showed up and demanded he hand it over. Lying didn't go down well at Court; lying by omission or letting people assume was another matter.

He walked over to Lydia. "Are you okay?"

She shrunk back against the door frame as if his touch was poison and her eyes were full of suspicion and fear. "What are you?"

He had to be honest. Shea had already spilled the truth and lying would only make it worse. "You know what I am. My father took my soul in exchange for the Window."

Her lips moved but no sound came out. But she didn't

need to speak; he could see the distrust in her eyes. "You're a Grey, like him."

"It's temporary, if I return the Window." But it was also clear he couldn't protect her from his family or fairies in general. Maybe a life in Annwyn was the only chance he had. While he missed the beauty, that was all he missed. Beneath the dancing and partying there was an edge. A razor constantly held to throats just waiting for an opportunity to slice. When he looked at Lydia, he didn't want to live at Court. He wanted to be human and with her. She made him feel like he had a chance at living again.

"You should have told me last night."

"Does it change me?" He already knew it did, but had she noticed?

She nodded and his worst fears were confirmed. He swallowed down the rising ache. What would he do if she never wanted to see him again? Would he have the strength to say no to his father when the Prince asked if he wanted to live in Annwyn?

"Is he gone?" She pointed to the broken mirror.

"I think so." He picked the pieces up and placed them on the table. How did he ask for the other piece? Straight up. It was the only way. "While I was in Annwyn I saw you in this piece. I think you have the other half." He turned to look at her. "I think it was here all along, but no one, not even the ghost, knew what it was."

"The ghost followed me home after I'd packed up some of my grandmother's personal things. I think I have it."

"Do you have it here?"

"What are you going to do with it?"

"Return it to my father and get my soul back, hopefully."

She looked at him as if trying to work out if he was lying. "How do I know you aren't trying to trick me? Isn't that what Greys do?"

"A Grey will do anything to get back to Annwyn and stop the fading of looks and power. I didn't fight Shea because if I did I would have weakened myself and I am already weaker than most Greys because I am half-human. I want my soul back. I want you. I love you." He wanted to reach for her, but he knew he wouldn't be able to handle her reaction if she pulled away again. While he could glamour her into helping, he didn't want to do that either. He was trying his hardest to prove to her he was human, but it felt like everything he wanted was slipping through his fingers and he couldn't stop it. He waited for the rejection. For the denial of affection.

She took a breath. "I love you too." Then she walked through the kitchen to her handbag and pulled out an iron bolt and a silver compact. She placed them on the kitchen table next to the broken mirror. "When I realized this might be fairy I put it in my bag next to iron to try and keep it safe. I wanted to give it to you last night but you weren't in any state to do anything." Her cheeks colored as if remembering the rest of the details from last night.

When he got back it had felt like he hadn't slept for three days, that and the loss of his soul and the lack of connection to Annwyn had taken a toll. But Lydia made him feel alive.

"It's okay. I didn't know how to ask if you had it. I suspected it must have been something of your grandmother's."

"It was a gift, but I think the man was just hiding it

here." She touched the silver case. "Will that Grey be in there, in the mirror?"

"I don't know." They both looked at the compact as if expecting Shea to burst out at any moment. Nothing happened. He needed to know if the compact was what he was searching for. "Can I?"

She nodded.

His fingers brushed the silver casing and he got nothing from it. The metal told him nothing of the mirror's past. He bit back his frustration. How was he supposed to find the damn Window when he couldn't see what an object was?

"Well?" Lydia raised her eyebrows.

"I don't know." The compact was a lump of dead metal in his hands. Then he remembered what Shea had said. A fairy couldn't sense the Window. Because he was a soulless fairy at the moment it felt like a normal mirror. But the silver case was decorated in a vine-like pattern which was very Annwyn. He opened the catch. The mirror was broken into three, the same as the Counter-Window. Pressed against the silvered glass was Shea. Blue blood stained the cracks as if the mirror was weeping.

"Is that it?" Lydia stepped closer. "Is that… ?"

He let out a slow breath, then shut the compact. There would be no funeral games for Shea in Annwyn. But he'd also been saved the slow death of a Grey.

"It is the Window," a voice said behind Caspian.

Caspian turned. His father stood in the kitchen. His elegant clothing too bold and bright for the mortal world. He'd heard the call for the end of the deal and crossed the veil to be here.

Felan looked at Caspian, then Lydia. "I'm sorry for this intrusion. I trust you haven't been harmed?" Felan inclined his head and smiled.

Caspian waited for Lydia to glide toward his father and melt into his arms. But she didn't move. She was immune to Felan's charm, that or he wasn't turning it up to full volume.

"I'm fine…" Her gaze flicked over the Prince's clothing. "Sir."

The Prince turned his attention to Caspian. "Thank you." He held out his hand.

Caspian handed over the compact. The Prince opened it, nodded, and closed it. Then he gathered up the broken pieces from the table.

"Well played, son, although I wished you hadn't destroyed it." Felan slipped the pieces into a pocket in his silvery blue coat. The collar was turned up, sharp points jutting under his jaw. With careful movements he pulled the ring off his finger. "This belongs to you."

"That simple?"

"That simple." He almost handed Caspian the ring. But closed his hand at the last moment. "I ask you again, do you wish to remain in the mortal world?"

That would be twice he'd been asked. The first time he'd known the answer. Caspian looked at Lydia. She loved him. He had a chance at the life he'd always wanted. The pause stretched out. Felan raised his eyebrows as if he'd won.

Caspian smiled. "I choose to remain."

Felan gave a small nod, his lips curved up at the corners. "Very well. The next time I ask, you'll be drawing your last breath."

A shiver raced down Caspian's spine. Would he be able to refuse when death was imminent?

The Prince handed over the silver ring with the green and red stone that held his soul and all of his humanity. As soon as it was in his hand there was a change. Nothing he could name directly, but from the ring he received an impression of love and pride. He smiled, his smile, without the fairy edge. "Thank you."

Caspian put the ring on, not surprised that it fit perfectly.

"You don't have to wear the ring."

"I want to." It would be a reminder of what he'd almost lost. The red line that had split the stone like a cat's pupil was gone. But it would also remind him that his father had stayed away out of love, not because he was an unwanted changeling.

Felan nodded to Lydia, then to Caspian. "I shall leave you. I have other business to attend at Court." A flicker of anxiety crossed his face but was quickly masked.

No doubt news of Shea's death would rock the Court. Those who aligned with him and the Queen would rapidly shift their game. Whatever happened Felan was going to have to make some dangerous calls to save Annwyn. Caspian didn't envy him at all. For all the privilege, wealth, and status, it wasn't worth the cost.

"Good luck." He went to shake his father's hand, but Felan pulled him into an embrace. They might scheme and carry on as if life was one long party, but fairies did feel and weren't as cold as he'd thought. He'd learned that in the short time he'd been truly fairy.

Felan drew away. "The family reunion is over. Next time I hope we meet under better circumstances." Then he turned to leave.

"Wait, sir." Lydia took a step after him. She should be letting him leave. This man, this fairy, was dangerous and powerful and Caspian's father. Something she was still trying to grasp, but he was about to walk away with her grandmother's compact, something her gran had treasured and kept safe for years.

The fairy turned to look at her. His expression was one of puzzlement, as if he didn't expect to be questioned. There was a similarity between Caspian and the fairy. The eyes. They were the same ice green.

"I just want to know about the mirror and the man who gave it to Gran. I don't want it back." She rushed on. This was a bad idea; she shouldn't have asked. She half-expected anger or some reaction like she had from the Grey, or the sense of menace from the Hunter.

Instead he nodded and drew the compact out of his coat and handed it to Caspian. "Answer her question. I'd like to know too."

As soon as Caspian's finger's touched the mirror he smiled. "A fairy gave her the mirror, he loved being the center of attention at her parties, but he gave her the mirror to hide it as well as to thank her. They were more than friends."

She'd been right. The singer had been Gran's lover. Go Gran.

Felan pressed his lips together. "Which fairy?"

"He was a singer... wait," Lydia darted out of the kitchen to the parlor and Gran's collection of photos. She knew exactly which picture it was, the one that had made Caspian look twice, because he'd recognized the man as fairy. Looking at it now, he was more than pretty. There was something in his eyes and his cheekbones that gave him away. She picked it up and brought it back to the kitchen where Caspian and his father waited. "Is this him?"

The fairy peered at the photo. "Riobard, up to your old tricks. How did he get his hands on it?"

Caspian frowned, his focus on the mirror and the past no one else could see, then spoke. "He stole it from a female fairy some time ago. There was bitterness between them. Did he know what he was stealing?"

"Oh yes, and I have no doubt he'll be showing his face at Court very soon." Caspian's father took the compact back. "We're done." He turned on his heel and left.

This time Lydia kept her mouth closed as the handsome man in the odd clothing walked out of her kitchen as if he owned the place and was giving them permission to get back to their lives.

She'd been speaking to Caspian's fairy father, Gran had entertained a fairy. She'd seen a Grey get killed by jumping through a mirror. The adrenaline left her feeling sick and weak. She leaned against the kitchen counter for support. Could she deal with having fairies in her life? But when she looked at Caspian she knew she could. It wasn't his fault he was related to a bunch of immortal, immoral beings.

"Your father's not any just any fairy, is he?" Her voice was low in case somehow he was still around and listening.

"He's the Prince."

"Right." Of course he was. "Were you ever going to tell me you were fairy Prince?"

"I'm not a prince. I'm just a changeling of no

significance to Annwyn. My parentage has been kept secret because others might try to use me to get to him."

After what she'd seen over the last few days of fairies she totally understood that. "I won't tell anyone."

He walked around the kitchen table and drew her into his arms. "Thank you for believing, for understanding."

Lydia let herself sink into his embrace, just glad to have him back and the other fairies gone. "You don't get to choose your family."

Chapter 23

CASPIAN LAID OUT THE WAFERS AND FILLED UP THE teapot while Lydia topped up the sugar. Since bringing the fairy-made silver tea set to Callaway House the place was immaculate. All the dust had been cleaned away, and while Lydia was amazed, he warned her not to say anything as that would be breaking the unspoken agreement between Brownie and tea set owner. That his Brownies had followed him to Callaway House made him suspect there was a deal he didn't know about, one he didn't want to know about.

Dylis had agreed to help him keep the promise to the imp who had been nothing but helpful at the shop—Bramwel was used to the idea and was glad not to be doing the dusting himself.

"Do you regret selling your house?" She lifted her gaze.

"No." They'd needed a mortgage to do the repairs, but with two incomes that hadn't been hard—if he sold his house and she sold hers and they moved into the house. The closing on his place had been today. He was now bound to Callaway House financially as well as emotionally, and he couldn't be happier.

Since Bramwel was running the shop Caspian had spent more time at the house making sure the repairs were done in keeping with the house's history. But he missed his shop, even if he was still going on buying trips. Also given the news of late, he hoped Bramwel would be going back sooner rather than later. The disease outbreaks were getting worse, which meant the situation in Annwyn was, too. He tried not to think about it as there was nothing he could do.

Caspian slipped his arms around Lydia's waist and kissed the back of her neck. He remembered doing that before—while he hadn't been quite himself—but she liked it and he'd realized that the fairy side of him was part of him. Instead of trying to control or suppress it as he once had, he'd embraced it and found living with it was much easier. But then Lydia knew him better than anyone else.

She leaned back against him. "Are you ever going to make an honest woman out of me?"

"Maybe one day." He wasn't in a hurry, not because he expected his relationship with Lydia to fail, but because the paper didn't prove anything.

She turned her head. "You know I'd keep my name."

"Yep." He moved the collar of her shirt aside and kissed the side of her neck. His hands splayed over her hips, drawing her closer so she could feel him hard against her butt.

"You don't care?" She gave her hips a wiggle that felt entirely too good.

"No. Fairies never change names, and the children take the name of their fairy parent." His thumbs slid under her shirt, sweeping across the bare skin of her stomach. "Do you want to go upstairs?"

"If I say no?"

He undid the button on her black trousers. "I'm happy to keep going here."

She covered his hands with hers, guiding them lower. He smiled as he kissed her earlobe, and raked the skin softly with his teeth. She gave a little moan, but made no effort to move.

"You want to stay here in the kitchen?" His fingers traced her inner thigh.

With every breath and every kiss they were creating new memories in the house. It was feeling more like a home. A place where he belonged. Where she belonged. And while the past could never be erased, the present could be written over the top, creating a future he hadn't thought possible.

"Only if there are no fairies watching."

He laughed. "Only me."

Read on for a look at the first book
in the Shadowlands series, *The Goblin King*

Chapter 1

THE SUMMONS PULLED AT EVERY CELL IN HIS BODY,
tearing the bonds that held him together and dragging
him from the Shadowlands. He fought the compulsion to
answer, as he did every time. And lost. As he did every
time. The urge to obey his summoner's orders he'd tamped
down long ago. Yet he attended, as he did every time.

The beads in his hair jangled and chimed, lifted on the
breeze created as he moved from one world to the next,
like golden music in his ears. He moved into the Fixed
Realm wrapped in shadows to hide from the eyes of his
would-be commander. Then he paused and looked around.

A bedroom. Not the first he'd been summoned to.
The only light spilled from the nearby bathroom. His
nose wrinkled at the smell of wet dog and wine. He
frowned. No summoner stood before him, demanding
an audience with the Goblin King. The human who'd
called him from the Shadowlands and sought to control
him lay on the floor at the foot of the bed. Immobile.
Wounded. Female.

The goblin kept his hand on his sword and stepped
forward. As he did, the shadows sloughed off him and
slid away to the corners of the bedroom. The tension in
his skin eased as the compulsion to obey faded. He'd
attended. He could leave. Yet he couldn't look away.

The woman breathed, her breasts lifting with each
inhalation. Her black silk dress clung to each curve,

hiding and revealing without ever moving. His fingers rubbed together as if feeling the glide of silk on skin.

His concentration was broken by a knock on the door. The handle turned slightly. He raised one hand and metal jammed, securing the room. The door would hold until he was done.

"Eliza, you have to come down." A man's voice came from the other side of the door, the words just shy of an order. The handle jiggled, then a fist pounded on the door as the man tried to get into the bedroom. Could he sense the darkness creeping under the door, leaking from the goblin?

The goblin squatted and studied the woman the man had called Eliza. *Eliza*. Her name echoed in his ears as if he should know her. Her head was bleeding, the dark blood seeping into the darker carpet. He reached out to touch her, drawn to her beauty the same way he was drawn to the gold hanging from her ears. The light from the bathroom cut across his mottled gray skin. He jerked his hand back as if he'd been burned. It was this body the woman would see if she woke now. A body not even he could bear to see. He should unlock the door and leave. Let the man who kept knocking tend her cut feet and bruised head.

He hesitated. Eliza had called the Goblin King.

"Open up, Eliza." The knocking became more urgent. The tone less caring. "You look like a fool hiding from your own birthday."

Charming. *She is unconscious, you fool. And drunk.*

Something was amiss. He rocked back on his heels as he assessed the woman and the bedroom. Glass and wine covered the bathroom floor. Eliza lay unmoving.

Yet the man demanding her presence knew none of this. He shook his head and the beads rattled. This wasn't his problem. The gods knew he had enough of his own.

But Eliza had wished. Wished to be taken away. And he wanted to obey. Her words pulsed in the air and shook in his presence. The goblin let her wish settle around him like a cloak made of the darkest dreams—where hers ended and his began. He forced out a breath. No good would come of this.

The door vibrated under a fresh onslaught of hits this time accompanied by muttered swearing. His fingers brushed over the ends of her blond hair. There was something disturbingly familiar about her. Her face, the curve of her lips. Where had he seen her? Had she summoned him before? There was something about the magic, her words…His eyes narrowed and he glanced back at the door. He couldn't think through the thousands of summons he'd answered with that incessant noise. Couldn't the man give him some peace?

"What am I supposed to tell the guests?" The man's silence seethed with fear. "Fine, have it your way. We'll talk tomorrow." He gave the door a final slap before his footsteps faded away. No fight to be had.

The goblin smiled. Eliza was his.

He scooped up her limp body. Her fair skin was scented like summer blossoms. It had been so long since he'd felt the summer sun on his skin. So long since he'd been able to touch a flower without killing the bloom. So long since he'd had company, female company.

Her head lolled against his arm. He cradled her closer and murmured against her hair.

"You should be careful what you wish for, Eliza."

Her name rolled easily off his thick tongue. "For I am all too happy to oblige," he said with a laugh that held no joy.

The shadows closed around the Goblin King, drawing him, and his prize, home to the Shadowlands.

Eliza was warm against him. She glowed as if lit from within, a radiance not usually seen in the Shadowlands. He hesitated, not wanting to lay her down and lose contact. He liked her weight in his arms and the touch of her skin against his. If she woke now, in the Shadowlands, he would look human with a face he had no qualms about Eliza seeing. He inhaled her delicate female scent once more. His body responded as any man's would, and the lust for something other than gold burned through him as unfamiliar as it was pleasant.

Soon enough. He preferred women who participated, eagerly.

He placed her on his bed, and her dress rode up over her thighs, revealing long, smooth, creamy white legs. He ran his thumb over the scar on her inner knee. Like dew on a spiderweb, it accentuated the perfection of her body. He brushed the scar again. Years he chose not to count had passed since any woman had called the Goblin King, and he intended to make full use of the summons.

Who was he to disobey her command?

He fanned her hair over the sheets on his bed, an old four-poster taken from a palace. The posts were cleverly carved with a hunt, the prey forever chased by the hunter. He doubted the French king who'd originally had it noticed its disappearance.

He'd gathered beautiful objects from all over the world to fill his caves. Authentic Persian carpets, Ming vases, silk drapes, gold statues, gold mirrors, gold coins. Yet…something was always missing. So he followed his goblin nature—when in doubt add more gold. It was an easy way to decorate.

But an empty way to live.

Now he had another beautiful object to entertain him while he wasted eternity. His knuckle traced her cheek. Eliza didn't flinch and her eyes remained stubbornly closed. She would look upon the king she'd called and have her audience on her knees.

He tore his gaze away and stared at the cavern's ceiling. The beads in his hair hit his back like hail as they resettled. He was hard, ready. He fisted his hand, fighting the urge to possess the woman he had taken, and drew in three deep breaths. They did nothing to settle the rough lust riding in his blood.

Did he want her with the need of goblin, or the desire of a man?

Did it matter anymore?

Yes.

He still had a human soul, if only barely. If he were truly goblin, he would already be buried to the hilt, enjoying his first root in a couple of centuries.

His nails broke the skin on his palm. The pain grounded him and gave him something else to think about besides his daily battle with the curse. He uncurled his pale fingers. Scarred knuckles, callused palm. His hands. Warrior's hands. Not the gray, gnarled hands of the monster he was cursed to be. He ran the palm of one of those hands over his groin as he got up. The jagged need didn't slacken, but he wouldn't be the monster today. He didn't need to be.

She would awaken soon enough and realize what she'd summoned.

He pulled back the gold, embroidered silk curtain and found his subjects waiting for him on the other side. He truly never got any peace. His brother, Dai, and Anfri stood, arms crossed, in the hallway. They would've known the second he'd returned.

"She's mine." It was all he needed to say. He had been their king in life, and he was their king in curse. They were all who were left. The others had been granted the mercy of death, except the one who had faded to goblin.

He glared at Dai, then at Anfri. Anfri held his gaze for just a moment too long before looking past his shoulder to Eliza.

"A woman, Roan?" Dai acted as if they had never brought women to the Shadowlands before.

They hadn't. Not like this. In the past they had parted with gold, then silver, for a woman's company. Now they would rather keep the coin. A reminder of how far they'd come from being men who'd fight and drink and fuck, to becoming misfits so almost goblin they'd rather the glittering lure of gold.

"Only one." Anfri moved for a better look at Eliza.

Roan blocked his view. He placed a hand on Anfri's arm. "The woman is mine."

Anfri's face contorted as his eyes yellowed and bulged. The gold heart in Roan's chest ached in response. He could no longer ignore the change in Anfri.

He knew the signs too well and it was happening again. Anfri was fading.

"Roan, this isn't wise," Dai said. "What about—"

"This is different." Roan glared at him.

"Yes, brother, you kidnapped her." Dai pressed one hand against Roan's chest where his heart should've beaten. Concern deepened the lines in the younger man's face. Dai should have been the older sibling—he was always watching, making sure Roan didn't slide into the curse without noticing. His men's lives would have been so different if he had died that day on the battlefield.

Roan removed Dai's hand. "She asked."

"She didn't know what she asked."

"Too late." Too bad. Eliza was his. A prize fit for a king.

"She is injured," Anfri said, stopping Dai's arguments.

Roan turned away, not wanting to see the judgment on his brother's face. Instead he focused on the cuts on her feet, where blood stained her soles and spread to his sheets. His gut tightened as the magic of the Shadowlands ran through him, begging for use, urging his surrender. He hissed. He didn't want anyone else touching Eliza, but her wounds weren't life threatening, so no magic was required. He had to let Anfri tend to Eliza. He was the closest thing to a doctor they had, patching their injuries hundreds of times over the centuries.

"Get your kit," he said to Anfri before turning to his brother. "I didn't do it." He knew exactly what his brother was thinking, the same way Dai knew his thoughts too well. "I'm not that close to succumbing."

Dai nodded. They both knew. Not this time. Maybe not next time. But soon.

———— ∿ ————

Milk dropped into Steven's coffee like a turd. It splashed onto his hand and the cuff of his shirt. He swore and tipped the foul brew down the sink. Then he pulled out another carton, the low-fat, high-calcium crap Eliza liked, and gave it a trial sniff. He gagged. Every drop of milk in the house had soured overnight. It would have to be black coffee, the perfect end to the perfect night spent in the guest room after Eliza's little temper tantrum.

He drank the coffee fast even though his stomach complained, still struggling with the after-effects of last night's alcohol. Last night, what a nightmare that had turned out to be. He'd made excuses for her not being there to cut her cake. A migraine. His knuckles whitened. She was giving him a fucking migraine.

Steven left the cup in the sink and stalked upstairs. He'd break the door down to get in if he had to. He should've hauled her out last night. He shook his head. No. Better she acted the fool in private. In public they were perfect, the soon-to-be Mr. and Mrs. Slade, heirs to the Coulter legacy.

He twisted their bedroom door handle. The metal groaned and opened. Last night the handle hadn't budged. He shrugged off the faint sense of unease gathering around him like whispered accusations. She must have jammed the door and then felt repentant this morning. Pity he wasn't in the mood to forgive.

He stepped into the room, then reared back at the appalling stench. His bedroom smelled like a party of drunken rats had drowned and then dried under a relentless sun.

"Jesus." It was worse than the milk.

His wardrobe door hung open. The rails where his suits and shirts had hung were gappy and grinning like an old man missing teeth.

"What the hell?" His face twisted with rage. Every suit was gone.

Steven turned. The bed was empty and un-slept in. Where was she? He spun. She wasn't in the bathroom but the bath was full. Every one of his suits was stuffed into the tub.

"Fuck, no."

The stink was wet Italian wool and wine. And was that wine or blood on the white tiles, pooling in the grout?

Steven snatched up the phone from his side of the bed and dialed Eliza's cell phone. This little stunt was too much. She had no right to do this, after everything he'd done...

A chirp answered his call. Anger congealed into a sharp-edged brick that wedged in his gut. He stomped around the bed and flung open her wardrobe door, knowing what he'd find. Her handbag. He pulled the little black bag down from the shelf. Her phone lit up the interior. Keys. Wallet. Sunglasses. All still inside. His rage exploded. The phone slid out of his fingers and bounced in the soft burgundy carpet.

It could have been the hangover, or the smell of his ruined suits, or that Eliza was gone and he would have to involve the police. His stomach heaved and acid coffee scratched his throat. Steven ran for the bathroom, stepping on the smashed wine glass and slicing his foot. He didn't have time to curse. He barely made it to the toilet.

If she ruined his plans, he'd kill her, he swore as he threw up.

Chapter 2

ELIZA'S HANDBAG SAT ON THE TABLE, SMALL AND NEAT and expensive. But then he'd bought it for her, and it perfectly suited his tastes. Steven had brought it downstairs and placed it in the cloakroom for the police to find. She may be missing, but he didn't want the police in the bedroom. Not until he'd finished cleaning up. Partners were always the first suspect. Given the spat last night, a giant novelty neon-yellow sports finger was pointed his way, declaring him guilty of a crime he hadn't committed.

He didn't need the police uncovering the ones he had.

"So you had a fight at eleven," the cop read from his notes.

"Approximately." Steven folded his hands. He stopped short of wringing them; that would be too much.

"Then Ms. Coulter disappeared."

Steven nodded. "I thought she'd gone upstairs to tidy up."

"Tidy up?" The cop raised his eyebrow.

"Fix her makeup. She was upset."

"Give her twenty-four hours." The cop closed his notebook. "She's probably at a friend's."

Which friend? He knew all her friends and none of them would hide her from him…except the bitch sister-in-law, but she wouldn't involve her precious brat. Eliza should've been in the bedroom. How had she left the party without being seen by anyone? Without taking her car, or cell, or purse? Yet she'd vanished, leaving everything behind, but taking everything she knew about him and his business dealings. For all he knew she was having a chat with the Major Fraud Squad now. His throat constricted.

"I'm worried." What if she'd planned this and faked her own disappearance just to get the police involved? "She's never done anything like this before."

And wouldn't again, once he got his hands on her. His mind raced. If she didn't turn up, maybe he could still use it to his advantage. The paperwork pointed at her…that alone gave her motive to vanish with the cash.

"It happens more often than you'd like to think." The cop made to leave, then turned. "What was the fight about?"

Steven hid his frustration at the cop for lingering. Who cared what they fought about? He fabricated a lie around enough truth that it was plausible.

"She saw me talking to another woman. Got jealous. Women on their birthdays—they just don't like getting older." Steven walked toward the door.

He didn't want to seem overly eager to get the cop out, but if the constable looked hard enough, there would be something that would earn a more detailed investigation of the house. He couldn't afford that. He was working a balancing act. He wanted Eliza found *and* he wanted his privacy.

Did he want too much?

"She'll be back by dinner," the cop assured him.

She'd better be. But already he was making a contingency plan. Eliza wouldn't catch him with his pants down twice.

Steven opened the front door and winced. There was

probably glass embedded in his hand. It had been everywhere else—in the bath, in his suits, on the floor. One
glass in a hundred pieces.

The cop had noticed and paused. "What did you do
to your hand?"

Steven held it up for inspection. "Broke a glass while
I was cleaning up the lounge room."

"Looks like you've got more to go."

"I've got cleaners coming in to help." He'd left enough
mess to make sure he looked like the anxious fiancé. The
bedroom he was going to have to finish himself. It was
too much of a crime scene. Like Eliza was trying to frame
him and make sure the police would search the house and
office. Was she hoping they would find what she couldn't?

Whatever Eliza was trying to pull would fail. He'd
already bagged his suits and put bicarb on the stained
grout. Getting rid of the stink was going to be harder.
But by the time he was done, there would be no reason
for the police to suspect him of any wrongdoing at home,
or at work.

If she came back, he would be teaching her a lesson. He
needed to pull her into line. And fast. A performance like
this at the wedding wouldn't fly. It would ruin his reputation.

Steven held the front door open. "Look, don't take
this the wrong way, but I don't want to see you again."

If Eliza didn't come back, he would have to file a
missing persons report just to look the part. A flicker
of doubt surfaced. What if she were really missing? He
pushed the thought aside. Who abducted a woman from
her own birthday party?

———

Roan watched the rise and fall of Eliza's chest. Her lashes lay against her cheeks as if she were a doll waiting for life to return and reanimate her body. A purple bruise and patterned graze marred her forehead, and her feet were bandaged. Anfri had worked under his supervision, touching only where told, yet still it had been too much.

Now he waited, stretched out on the bed next to her. Over the span of two thousand years Roan had become very good at waiting. And watching.

Her black dress tightened then eased with each breath. Women hadn't changed that much over his long and unnatural lifetime. The clothes, the jewelry, the makeup—of which she wore too much—were all irrelevant. And he was sure the blond of her hair was false. He smiled and ran his hand up her thigh, nudging the dress a little higher. He was looking forward to finding out.

He pushed the soft silk until it just covered her underwear. The beads in his hair whispered in his ear as he moved. Would she fight or submit?

Over time he'd learned how to avoid being commanded by his summoner; after answering their initial call, he simply left. Some tried again. Most laughed and had another drink. Yet, ignoring their demands hadn't always been so easy. He wore the scars of being called by history's worst—weak-willed commanders, paranoid rulers, men who didn't deserve respect. He had committed atrocities in their names.

Decades had passed since anyone had offered him anything of value other than gold. The last summoner to give him something had been a child wanting to be a young woman. In helping her, he had remembered what it was like to be human again, something that happened far too rarely these days. For a while she'd thought of him, he'd felt her dreams on his skin, not quite a summons, more of a hope of seeing him again. He'd never responded. It was better to avoid temptation than fall headlong into something he knew he couldn't resist.

He glanced at the woman in his bed. For a moment he almost considered taking her back to the Fixed Realm. But taking her back wouldn't return his humanity. He might as well enjoy what he had left. She'd wished to be taken away. The words of the wish tugged at his soul like a half-forgotten dream. He pushed them aside. Her wish was granted and his would be too. Roan ran his palm down the woman's leg; the touch of human skin warmed his hand but didn't reach his heart.

"Silly, silly girl," he murmured, wanting to hold on to the moment before she woke and the fantasy shattered.

Her eyelids flickered.

Expectation tightened every one of Roan's nerves to battle ready. Starved for too long, he refused to rush. Anticipation was half the delight, half the torture.

Her eyes opened. She blinked and turned her head. Her eyes widened in fear when she saw him.

Roan placed a finger over her lips. He didn't want to hear her scream. Not until he was deep in her, her legs around his shoulders. "I've been waiting, Eliza."

Her lips parted for speech. Or was it a kiss? He took the latter, leaning over to brush his mouth against the red of her lips. She shoved away, denying him a taste in her scramble to escape. Power thumped through his body and his skin tingled.

A fighter. Always more entertaining than a simpering miss who'd cave to his every request.

Roan snapped into action, catching and trapping her beneath him. Eliza kicked her legs, trying to throw him off. One knee connected with his back. Roan grunted and shifted to sit on her thighs so she couldn't repeat the blow. She bucked and wriggled, all without a sound, then she struck out with her nails. He leaned back, dodging the cat scratch, and grabbed her wrists. He pulled her hands to his chest.

Eliza became as still as a corpse. Realization spread over her face, stretching her features. She knew she was his for the taking.

Roan kissed her hand. He didn't want fear. Without warning she lifted her hips, trying to throw him off. He hooked his feet around her legs and spread them. Her hands were trapped beneath his on the bed. Body to body. Hip to hip. The gold and amber beads in his hair danced above her skin. The clothing between them could be gone at his will, but he waited. What were minutes in the face of centuries?

The torment of being unable to taste her skin filled his thoughts. An eternity, that's what it was. An eternity of flesh-hardening agony with no release. And he no longer had an eternity to wait.

Beneath him her heart raced, and the echo resonated in his body and reminded him of what he wasn't. That he only pretended to be a man when it suited him. But he wouldn't inflict the curse, or the goblin, on any woman.

"I'm not going to hurt you," Roan promised as his thumb stroked her skin. He lowered his head to take a kiss.

She turned her head away, the only movement his

body allowed her. His gaze followed hers to her imprisoned hand. He froze.

Around her wrist was a plain gold bangle. On the bangle was a bead.

One amber bead.

Identical to the hundreds in his hair, the carved pattern was unmistakable.

If he'd had a beating heart, it would've stilled. He'd removed a bead only once and given it to the young woman who'd called on him for help. He glanced at the face of the woman beneath him. Her eyes gleamed golden-hazel. The same eyes that had gazed at him when he'd taken the girl to the Summerland so she could see him as a warrior and not a goblin.

Surely so many years couldn't have passed?

Time had no correlation between the Shadowlands and the Fixed Realm, but still this woman couldn't be the same girl. Eliza lay acquiescent beneath him, his hips hard against hers. No. It wasn't possible. He'd warned her not to summon him again. There had to be another explanation.

His fingers gripped the bangle. He tried to tug it off, but it was tight, too small to work over her hand. As if it had been put on before she'd finished growing. Her eyes, his amber bead. Why did it have to be her? Of all the women in the world who could have summoned him, it was the one he knew he would be helpless to resist and powerless to release. After all these years she was finally his. Cold crawled through his veins, smothering the heat of lust.

"Where did you get this?" He forced calm into his voice, but he felt like a strand of wire pulled too tight, his control held by the flimsiest thread.

She pressed her lips together and refused to meet his gaze as if she was a queen refusing to entertain the pleas of a servant.

His grip tightened. White bloomed on her skin under his fingers. "Where?" He knew the answer. Wished he didn't. He'd left it for her, a token to a child he shouldn't have bothered to help.

"I was given it." Her voice broke, but no tears glassed her eyes. She lifted her chin and met his gaze without blinking, her gold-flecked eyes glinting like polished stone.

"By who?" He shook her hand, holding the gold bangle, wishing he could tear it off and forget the child so he could enjoy the woman in his bed.

Her eyes flicked from his face to his shoulders and then back to meet his gaze. She shrank into the bed away from him. Her eyebrows drew together in puzzlement.

"It's yours." The words hung in the air. Her gaze darted around the cave masquerading as a bedroom. "Where am I?"

"Where you wanted to be." He released the gold bangle, but he couldn't pull away.

Eliza lay still, her breathing shallow, but she made no effort to escape. If she had, he may have let her leave the Shadowlands.

Her frown deepened and her eyes lost their focus. "I...I called..." She looked back at him as if seeing him for the first time and realizing who he was. "You're him...but you don't...don't look like a goblin." Her voice steadied as she tried to rationalize his existence.

"Looks are deceiving." He should have recognized her straight away. Maybe if her eyes had been open, he would have…or maybe he would've been sucked in the golden gleam and taken her anyway. Eliza was no longer a child who didn't know what she was asking. She was a woman who should know better.

"You're the Goblin King." Disbelief tainted her voice. She could have been calling him the tooth fairy.

Roan moved his hips against hers. "At your service."

Eliza drew in a breath, and her tongue stuck to the roof of her mouth. She needed a drink. She needed to get him off her. She needed to keep the crazy man talking long enough to get away.

"Where did you get my bead?" The nutcase who thought he was the Goblin King lay over her, speaking through clenched teeth as if he was the one being inconvenienced.

Eliza had never told anyone about the night she'd called the Goblin King. Yet beaded-crazy-man knew, and she was just as crazy for wanting to believe in child-ish nonsense. Goblins. The indulgence of a terrified child. Yet her heart refused to believe her head.

There was something about this man, something just beyond her memory, trapped in a dream she'd never forgotten but couldn't quite remember. Summer skies and the warrior who'd helped her. No matter how hard she'd tried to hold on to what he looked like, his image had faded so only the outline remained. Was this really the same man? Where was the smiling warrior who'd handed her the bead and fixed her torn top?

She twisted her wrist, trying to free her hand with-out success. Her body was expertly pinned down by a man who looked like a cross between a Special Forces operative and a rock star. Dreadlocks filled with gold and amber beads that glinted in the candlelight and rustled musically with each movement. The sound was so distinctive and so familiar—heard only once and then repeated ever after in her dreams—that she shivered.

The man who called himself the Goblin King waited for an answer.

Keep him talking, make a bond, and he'll be less likely to kill me.

She swallowed and played along with his delusion, not wanting this man to be the kind warrior she could barely remember from a dream brought on by too much beer. Her mother had given warnings about being greedy and ending up like the man who'd longed for gold and been given a heart of gold instead. Cursed to be a goblin, he was compelled to answer other people's wishes.

Nine years ago she'd tested the story and summoned the Goblin King.

Eliza stared into his eyes. Aching blue. How could she forget? "You gave it to me when I was a teenager."

His face went blank. Her heart skipped, then raced. The unchecked lust was less terrifying than this new, unreadable expression. At least she'd known what he wanted. Now...

She let the words spill out before he could shut her up for good. "I called you, you broke up the party. Do you remember? You sent the boys running." The lights had gone out and goblin howls had filled the house. For a few minutes she'd lived in a nightmare full of screams and darkness. She'd never told her brother it was she who'd called the monsters. She'd never told him why, or what his friend had done.

"You protected me. I put the leftover beer outside to thank you. Do you remember?"

She remembered him. The faded dream grew stronger and the features of the man who'd saved her nine years ago became the features of the man above her. The full lips, straight nose, and blue eyes that would always be hungry. This man was the Goblin King.

"You took me to the Summerland and gave me the bead." He'd given her the bead to make sure she didn't forget. Had he? "Do you remember?" She willed him to remember.

The man didn't blink. His eyes burned into her soul as if he was searching for a lie that didn't exist. She'd gone to the Summerland many times in her dreams as a teenager waiting to see if she'd see him again. Not sure if she'd dreamed him into existence, but too scared to directly summon him and find out.

Eliza sucked in a breath but couldn't release it. Panic swelled until her chest hurt. "This is a dream."

It had to be a dream, but he had never been in her dreams no matter how much she thought of him. If not for his bead, it would have been easier to think she'd imagined the whole thing. But he hadn't allowed her that illusion. And she hadn't been able to let go of the memory. Now the warrior she'd dreamed of was made flesh.

"Why did you call me?" he demanded.

She squeezed her eyes shut. Steve. The party. The woman. The suits. The wine. Oh God. She had called him. She had called the Goblin King.

Again.

"Why?" He released her hands but still caged her

body. He was a prison made of flesh, and he demanded answers like a lawyer cross-examining a witness. "I warned you."

She hadn't thought of his warning at the time, but the words echoed through her mind now: *Next time I may not return you.*

She looked up at the man she'd often thought of before life had gotten in the way and she'd given up on childish fantasies and fairy tales. His gaze was hot, the lust simmering behind the frown that scarred his brow.

"I wanted to escape." It was the only answer she had. Living with Steve and his lies was like suffocating—it was only a matter of time until she died.

"Then you got your wish." His mouth closed hard over hers, stealing the air from her lungs.

She pushed against him, fighting the kiss. The first time she'd called him, he'd protected her. That's what she longed for—someone to make her feel safe, to care about her and listen to her. Not another man to use her for whatever he wanted. She hiccupped on a strangled sob. How could she have messed this up so much?

He jerked away as if her tears burned his skin. Freed, she lurched to her feet and ran. Ran because the memories couldn't be real, ran because she wanted to wake up, ran not caring where she went. Her memories didn't mesh with reality. Her warrior had been caring, where this man was harsh and dangerous. Eliza passed another man in black and gray camo. He reached for her and she twisted away.

"Let her go," the king called out, his voice ringing down the rock halls.

She ran through candlelit tunnels. Her lungs ached,

her head pounded, but then she saw the cave opening and ran faster. This was just another crazy dream, the dangerous imaginings of a desperate woman.

Fifteen feet beyond the cave Eliza stopped. He hadn't brought her to the Summerland. This place was empty. There was no sun. No stars. No moon. Just a gray twilight that was both oppressive and endless. Twisted trees grew out of gray dust, their limbs a tangle of blackened fingers. An oily river snaked into the distance. She squinted. Did it move, or was that an illusion?

As she stood there staring at the bleak scenery, her feet and legs became heavy and cold, as if the ground was sucking the warmth from her body and making her muscles sluggish. She looked down. The gray dust that was the ground stained the white bandages on her feet. Someone had tended to her, yet she couldn't remember hurting herself.

Eliza turned around. The entrance to the cave was nothing more than a crack in the face of a sheer cliff that rose with no end. There were no clouds to hide its harsh lines and no plants to soften the angles. Her beaded captor leaned against the rock, his arms folded, as impassive as the rock he had made his home.

"What is this place?" Her voice echoed in the empty world.

"The Shadowlands." His voice didn't echo. It dropped like a weight and was absorbed into the ground as if he were part of the strange landscape.

The Shadowlands. The name should mean something to her. She shook her head, unable to find the thought.

"This is a dream." It had to be. She would wake up with a hangover at home with Steve.

"No." His lips turned into a smile that cut her to the bone. "A nightmare."

Eliza's breath slid from her body and threatened to never return. She did know this place. So alien, yet so familiar. Every nightmare she'd ever had was created here, sired by goblins. The screeching and yells that had broken up the party had haunted her sleep, but it was a nightmare she'd thought she'd grown out of, the same way she'd put aside her dreams.

She glanced at the Goblin King. The first time she'd called him, someone had died. Her brother's friend Ben, the boy she'd been so desperate to escape, had fled the party in fright. He ended up wrapping his car around a tree on the way home. Whether it was the Goblin King directly, booze, or just reckless driving, she couldn't help feeling that her wish had caused his death.

Without sound or warning, the dust beneath her feet bubbled and swelled and grew. Eliza stumbled backward. Out of the blister burst Ben.

"You killed me," Ben accused.

Eliza stepped back again. "This isn't real." Yet he looked real. The same as he had on the night of the party— leering and drunk. "None of this is real. It's a nightmare."

All she had to do was wake up and all of this would be gone…including the Goblin King. She'd forgotten about him once before. Could she do it again?

She glanced at the warrior leaning against the rock. The memory of his touch lingered on her skin, cool and firm.

Ben moved closer as if he was stalking her once again.

Eliza covered her mouth and shook her head. No. No. No. Not possible. This was a nightmare created by the

Shadowlands to torment her. To awaken the guilt she'd thought long buried over Ben's death.

"It was a car accident. It wasn't my fault." She'd never believed those words before, even though she'd wanted to. The old guilt hadn't gone. It had grown stronger with time.

Ben reached out, almost close enough to touch her. His hands ready to paw at her the way he once had.

She forced out a breath and tried to be calm. None of this existed. It was just a nightmare more vivid than any other she'd ever had. But not real. Ben's chant closed in around her.

"You called. He came. He killed. For you." Ben pointed at her, his eyes lit with malice.

Had the Goblin King killed for her, to keep her safe? Or had it been for payment? It was a question she'd never gotten the chance to ask. One she wasn't sure she wanted to have answered.

Eliza pinched her arm, twisting the skin into a bleached white peak. She didn't wake.

Two other men joined the watching warrior as Ben drew closer, circling, closing in. There was nowhere for her to go...except back into the rock spire and the embrace of the Goblin King.

"Make it stop." She twisted away, not wanting Ben to touch her.

The goblin-man shrugged. "Maybe I could, if I were real. If I'm not, then I can't. If I'm a dream, you should have power over me. If I exist, then I have the power to make every day a living nightmare." He uncrossed his arms with the grace of a warrior readying for battle. "So, Eliza, do I exist?"

Her lips moved without sound. Did she really want to know what had happened that night? Would she be able to look the man who'd saved her in the eye, knowing he'd killed for her?

She glanced at the man who looked nothing like a goblin and stared into his unforgiving blue eyes, daring him to admit the truth.

"Did you kill Ben?" Was it her fault he had died?

"No," he answered without pausing for thought.

"Swear you didn't kill him."

"If you don't believe I exist, what do I swear by?"

Ben reached for her hand, the same way he had when she was sixteen. She knew what would happen next. The first kiss had been fun, the next not really. The scent of beer on breath still made her stomach turn.

"You win. You exist." *Goblins exist.* "Just make it stop."

Ben disintegrated into nothing more than dust settling on the flat barren landscape.

"I didn't kill Ben. And I didn't bring you back to the Shadowlands that night because you didn't know what you were wishing. But I warned you. You should've known better this time." His words were soft as he picked up a handful of dust. "Listen carefully, Eliza. Everything here is real. And everything here can kill you." He blew the dust into her face.

Her muscles went lax.

His hands caught her.

"Everything."

Acknowledgments

I could write a whole list of everyone who touched this book and helped its progress along, but you know who you are. From reading the first draft, to tightening the romance, fixing my commas, giving it a lovely cover, and then marketing it. This book wouldn't be here without you. Thank you.

About the Author

Shona Husk lives in Western Australia at the edge of the Indian Ocean. Blessed with a lively imagination, she spent most of her childhood making up stories. As an adult she discovered romance novels and hasn't looked back. Drawing on history and myth, she weaves new worlds and writes heroes who aren't afraid to get hurt while falling in love.

Lord of the Hunt

by Shona Husk

—⁓—

Raised in the mortal world, the fairy Taryn never planned on going back to Annwyn, much less to Court. But with the power shift imminent, she is her parents' only hope of securing a pardon from exile and avoiding certain death.

Verden, Lord of the Hunt, swore to serve the King. But as the magic of Annwyn fails and the Prince makes ready to take the throne, Verden knows his days as Hunter are numbered.

When Taryn and Verden meet, their attraction is instant and devastating. Their love could bring down a queen and change the mortal world forever.

—⁓—

For more of the Shadowlands series, visit:

www.sourcebooks.com